BLOOD OF THE PHOENIX

RISE OF THE PHOENIX, BOOK 2

JESSICA WAYNE

She fell.

She crashed.

She broke.

She cried.

She crawled.

She hurt.

She surrendered.

And then…

She rose again.

-Beautiful Minds Anonymous (a book of poems)

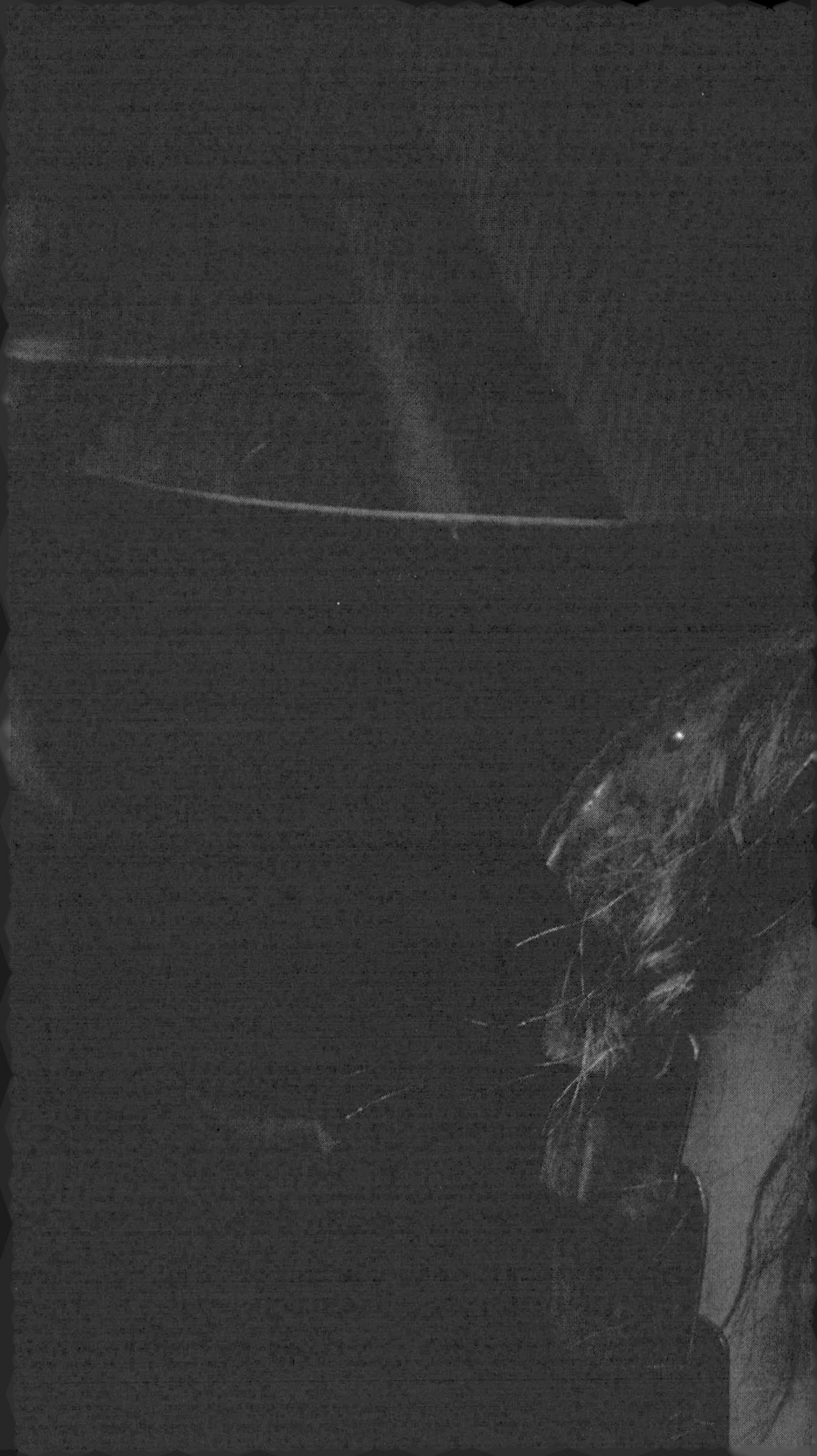

Blood Of The Phoenix

Rise Of The Phoenix book 2

by Jessica Wayne

Edited by Jessa Russo of Russo's Editing Services

Proofread by Dominique

Proofread by Rachel Cass

Cover Design by Fay Lane Graphic Design

CONTENTS

1

TERRENIA

ANASTASIA

Anastasia tightened her grip on Dakota's hand as her pulse accelerated. Where the hell were they? Had she accidentally sent them to another world without realizing it?

Smoke billowed up from piles of rubble, collecting in dark clouds high above the obliterated landscape. Hundreds of broken bodies lay strewn across the shattered bricks and crumbled rock. So much death and destruction… the force of it hit her like a punch to the gut. She bent forward, fighting to catch her breath.

As far as their eyes could see, no buildings stood, no remnants of the city she'd grown up in remained.

As much as her heart cried out in defiance, she had

taken them right where they'd meant to go, but Seattle —as they knew it—was gone.

"Holy shit," Dakota said.

The blood drained from Anastasia's face. "Oh my God."

The destruction burned itself into her memory. She would never forget what her city looked like in ruins.

"Ana." Dakota gently touched her hand, and she looked down between them. Her skin glowed, a bright, blinding white, a direct result of the power building in her blood. She closed her eyes and did her best to push the anger aside.

She couldn't lose control until she got close enough to Vincent that the backlash would destroy him. Then, if needed, she would allow her anger to consume her.

Hot tears streamed down her cheeks as she and Dakota stepped carefully over the rubble. The images from her nightmare flashed through her mind.

A city in ruins.

Bodies everywhere.

Her fault.

No, not her fault. This was Vincent's doing. She clenched her fists at her sides.

"Fuck, this is horrible." Dakota knelt to check the pulse of a man whose dark hair was matted with blood. "Dead." Dakota stood and wiped his hand on his dark pants. "Why the hell would he destroy the entire city?

Was this his fucking plan all along? Just to kill everyone?"

"I don't know."

"What the hell did he have to gain from this?" Dakota ran his hand down his face.

Something moved behind them, and as they spun to face the sound, Anastasia drew her sword and Dakota raised his gun.

"What are you idiots doing? Get out of there before they see you!" a man whispered loudly. He slipped back behind what was left of a building before they could get a better look at him.

Curious, they followed him behind a half-crumbled brick wall, where he joined a small group of men sifting through the rubble.

"What the hell happened here?" Dakota asked.

"How about you start by telling us who you are." The man was short, probably only about four inches taller than Anastasia, and not in shape like the other two men with him who were tall and heavily muscled, as if they spent a lot of time in the gym. The man they'd followed wore a Seattle Seahawks baseball cap, tufts of bright red hair sticking out from the sides.

His face was dotted with freckles and bright red, making her wonder how long they'd been searching.

"My name is Dakota. This is Anastasia." Dakota holstered his gun, trying to show peace to the strangers.

"We saw you step through one of those blue lights," the taller of the man's two companions said.

"Is that what happened here?" Anastasia asked. "Did someone come here through a portal?"

The man with the Seahawks hat raised an eyebrow. "Portal?"

She nodded. "Who are you?"

The man took a deep breath. "I'm Robbie. This is my son, Edgar, and my other son, Zeke." He gestured to the younger of the two who bled from a wound in his cheek. Both boys had dark brown hair, rather than their father's red "Want to tell us how you came through one of those lights just like the monsters? And why we should trust you?"

"I'm from here," Dakota told him.

"We came to help you," Anastasia added. "Those monsters are called Brutes. They came from a place called Terrenia, a world that runs parallel to this one."

"A parallel world?" Zeke scoffed. "You can't be serious."

Robbie shot him a glare. "Really, son? That's what you're grabbing onto? You saw the light, the beasts, and we're standing in the middle of what *used* to be Seattle, and you're struggling with the idea that there are worlds outside of this one?"

"Has no one come to help?" Dakota asked. "The National Guard? Homeland Security? Anyone?"

Robbie shook his head. "It's honestly like the rest of

the world forgot about us. Either that, or the destruction is not limited to Seattle."

"I wonder if he blocked the city," Anastasia murmured to Dakota.

"He can do that?"

She nodded. "He'd said he would once they moved on to the next step in their plan."

The older of Robbie's sons, Edgar, stepped forward. "Who are you talking about?"

"The man in charge. His name is Vincent. He's who we're here to stop," Dakota explained. "Can you tell us exactly what happened?"

Robbie nodded. "Last night, those portals, as you called them, opened all over the damn place. Beasts came pouring through, grabbing up who they could and slaughtering the rest." Robbie's jaw was set and he ran his hands over his face. "A few hours later, explosions went off, and the city just fucking… well…" He sighed, looking at the destruction around them. "You get the picture."

"How many are left?" she asked.

"There are thirty-seven of us. We've been looking for survivors, but so far…" He shook his head sadly. "It happened so damn fast. We barely had time to get out."

"Do you know where the beasts took the survivors?" she asked. "Is any part of Seattle still standing?"

"I have no idea. We only came out to look for supplies. Haven't made it past here."

Something growled deep in its throat, and Anastasia spun, moving quickly into a fighter's crouch and bracing for a fight. Two Brutes rounded the corner, looking down at her with hunger in their onyx eyes.

She glanced at Dakota, who was also ready, his sword drawn and at the ready. With a curt nod, they charged. Saving her magic for Vincent, she attacked the beast on the right with her sword, dodging its large fist and driving the blade into the beast's chest.

Dakota had taken the other Brute down, and in unison, they brought their blades up and removed the Brutes heads from their shoulders.

"We need to get going," she told them. She stepped toward the Brute closest to her and wiped her blade off on its pants. "Brutes always come for their dead." She sheathed her sword and Dakota did the same.

"You are more than welcome to come back with us," Robbie told them.

Anastasia hesitated; they really needed to get going. But with the city in ruins, where did they even start? It wasn't like they'd be able to move amongst the crowds of people in secret like they'd planned.

"Maybe someone saw something that might help you."

"That would be great, thank you." She offered a small smile to Robbie as he and his sons turned to head back the opposite direction.

"You all right?" Dakota's voice was just above a whisper.

"I think this is my fault," she said, voicing her biggest concern

Dakota gripped her hand, looking intently into her eyes. "This was not your fault, Ana."

"I dreamt this."

"What do you mean?"

She stepped around the body of a woman in a red dress. Had she been getting ready to go on a date? Anastasia's heart ached. So much death. So much destruction. And for what? So a power-hungry man could rule?

"My nightmare last night was *this*." She motioned to their surroundings. "Well, almost like this." The only difference? Dakota was dead in her nightmare.

She squeezed his hand tighter.

"There was no way you could have known."

"How did I dream it, then? If I was not meant to stop this, then why did I see it?"

He shrugged. "I have no clue. But I do know that there was nothing you could have done."

"We should have come back yesterday. Then maybe we could have stopped it."

Dakota didn't say anything; he just held her hand as they walked.

2

SEATTLE

ANASTASIA

They reached the crumbled remains of what was once a small house. Robbie lifted a large piece of plywood, revealing an old cellar door, reminiscent of the cellar where Anastasia discovered the bodies of Ophelia's family. For a moment, the scent of death surrounded her and she couldn't bring herself to follow the others down into the cellar.

"Are you okay?" Dakota whispered.

"Yes, just a bad memory is all." She took one last look around at her surroundings and, with a deep breath, descended the stairs.

Anastasia and Dakota followed the men through a labyrinth of hallways, eventually emerging into a large common room. Survivors lined the walls, some bleeding from head wounds, others barely breathing, all coated in a thick later of dirt and blood. A handful of children sat in one corner, listening intently to an older gentleman as he told them a story.

Eyes watched them as they moved further into the room, and rage had her magic blazing again.

Dakota squeezed her hand, a silent reminder to keep control, so she breathed deeply and tried to focus on the task at hand: finding out whatever they could about the state of Seattle.

Edgar and Zeke broke off and disappeared into another room, and Robbie cleared his throat. "I want to introduce you all to Dakota and Anastasia. They are here to help us."

The men and women nodded in their direction, welcoming them with smiles and small waves, and a few murmured amongst themselves.

"Hi, honey." An older woman stepped forward and kissed Robbie on the cheek. She was petite, her soft features framed with dark bangs. The rest of her dark brown hair was braided down her back.

"Hi, Tilly." He kissed her back, then turned her to face Anastasia. "This is my wife, Matilda."

"It's nice to meet you," the woman said, shaking Anastasia's hand.

"You as well, Matilda."

"Oh, honey, please just call me Tilly."

"They came through one of those lights," Robbie whispered.

Tilly's eyes widened with surprise. "So, you know how to stop those beasts?"

"They are called Brutes," Robbie corrected.

"Fitting title," she responded tightly. "What can we do to help you?"

"We need to know if anyone has any idea where they might be hiding," Anastasia said. "If any part of the city is still standing after the attacks last night, that's probably where they'll be."

Tilly turned to address the survivors. "Does anyone know if there was any part of the city that wasn't destroyed last night?"

The survivors muttered amongst themselves and shook their heads morosely.

So much for getting any useful information. Not that she could blame them; what they'd gone through had likely been more than traumatic.

"I'm sorry." Tilly offered them a sad smile, then turned and walked back through the doorway her sons had disappeared into moments before.

"Can you give us a minute?" Dakota asked Robbie.

Robbie nodded, stepping aside to speak to a small group waiting off to the side.

"These people aren't going to last long," Dakota whispered once Robbie was out of earshot.

"I know."

"What are we going to do?"

She let out a breath. "We can send them to Terrenia."

Dakota raised an eyebrow. "You want to send thirty-seven people from this world into Terrenia without warning the others?"

She shrugged. "What other option do we have?"

"What about your magic? The more you keep doing things like that, the more it's going to drain you. We need to save all the strength we can."

"I agree, but we can't just let them die."

A baby cried somewhere in the room and Dakota pursed his lips, nodding slowly.

Anastasia turned to search for Robbie, and smelled sulfur moments before the thudding of footprints.

"Robbie!" Anastasia called.

The door splintered and at least a dozen Brutes ran inside. They headed for the weakest first, the ones who could do no more than crawl away. Screams ripped from the throats of the survivors, and those with weapons drew them.

"Get them out of here!" Dakota yelled, lunging for the nearest beast.

Anastasia raced to Robbie and closed her eyes to conjure a portal. When she opened her eyes, blue light had filled the room. Robbie stared at her wide-eyed, then his gaze flicked back and forth between her and the portal.

"You need to go now," Anastasia urged. "Get your people out of here! Ask for Tony. He will keep you safe."

"What? Where will we go?" Tilly asked, her eyes filled with fear.

"Terrenia. I promise you'll be safe."

Not having any more time to argue, Anastasia raced back to Dakota. "Duck!" she shouted as a Brute drove his dagger through the air toward Dakota. Dakota jumped just in time, but the distraction was just long enough that she felt the gripping fingers of a beast on her arm. It crunched down on her bones, and Anastasia cried out.

The sword clanked to the ground from her now injured arm, and she conjured a ball of light to slam into the beast's chest, who after the impact, crumpled to the ground.

Anastasia looked over as the last of Robbie's people fled through the portal. She closed it seconds after, breathing a sigh of relief. At least Robbie and the other survivors were safe now.

"Ana!" Dakota called out and she saw three Brutes closing in on him. The others tore through the building, searching for anyone who might have gotten free.

Anastasia threw her head back and screamed, allowing the power to seep into her bones. Saving energy wouldn't mean shit if she died in the process.

A blast of light shot through the room, and each of the Brutes evaporated into dust.

"Ana!" Dakota slid to his knees beside her, reaching for her arm. She glanced down, her eyes widening. The pain was well deserved. The Brute had crushed her bicep, and she would be willing to bet nearly all the bones were broken.

Her vision wavered from the pain, and she heard Dakota say her name one last time before she passed out.

3

DAKOTA

"Fuck!" Dakota leaned closer to Ana and checked her pulse. Unsure of what to do, he pulled one of the orange vials from her bag, and a knife from his waist. "I'm sorry," he mumbled as he sliced the inside of her bicep, cringing when the blade split her skin open.

Blood poured from the new injury, and Dakota opened a vial to release its contents into Ana's arm. He ripped a sleeve from his shirt and wrapped it around the wound, hoping that between the healing tonic and the pressure, the bleeding would stop.

Dakota stood and surveyed the damage around him. Splintered wood, overturned tables, abandoned toys, and weapons littered the ground. There were no bodies, though; whatever Ana had done completely obliterated anything and anyone.

Except for him.

Dakota rubbed his hands over his face. Why the hell hadn't that blast of power killed him too?

He walked the space in search of any supplies that might come in handy, but Robbie's people must have cleared them out before going through the portal. He made his way back over to Ana, who was still unconscious, and lifted her into his arms.

He wasn't sure if the Brutes would come back now that there was no one here, but he couldn't take that chance, especially with Ana completely helpless.

After stepping onto the street, Dakota headed back out of town toward his family's cottage. They couldn't go back to the cabin, not after Vincent had found them there before, but maybe if they could get far enough out of town, they'd stand a chance until Ana came back around.

If the healing potion worked to fix her bones…

Wetness soaked his hand and he glanced down at the blood seeping through the makeshift tourniquet on her arm. His stomach sank. He looked up at her face, completely void of color. What if she died from blood loss due to the gash he'd made in her arm? He swallowed hard and pushed the thought to the back of his mind.

She was *not* going to die.

As it turned out, carrying an unconscious woman five miles was a lot harder than he'd considered. His muscles screamed in agony with each move he made, and when he stumbled, nearly dropping them both, Dakota decided it was time to find a place to camp for the night.

After searching for a safe place, Dakota sighed with relief when he spotted a half-standing building. Dirt and grime coated the once polished flooring of what appeared to have been a fancy apartment building of some kind, but at least there were no dead here.

Dakota set Ana down gently in the corner, using his backpack as a makeshift pillow for her head. After checking to be sure she was breathing steadily, he stood and stretched.

Bones popped and muscles screamed, but he didn't rest yet, instead he did a perimeter check just to be sure they were alone.

The partial brick wall would block them from anything passing by, and the overhang would do the same on the off chance their enemy had a way of looking down.

Hopefully Brutes couldn't fucking fly. Wouldn't that just be the cherry on top of the ice cream sundae that today had been?

He tucked Ana closer to his body and pulled out a

pouch they'd filled with water before leaving Terrenia. After drinking just enough to satisfy the burn in his throat, he replaced the cap and leaned back against the wall.

What the hell were they going to do now? One minute they'd been here to kick some ass, and the next they'd had their asses handed to them by a dozen Brutes in a random ambush.

But was it random?

How had the beasts known where to find them?

Was Vincent tracking them? Or had it been coincidental?

Either way, they were screwed if Ana didn't wake up soon. He pulled her closer and closed his eyes, breathing in the scent of her hair as he drifted off.

4

ANASTASIA

Anastasia woke to the sound of the rain. Her eyes fluttered open, adjusting to the darkness that surrounded them. What happened? She sat up quickly and looked for Dakota, who slept soundly beside her, propped up against a half-crumbled brick wall.

Rain poured down on the death and destruction that Seattle had become. She quietly got to her feet to survey the area and figure out where they were.

She reached out to let the raindrops fall onto her palm. The water was cool and sent a shiver down her spine.

Dakota shuffled behind her, and she turned to see

him stretch. His eyes fell on hers, and he smiled. "Thank God. I really didn't want to have to carry you anymore."

"Where are we?"

"About five miles away from where we were."

Her mouth fell open. "You carried me for five miles?"

"Hence the not wanting to carry you any further."

"Shit, Dakota. What happened?"

"You exploded with light, turned everything and everyone in that room besides me to ash, then passed out."

"My arm." She lifted her arm and looked at the blood-stained bandage. It didn't hurt anymore, but she knew without a doubt bones had been broken. After removing the makeshift bandage, she studied her now unmarred skin. Blood had dried on the surface, but the skin beneath was in perfect shape.

"Sorry about the blood." Dakota grimaced. "I had to slice you open."

"You did what?"

"To get the healing potion deep enough into your arm to fix the bones. That Brute shattered it and you passed out from either the pain or the magical overload."

"Damn." She flexed her muscle that still felt somewhat weak. "I left you completely defenseless. I'm sorry."

Dakota shook his head. "Seeing as how you saved

both our lives, you're forgiven." He stood and wrapped his arms around her. "You scared the shit out of me," he whispered against her hair.

The warmth of his body was a comfort to her and she held on as long as she could. Lightening split the sky, and they stepped further beneath the overhang.

"We should stay here through the night and head out first thing in the morning." Dakota took a seat and handed her a sleeve of water.

"I agree." She took a drink and savored the coolness of the water as it slipped down her throat. "Once we're rested, we need to head deeper into town. Vincent has to be somewhere."

"Ana, do you really think he's still here? I mean, it's already been destroyed. Is it possible he's moved on?"

She shook her head. She had to believe he was still here, somewhere, waiting for his next move. "He has to still be here."

"Why destroy it, though? What did he have to gain from this?"

She shrugged. "I don't know, but it had to have been something."

Still feeling the strain from her magic, Anastasia leaned against Dakota's shoulder and closed her eyes. "We have to stop him."

"I know." Dakota kissed her head. "Get some sleep. I'll keep watch."

Anastasia drifted off, listening to the first Seattle rainstorm she'd experienced in half a decade.

"UM, EXCUSE ME."

Anastasia opened her eyes and jumped. A woman in a flowery dress with white hair, stood directly in front of them.

"Thank goodness. Are you two all right?" she asked curiously.

Anastasia looked around, her eyes widening as she took in the pristine marble all around them, from the clean, shiny floors to the pillars erected along the walls. She jabbed Dakota in the ribs with her elbow, and he snapped awake.

"What is it?" he asked gruffly.

"Look." She rose to her feet, pulse racing as she gaped at the gorgeous lobby. The old brick wall they'd fallen asleep against was now solid and not at all crumbling.

"What the hell?" Dakota murmured. He pushed to his feet and stood beside Anastasia.

The woman beamed. "Isn't it lovely?" she exclaimed happily. "He fixed it all!"

He? Anastasia frowned as she pushed the glass door open and stepped out onto the busy street. People smiled and embraced, greeting one another as if nothing had happened. There was no evidence of the prior destruction as far as the eye could see. This quaint suburban neighborhood—and Seattle beyond—had been completely restored while they slept.

Nothing was right about this. Ana's muscles tensed.

"Who fixed everything?" Dakota asked, his eyes displaying the same unease that had begun to settle in Ana's stomach.

"Mr. Vincent! He put the entire city back together! With magic! Can you believe it? I wouldn't have believed it myself if he hadn't rescued us from those terrible Brutes in the middle of the night!" She clapped her hands together. "I'm going to go find my daughter and son-in-law." She bounded away from them, pure joy giving her body the agility of someone half her age.

"Here." Dakota handed Anastasia a bundle of cloth they'd planned to wrap their swords in so they could carry them around modern-day Seattle. They, of course, hadn't needed to hide their swords once they'd arrived, but standing out now could prove deadly.

After strapping her swathed sword to her back, she walked further outside and onto the sidewalk. The sky was clear, and the sun shone down on the city that had been reduced to ruins only hours ago.

"There is no way he has this power, Dakota."

"What do you mean?"

"I mean, he had to have gotten it from somewhere.

The amount of magic it would take to do this, to *fix* all of this… it would have killed him."

"So you're saying he's weak?"

"He has to be." She turned to him. "That is, if it didn't kill him."

"How about we go see?" Dakota held out his hand to her, and they made their way down the sidewalk. "This is a much easier walk than it was carrying you through rubble," he joked.

But Anastasia didn't laugh. Something wasn't adding up, and unease sat heavy in her belly. Why destroy everything, only to put it back together again?

"Let's stop at my apartment. If the rest of the city is restored, it should be too. We need to grab some food and change clothes."

Anastasia looked down at the leather pants and vest she wore. Aside from the blood still crusted on her arm, her outfit could pass as normal, but Dakota's blood-stained and ripped shirt definitely stuck out.

"Okay." She followed him through the bustling streets, past people who were ecstatic to be alive. Some were still dirty from the attacks, but others were already in freshly-pressed clothing.

Her mind whirled; she couldn't grasp a single logical reason for what had happened to Seattle.

Or, why no one even seemed to question that the man behind the destruction was also the one who restored the city.

They moved quickly, not wanting to risk getting caught by Vincent or any of his beasts, but as she looked around, there were no monsters among the people. All the Brutes were gone.

"Here." Dakota opened the door to a cab that was parked on the street and they climbed inside.

After giving the driver his address, he leaned back against the seat.

"You guys grateful to have everything back?" the driver asked.

"Yeah, man, it's insane," Dakota replied, raising his eyebrow as he looked at Anastasia.

"I'm so glad that man fixed it. It was a pretty brave thing he did driving out those aliens."

"Aliens?"

"Yeah! You saw them, didn't you? Or were you two some of the few who managed to evade them? We heard about a few clusters of survivors back at the camps."

"What camps?" Anastasia asked.

"The ones the aliens took us to. They pushed us through a blue light and into this weird ass place with nothing but mountains." He shivered. "When we got back, I found my cab and went out to start helping people get home."

"Damn, man, I'm glad you're okay," Dakota offered.

Anastasia met the man's gaze in the rearview mirror. Tears glistened in his eyes.

"You and me both," he said. He pulled the cab to the curb and Dakota leaned forward to hand him some cash.

"No, you keep it. I'm doing this to help."

"Are you sure?"

"Absolutely. Hold the ones you love and be glad we're home."

As he pulled away from the curb, Anastasia looked over at Dakota, who stared up at his building.

"Still looks exactly the same."

They made their way inside and up to his apartment. Everything was exactly the same as they'd left it, right down to the half-drank cup of coffee she'd left behind the night she was attacked.

Dakota flipped the TV on and Vincent's face took up the screen.

He smiled brightly, his silver eyes alert as he listened to whatever the newscaster was asking him. Anastasia couldn't focus on anything but his face—until he started speaking.

"Well, you see, Gwen—may I call you by your first name?"

"Oh, honey, you fixed the entire city; you can call me anything you'd like."

They laughed and Vincent looked back into the camera. "I hid who I was for a long time, afraid of being cast out or tormented for being different." His eyes glistened with unshed tears and Anastasia shook her head.

Had she not known what a murdering psychopath he was, she might've believed his performance.

"But when those beasts tore through this wonderful city, I couldn't stay hidden any longer. I came out of hiding and did what any good person would do. I drove those monsters out of our city."

"I would say you went above and beyond what most people would do." The reporter reached over and touched his hand on screen. "And I only wish we had more to give you."

Vincent covered her hand with his other hand. "You have given me so much already. Just knowing I can be free to be who I am is enough."

"This is disgusting." Dakota flipped the channel.

Then he changed the channel again. And again. Every single station only played one thing: Vincent.

Anastasia's lips curled into a cynical smile as she watched. "He isn't taking this world by force. He's doing it by pretending to be a hero." She shook her head in disbelief as Dakota continued to flip through channel after channel of Vincent's face.

"Surely no one is stupid enough to buy that."

"Think about it. There's no one to corroborate his story of 'driving the beasts out', and no one to refute it because everyone was *gone*. He just"—she shrugged—"called them off. Then, Vincent the Savior went to wherever the hell they'd taken the survivors and brought them back." She raised her hands up, palms out, then paused, tilting her head as she considered. "But that still doesn't explain how he fixed things. Especially when he is sitting right there, in peak condition."

"Is it possible he *is* that powerful?"

She looked up at Dakota, eyes wide. "I sure as hell hope not. Otherwise, how am I supposed to stop him?"

5

DAKOTA

Dakota stared out at the city beyond the glass of his window. How strange it was to be back here in his apartment after the events of the last few days. It felt like a lifetime ago when he'd stood in this exact spot and watched the beasts pour into the alleyway below.

He took a drink from the bottle of water in his hand and placed one hand against the wall.

Since that night, Ana had reappeared into his life, his partner was murdered, he was sent to another world after being attacked by a psycho sorcerer—or whatever the hell Vincent called himself—he was returned to a destroyed city, witnessed Ana nearly dying, and woke up today in a world completely unharmed as if nothing had ever happened.

Shit, it had been a long few days.

He knew they had to move forward with their plan of finding Vincent, but he couldn't help himself; part of him just wanted to take a day—a month, even—and just relax with the woman he'd loved his entire life.

A woman he barely knew anymore.

She stepped into the living room and he turned around to face her. Ana wore one of his large t-shirts, and it fell to her knees. She smiled as she met his gaze. Her hair was wet from the shower, the dirt and grime from the last twenty-four hours washed away down the drain.

She looked absolutely stunning.

"Good shower?"

"Great shower." She groaned. "I haven't had one in five years."

He made a disgusted face.

She let out a small laugh. "You know what I mean."

"Do I? I thought I smelled something."

"Probably yourself. You planning on showering anytime soon?"

He drank the rest of the water and tossed the bottle into the recycling bin, then shook his head at the absurdity of recycling after everything they'd just been through. But, damned world or not, old habits die hard.

“I hope I didn’t use all the hot water.” The grin on her face let him know she didn’t really care.

“I’m used to cold showers.”

“Oh?”

“You know what I mean.” He winked and stepped past her.

“Hey, Dakota?”

“Yeah?” He turned to face her again.

“Don’t shave.”

“You got it.”

He walked away with a smirk and stepped into the bathroom. The water was still warm, thankfully, but as he stripped off clothes he never intended to wear again, he wondered just how far up shit creek they were.

With Vincent on everyone’s Christmas card list, how were they supposed to get to him? He’d have unlimited resources, if need be, and he’d been powerful even from the shadows.

So how would they defeat him now that he was the poster boy for Seattle’s salvation?

6

ANASTASIA

"I completely forgot how freaking delicious pizza is!" Anastasia exclaimed. She took another bite of the triple pepperoni Dakota had ordered after his shower.

"It is hard to match it."

They sat on his couch, enjoying pizza and watching TV reruns like they had so many years before. Dakota convinced her another night of relaxing would be beneficial, giving them time to prepare for their assault.

She itched with the need to find Vincent and finish him, but she couldn't deny the appeal of spending an evening with Dakota. Surely saving the world could wait one night.

They still had no clue where to find Vincent, and so

far, looking for Mitch had been futile. It was as if he'd fallen completely off the radar. She honestly wondered if Vincent hadn't just killed her former "father" since Mitch's usefulness had likely run its course. Vincent already had the city of Seattle hanging on his every word; what more could an alcoholic child abuser have to offer him?

"Where are your thoughts?" Dakota asked from his side of the couch.

She looked up and shook her head. "Just going over everything."

He set his plate down and leaned back. "I wish I knew where to even start. I figured I could check in with my lieutenant at the department. I'm technically on leave, so it's not like I'll be reprimanded for being gone three days." He laughed. "But I'm concerned he might be in Vincent's pocket at this point. I don't even know who to trust."

"I agree."

"We have to make sure he doesn't know we're here, but in doing so, we'll cut off every potential thread of information we have available." He ran a hand through his hair, the muscles in his arm flexing from the movement.

Anastasia swallowed hard, forcing her gaze away from his arm. "We'll figure something out." She got to her feet, embarrassment heating her cheeks. She'd just been ogling Dakota—had he caught that? The timing was beyond inappropriate—it's not like they had all the time in the world. Vincent could find them at any moment. Or, worse, he could change his mind and rain destruction down on their city all over again.

Then again, not having all the time in the world meant no time to waste.

"I'm pretty wiped out." She yawned and stretched. "I can take the couch if that works."

Dakota shook his head. "You can take the bedroom." He rose to his feet and walked over to give her a hug. "Night, Phoenix," he whispered into her ear, sending a shiver down her spine.

She sucked in a shaky breath. "Phoenix?"

"That's what you are, isn't it? Besides, it's what the villagers call you behind your back."

"What? Seriously?"

Dakota smiled. "Night, Ana." He pulled a blanket and pillow out from a storage ottoman and laid them on the couch.

Anastasia made her way back to the bedroom and slipped between Dakota's soft sheets. She stared up at the ceiling fan as the blades spun around and around sending a delicate breeze through the otherwise still room.

She closed her eyes and allowed the power to surge forward. Focusing as hard as she could, Anastasia tried to sense Vincent. She wasn't even sure it was possible, but, given their current predicament, what could it hurt?

When nothing came, she pulled back and relaxed against the soft mattress. She ran her hands over her face, pulling them back to look at the tears on her palms.

She felt completely helpless and, despite the man sleeping in the other room, lonely. For as long as she could remember, she'd wanted a future with Dakota. Kids, a family, the whole nine yards.

When she'd been sent to Terrenia, she'd believed that future was over, had mourned the loss of those dreams and that man for all the years that followed.

Now that she was finally back with Dakota, back in a relationship with him, it felt so completely different than before. He was holding back and she couldn't figure out if it was because he was afraid of her, or if he still hadn't forgiven her for leaving.

Did she even forgive herself?

Her shoulders shook with silent tears for all they'd lost in the last five years. She cried for her mother, for his father, her father, the Terrenians who had been slaughtered mercilessly, and the Seattle residents who paid the ultimate price for a fucking show of power.

And she cried for herself: for the woman she could have been, and the Fighter she'd become.

7

ANASTASIA

Anastasia sat up quickly, the familiar destruction from her nightmare still lingering in her mind. She covered her face with her hands and breathed deeply, waiting for her thoughts to slow and return to the present.

They were not in a destroyed city anymore. Dakota was alive, and so was she.

The fan no longer spun above her; Dakota must have turned it off.

She put her bare feet on the floor and made her way to the kitchen for something to drink. After filling a glass halfway with water, she sipped the cool liquid and watched Dakota sleeping soundly on the couch.

She took a step forward and—

Footsteps in the hallway signaled someone approaching the door of Dakota's apartment. Anastasia's pulse raced and she quickly walked to the couch and shook Dakota.

"Dakota!" she whispered loudly. "Wake up!"

"Search the apartment."

Her eyes widened, and her blood iced. She recognized Mitch's voice immediately and shook Dakota harder.

"Dakota, wake up!"

The door opened and Anastasia stood, turning toward the entrance of the apartment as Mitch stepped inside, two large men flanking him.

"He won't be waking up anytime soon."

Anastasia looked down at Dakota, whose head faced her. His eyes were open, staring blankly at the ceiling.

"No!" She knelt again and checked for a pulse. "You can't be dead."

"I'm afraid he is, and it's all your fault."

"Ana, come back." Dakota called, and it was as if he stood beside her, but that was impossible! She cried into his shirt and clung to his limp body.

"Now, how about you come with me? Boss has some big plans for you."

"No!" she screamed, fighting against the two men as they hauled her to her feet. "Dakota!"

"Ana, I'm right here! Wake up!"

Hands shook her and she fought against them, desperate to get free.

"Ana!"

Anastasia opened her eyes to Dakota's face just inches away from hers. He searched her gaze franticly. She threw her arms around him and held on, as she shook.

"It's okay, Ana, just a bad dream." He held her while she tried to gain control over her body.

After a few moments, she gained control, and looked up into his familiar eyes.

"You okay?" he asked, his brow furrowed.

"Nightmare?" she asked. It had been different this time, so much more real than the nightmares she was used to.

He nodded. "Yeah, a bad one. I couldn't get you to wake up." He searched her gaze. "I'm going to get you some water, all right?"

She nodded, still trying to grasp that Dakota's limp body splayed out on the couch hadn't been reality.

8

DAKOTA

Dakota stepped out into the living room, leaving the door cracked behind him.

Waking up to Ana's terrified screaming was really starting to fuck with his head.

His own heart was pounding, and he pressed the palm of his hand against his chest as he pulled in some deep, calming breaths.

After taking a few moments to calm down so he could be the guy Ana needed him to be, Dakota made his way into the kitchen for a drink of water. When he turned around, he sucked in a breath, his hand hovering reflexively at his hip where his gun would be holstered if he wasn't in pajamas.

Mitch stood on this side of the front door, two large men flanking him on either side.

"Shhhh." Mitch put his finger up to his lips. "You bring her out here and we'll kill her on the spot."

The man to Mitch's right held up a pistol and aimed it directly at the doorway to Dakota's room.

Dakota swallowed hard, standing taller. "What the fuck do you want?"

"My boss wants to talk to you."

"I'm not going anywhere with you."

"You don't have a choice," Mitch said quietly. He nodded to the man on his left, who made his way to Dakota.

He could fight, could even probably manage to take this man down within seconds, but not fast enough to stop the bullet that would get Ana the second she raced out to see what the commotion was. Her life was more important than his own. Still, Vincent would use him as a trap; he was sure of it.

So was he really saving her by taking away her chance to fight?

He opened his mouth to speak and felt a stabbing pain on the back of his head, then everything went black.

9

ANASTASIA

Anastasia stepped out into the living room a few minutes later, searching for Dakota.

"Dakota?" she called.

"No need for that." Vincent appeared in front of her.

Her body went rigid and her blood chilled. "Where is he?"

"He's alive, if that's what you're worried about."

"What do you want?" she growled

"I want my family back."

"Little late for that, isn't it? You know, seeing as how your brother was murdered?"

He narrowed his eyes. They were blue tonight, but tendrils of silver had worked their way through the color. Was it the dark magic doing that to him?

"You are the last of my family, Anastasia. I do not wish to be at war with you."

"Really? Great. Then bring back Dakota and stop whatever plans you have for world domination."

Vincent scoffed. "Don't be so childish. You're better than that."

"You don't know me, not even a little bit. So let's not pretend."

"I only ever wanted to be a part of your life."

She thought she saw a hint of sadness in his eyes, but it was gone so quickly she was sure she'd imagined the emotion.

"You have a funny way of showing that," she muttered, disgusted. "You kidnapped me, forced me to spend my entire life being beaten, killed your sister-in-law, had your brother murdered… and that's only the beginning of the list of crap you have flung."

"Gregory brought that all upon himself. I only wanted to get to know you. He wasn't going to let that happen, so I took matters into my own hands." He crossed his arms over his chest.

"Then give me back Dakota."

"What happens to him is up to you."

"How's that?"

"You come to me willingly, and I might be persuaded to leave him alive. But you had better be quick, Anastasia, patience is not something I possess in spades." He began to fade, and Anastasia lunged.

"Where are you?" she yelled as he disappeared from her sight.

"Go to the docks."

Anastasia fell to her knees, tears welling in her eyes. The nightmare had been a distraction. It was meant to rock her so that she would believe her instincts were off about the intrusion into the house. If she'd been paying closer attention, she would have noticed it for what it was.

"Dammit!" she yelled into the dark as she rushed back into the room to get dressed.

Frantically, she packed clothes and weapons into a backpack, strapped her usual gear onto her body, and left Dakota's apartment.

She would be foolish to not see this for what it was: a trap. It was unlikely either of them would make it out of Vincent's grasp, but she would do whatever it took to save Dakota. She had to.

She would rescue him or die trying.

IT WAS LATE MORNING BY THE TIME SHE REACHED THE docks. The smell of saltwater mixed with the sulfur from the Brutes filled her lungs and her stomach churned.

She didn't see any Brutes, but they were nearby. Vincent probably just told them to stay out of sight.

Couldn't have them ruining his heroic reputation, now could he?

She stepped inside, and nearly walked straight into Mitch. He grinned at her, a sick smile of satisfaction and pride that he'd manipulated her into coming. "About damn time you started exercising some common sense, girl."

For the first time in her life, there was no fear when she looked at him. "I don't have time for you." She walked past him, and he gripped her arm.

Anastasia nearly spun on him, ready to conjure a ball of magic, but she paused. She had to play her cards right; she couldn't risk Vincent killing Dakota.

"You'll want to let go of my arm, Mitch." She smiled sweetly, but the threat was evident in her tone.

"You had better listen to my niece," Vincent commanded. Mitch released her arm with a huff.

She turned to face Vincent.

"I'm glad you came," he said.

"I wasn't given much of a choice. Where is he?"

"He's still alive, for now."

"I want to see him."

"Soon," Vincent promised, holding his arm out. "Let's take a walk."

She folded her arms over her chest. "I want to see him."

Vincent laughed. "You definitely got your stubbornness from your father's side of the family. Very well, let's go."

Anastasia followed him through a maze of crates and into a small room that had once been a shipping office. Dakota was tied to a chair, his head down, and there were no visible injuries. His chest rose and fell normally, and Anastasia felt a small relief in seeing him alive.

Now they just had to find a way out of here.

"You can speak with him later. Right now, he is suffering some of the effects of a calming potion."

"Why?"

"He was a bit anxious, naturally, and it was annoying."

"Nothing permanent?"

"No. I assure you, it will wear off in an hour or so."

Anastasia drew in a deep breath, trying to calm her nerves. Dakota was alive, and that was all that mattered.

Obviously, Vincent wanted something from her, or she would be dead, so for now they were safe. She would find a way to get them both out of there as soon as she could.

"Walk now? We have much to discuss."

She nodded and warily followed Vincent out onto the dock.

"Why all the guns? You were obviously able to keep anyone outside of Seattle from discovering your destruction here, so why do you need all these weapons?"

"My magic can only stretch so far. If I am to achieve my goals, then I will need the firepower to back them up. It's just a precaution."

"So, you did cloak the city."

"That I did. I have learned quite a bit over the course of my lifetime… knowledge I would love to share with you."

"Not interested."

"You will be."

"Unlikely."

Vincent laughed. "You are so much like your father."

Anastasia ignored his comment, afraid a conversation about Gregory might force her to snap. "So, what do you want?"

"To discuss an alliance."

"I don't want an alliance."

"That would be foolish," he said, dismissing her statement with the flick of his wrist. "Seattle is only the beginning, Anastasia. There will be nowhere for you to hide should you choose to become my enemy. The only reason you are still breathing is because I have high hopes for what we could accomplish together."

"You want the country."

"Think bigger, Anastasia."

"The world?"

His eyes flashed with delight. "All of them."

"Why?"

"Why else? Power. Isn't that reason enough?" He regarded her, his eyebrows raised. "I see that, in your opinion, it isn't. Not to worry, you will see soon."

"I will never understand how someone could murder innocent people just to gain power."

"Would you not kill in order to protect him?" he asked, gesturing toward the warehouse. "Did you not murder Ophelia and Maximus?"

"They were not innocent people," she growled. "For a guy who just lost two of his protégé, you don't seem too worked up about it."

"It is unfortunate that Maximus is dead. As I mentioned before, I would have killed Ophelia myself for what she did to my brother." He eyed her, his eyes more silver than they had been before. "You would do well not to push me, Anastasia."

"I am not a murderer."

"Did you not come here expecting to kill for something?"

"Dakota is not something, he is *someone*. There is a difference."

"Not to me. You love Dakota; I love power. People do crazy things for those they love."

Anastasia placed her hand on the railing and looked out over the water. "Power does not hold value the way life does."

Vincent shook his head. "You will see soon, Anastasia, just how wrong you are."

"You keep saying that, but I will never see things the way you do. I will never go dark."

Vincent laughed wildly. "Turn dark? Oh, child, how blind you truly are. There is no dark and light; there is only power and more power. My brother was too foolish to see that he could have had it all had he only embraced what he already was. We couldn't have been given this gift if we weren't meant to use it."

"What you have is not a gift. You sold your soul. Hell, you're weird ass eyes are evidence enough of that."

"So naïve," he spat. He looked past her, and she turned to see some Brutes standing behind her. "I have something to attend to. You may go and see your Dakota now, but don't be so foolish as to try escaping. I find my tolerance for you is wearing thin."

Vincent walked away, his Brutes following him like the good little lapdogs they were. The moment he was out of sight, she bolted for Dakota. She looked through the window as she passed, confirming that his head was still down, his bare chest unmarred.

When she stepped inside, however, the scene before her was entirely different.

She gasped and ran to Dakota's side. He was tied to a chair with his head down, but that was where the similarities ended. Blood covered his tattered chest. They'd beaten him, with a fucking belt. Bile curdled in her stomach. *They will pay.*

"Mitch," she growled, then she shook Dakota. "Dakota!"

His eyes, swollen from whatever beating had been inflicted on him, fluttered open and he looked down at her kneeling beside him.

"You shouldn't have come, Ana."

"Don't be ridiculous, Dakota, you would have done the same for me. Can you walk?"

She moved behind him and untied his hands.

"I think so." He tried to stand, and she secured herself beside him, then wrapped his arm around her shoulders to help carry some of his weight.

Securing herself beneath his arm, she whispered, "We have to go now."

They crept out the door, and Anastasia scanned the area for any Brutes that might try to stop them. Oddly enough, it appeared as if the entire warehouse was empty. Whether this was a trap or just a random stroke of luck, they had limited time, so Anastasia guided Dakota toward a side door that led into the woods behind the warehouse as quickly as possible.

"Where do you think you're going?" Mitch stepped into view, blocking their exit. "I told him you were more trouble than you were worth." He pointed a gun at her and smiled. "You have no idea how long I've wanted to do this."

"If you kill me, Vincent will not be happy," she said, trying to buy them some time.

"I'm not going to kill you. I'm going to kill him." He moved the gun over a few inches, aiming it at Dakota, then pulled the trigger—

Anastasia shoved Dakota out of the way, but the bullet tore into his abdomen, and he crumpled to the floor.

"No!" she screamed. Using her magic, she threw Mitch out of their way.

"Dakota, come on, we have to go!" She applied pressure to the wound in his side and lifted him again. He was miraculously still able to walk some, and she used that, coupled with a bit of magic, to move them quickly into the woods. She was beginning to feel the drain though, and knew if they didn't get somewhere safe, they were screwed.

"Leave me, Ana."

"I'm not leaving you! We just have to get back to the city. Someone will help us there." She cried as she pushed through the trees.

They walked for about ten minutes until they entered a clearing.

"No," Anastasia cried as she took in the scene before her. At least two-dozen Brutes stood in the center of the small clearing, and when she turned, she saw that more had moved in behind her. They were trapped.

She moved to the center and gently set Dakota down.

"Keep pressure on that, Dakota." He'd used the last healing vile on her arm, so there was nothing she could do to help him right now. Not unless they got to safety.

She unwrapped the brown cloth from her sword as two brutes charged toward her. Anastasia screamed and slashed out with her sword, catching one of the Brutes in the leg with the sharp blade.

It howled in pain and fell to its knees, and Anastasia swung up again, taking the head clean off. The other Brute lunged at her, and she slid in the dirt beside it to duck beneath the blow.

She pushed back up quickly, driving the blade into the beast's back.

Three more Brutes attacked, but Anastasia held her ground, taking each of them down in turn.

"Ana, you have to go!" Dakota cried.

She did her best to ignore him. There was no fucking way she would leave him. His life was more important than her own.

"Why do you fight, baby bird?" a deep voice grumbled from the sideline.

"You will die," another Brute said.

Anastasia dodged another blow and stabbed upward, splattering herself with Brute blood as she slit its abdomen open.

Not able to get her sword up in time, Anastasia

blasted the closer Brutes with magic, sending their ashy remains floating on the breeze.

"Anyone else want a piece of me?" she screamed. "Come on, you fucking cowards!"

She wasn't sure what had changed, but her power seemed deeper now, more available than ever before, and she dove into it, letting the pool fill her up and absorb the rage hammering through her body.

She blasted two Brutes who stood on the sideline, and smiled when they disappeared. Oh, the power! She dove further down into the recesses of her mind, reaching for what would help her destroy them all.

"Ana!"

Dakota's voice brought her back to reality for a moment, and she turned to face him. Blood had pooled on the ground beneath him; he didn't have long. Their mission wasn't complete, though. Vincent still lived, and she wasn't leaving until he was dead.

Anastasia conjured a portal and walked to Dakota.

"Get help," she said softly.

"Let's go."

Anastasia closed her eyes, the power was calling to her, begging her to absorb it. "I can't go with you, Dakota."

"Ana, you can't stay." He winced as she helped him to his feet.

"I have no choice." She refused to take what she was feeling back to Terrenia.

"Who cares?" A voice whispered to her. *"You are power, they should revere you!"*

Two Brutes charged, and Anastasia spun to launch twin orbs of power at them both. *I will kill them all.*

"Go!" She flung Dakota into the light, then quickly closed the portal behind him, turning to stare at the enemies that still surrounded her.

"Come on, then," she beckoned them.

As they stepped toward her, slowly closing the circle, she allowed the rest of her power to seep into her consciousness, the good, the bad, the light, the dark; it didn't matter. Everything she had blazed through her now and she was unstoppable. *I am power*.

"There you are." Vincent appeared in front of her, pride alight in his silver-blue eyes.

She smiled slowly. "You made a mistake." Her voice sounded alien, even to her.

"Oh? And what was that?"

"Now I can kill you." Anastasia held up her palm. Vincent's eyes widened slightly. "You could try. But then you'd never be able to learn from me. Don't you feel that power, Anastasia? Think about how much more you could have!"

"She is useless, Vincent. Didn't I tell you that?" Mitch stepped up beside him, and Anastasia cocked her head to the side.

"Ah, here it is, just in time." Vincent shoved Mitch forward and crossed his arms. "A gift. For my niece."

"What the hell does that mean?" Mitch looked back at Vincent, then turned to face Anastasia, his eyes as wide as saucers.

Anastasia took a step closer to him. "Tell me, Mitch, are you afraid?" No longer feeling like herself, but better. As if there was nothing holding her back. How freeing it was to feel powerful! She could practically taste his fear on her tongue, and it was *delicious*.

"Of you? Please." He pulled a gun from the back of his pants and aimed it at her.

Anastasia laughed as she flung her hand out and the gun was ripped away from him. She moved her other hand, motioning to the ground, and Mitch was forced to his knees.

"Do you have any idea what you put me through?" she asked. "Even after I moved out, I was still terrified every single day." Anastasia moved around him and gripped his hair in her hand. His head yanked back and she looked into those horribly evil eyes. Eyes that had tormented her every single day for the last twenty-six years.

"What the hell do you think you're going to do to me?"

"I'm going to kill you." Anastasia brought him back to his feet. "Goodbye, Mitch." She shoved her hand against his chest. Power flowed through her palm into his body, and with a flash of light, he turned into ash.

She stared for a moment at her hand. Why didn't she feel anything?

"Want more?" Vincent took a step closer.

Anastasia continued staring down at her palm, then turned to face the Brutes behind her. Her eyes landed on the bloodstain where Dakota had been only moments before.

Dakota.

What had she done? Her power pulled back, making her feel empty, and Anastasia fell to her knees.

"No." Vincent scolded. "Get up!"

She was exhausted, completely and totally drained, and when she tried to use her power against Vincent, it barely made a scratch.

"No!" He howled in rage and raised both hands, lifting her into the air, then promptly dropping her body back onto the dirt. She scrambled for her sword, but it was just out of reach. "I will bring you back," he growled. He raised his fist and brought it swiftly down through the air, slamming her body flat against the ground.

10

TERRENIA

DAKOTA

Dakota hit something hard, then slid to the ground. The movement drove the bullet deeper into his torso and he bit down on the insides of his cheeks to keep from crying out.

"What the hell?" Tony hollered.

"Dakota!" Elizabeth exclaimed. "Oh, Dakota! You're bleeding! Tony I need my kit! It's over by the desk."

Dakota groaned as pain throbbed through his body. "Ana. We have to go back."

"What happened? Where's Anastasia?" Tony asked him as he returned with the black medical bag.

Elizabeth went to work on his wound, and she

shushed them both. “I need quiet. We can talk in a minute.”

Dakota’s vision began to waver, but he shook his head slightly.

“Dakota, hold still!” his mother yelled.

“Stay with us, Dakota,” Tony pleaded.

“Go get Tilly; I need an extra set of hands.”

Tony disappeared and Dakota tried to stay focused. The pain seared through his veins, causing his entire body to begin to shake.

“He’s going into shock.” A woman rushed over; had he heard her voice before? “Shit, he’s lost a lot of blood.”

“Mom.”

“Don’t you say anything to me, Dakota George. You aren’t going any damn where.”

Dakota smiled slightly and lay his head back.

“Let me take over, Elizabeth,” the woman said.

“Yes, I think that would be best.” Elizabeth moved aside to cradle Dakota’s head. “You better not die, Dakota George.”

“Tony, give him some of that whiskey,” Tilly instructed, and the room stayed quiet as she worked.

“Agh!” he cried out when something dove into the bullet wound.

“I’m sorry, Dakota, I have to get this bullet out. Tony, hold him down.”

Tony pressed down on Dakota, but when she did

whatever the hell it was she'd done again, he writhed in pain.

"I need more help! Elizabeth, grab Shane and Andrew."

"We need to hold him down, Lizzie," Tony shouted. Dakota's mother must not have moved. "Your boy is tough; I can't do it alone."

"Okay." His mother's voice was just above a whisper as she gingerly lay his head on the floor.

A door slammed somewhere far away. .

"Shit, this is deep. And what the hell's with those marks on his chest?" Tilly asked.

"Belt," Dakota ground out through clenched teeth.

"Here, boy. Drink." Tony held the bottle of whiskey to his lips and he took a drink.

"Not too much," Tilly chided. "Let's not thin the blood."

Dakota barely noted the burn in his throat from the alcohol, the sharp pain in his side nearly too much to bear. He'd been shot before—once, after responding to a call regarding a domestic dispute—but the bullet had gone straight through his shoulder, and he'd had anesthetic when they'd stitched him up. This was much worse. *This shit hurt like hell*. It felt like every single nerve in his body was on fire.

The door slammed open and Dakota looked over to see his mother rushing toward him, Shane and Andrew in tow. Shane's eyes pierced Dakota, a silent accusation in them.

"What do you need?" he asked Tony.

"I need you both to hold a leg. Tilly needs to get that bullet out."

Dakota felt the pressure of the two men on his legs, since Tony held down his chest.

Elizabeth kneeled, lifting his head back into her lap. Tears streaked down her cheeks. She pressed both hands to the sides of his face and smiled down at him.

"Okay, here we go," Tilly said.

Sharp pain ricocheted through his body, stemming from his abdomen, burning from the inside out, but with the men holding him down, and his own stubbornness, he managed to stay still enough that he heard the plink of something metal in a container.

"Got it," Tilly said.

Dakota closed his eyes.

"Thank you," Tony said.

"Let's get you stitched up." As Tilly set to work on the bullet's entry wound, Dakota began to drift. Thoughts of Ana flooded his mind as the pain pushed him into the black depths of unconsciousness.

11

ANASTASIA

Anastasia stood in the center of her stone prison, a chain around one ankle holding her in place. Anytime she tried to access her magic, it failed. A spark that wouldn't quite catch flame, but physically, she was ready.

Magic or no magic, she would destroy them all.

The door creaked as it opened, and Vincent stepped inside. He was alone, his face a grim portrayal of what was to come. He wanted to turn her, to make her dark like he was, but there was no way in hell she was going down that path—not again. The dark mark from killing Mitch still remained on her soul, she had no intention of making it larger.

Vincent's silver eyes narrowed on her face. "You look well."

"Unchain me and I'll show you just how well I feel," she shot back.

Vincent's chilling laughter filled the room. "I'm not an idiot, Niece. I have no intention of unchaining you."

"Then why the hell am I here?"

"I'm going to use you. Sooner or later you will turn; you'll have to in order to survive. And when you, do I'll be waiting with open arms."

The way he studied her wasn't human, his head cocked to the side in an unnatural angle and it gave her chills. How much of his soul had he sold?

"Unlikely. I would rather die."

The door flung open, and four Brutes stepped inside. Each one smiled darkly at her, hitting fists against open palms.

Anastasia laughed. "Is that supposed to scare me? How many times have I kicked Brute ass in the past?"

Vincent smiled. "That was quite different, wasn't it? With your magic and boy toy to back you up. Now you have neither."

"Who says I don't have my magic?"

"I blocked all magic but mine, Niece. I assure you, unless I choose to allow it, or you access everything you're capable of, you will be helpless."

Anastasia swallowed hard, but worked to conceal the fear from reaching her face.

Vincent turned to look behind him. "Do what you need to, but don't kill her—yet." He stepped back and the Brutes moved forward.

She blocked the first blow, a crushing fist that would have otherwise connected with her jaw. The second smashed into her side, and Anastasia spun to land a kick with her unchained leg.

"Baby bird has some fight," one Brute laughed and brought its meaty fist down on the top of her head.

Spots exploded in her vision and she crumpled to her knees, dazed. The blows continued coming, and she briefly caught a glimpse of Vincent, only, he wasn't Vincent anymore.

A tall man with pale skin and amethyst eyes stood in his place, a slick smile spread across his strong face.

Anastasia rolled onto her stomach and pulled her knees up to protect as much of herself as she could. Pain radiated from every part of her body, making it impossible to gauge where the agony was coming from.

Eventually the blows stopped, and she let out a shaky breath.

Vincent had returned and knelt in front of her. "You will break, Anastasia. One way or another."

She spat and blood splattered the ground before her. "Not. A. Fucking. Chance. I will die first."

"Then you will die. Either way, you pose no threat to me."

Silver eyes flashed amethyst and he disappeared.

"See you soon, baby bird," A Brute said as he landed one last kick before they turned to leave.

Anastasia rolled onto her back, desperately trying to catch her breath.

"Bring it on, you fucking bastard," she cried to her empty cage.

12

ANASTASIA

Anastasia opened her eyes to survey her surroundings. She stood in the center of a cluttered living room. A calico cat rubbed against her leg. She turned slowly around, her breath catching in her throat. An elderly woman stood in front of a large bookshelf. The woman's back was to her, but Anastasia saw the steel in her old bones with the way she carried herself.

"Have a seat, Anastasia." The old woman turned and smiled kindly. "I've been expecting you."

"I'm not even sure how I got here… or where *here* is." Anastasia took a seat at the small table. *Why didn't her body ache?* She'd just had the shit beaten out of her; shouldn't there be some form of physical proof?

As the woman continued busying herself by the bookshelf, Anastasia scanned the room. There was a fireplace in the center of one wall and floor-to-ceiling bookcases lined the other. A small hallway jutted off toward the back of the living area, with one doorway at the end. The woman cleared her throat, bringing Anastasia's attention back to the shelves.

The room was familiar to her, although she knew that she'd never set foot there before; at least, not that she could recall.

"I can sense your confusion. We will get to that." The woman turned to smile at her again, and Anastasia was comforted when she looked into her hazel eyes. "I'm Carmen, and it is lovely to see you again."

"I don't understand. I don't think we have ever met."

"Sure we have." Carmen took a seat in a rocker near the fire and removed her glasses. "Although, I doubt you would remember. You were but a baby when your parents brought you here."

"Gregory and Annabelle."

"Yes." The woman's mouth tightened and her eyes softened at the sound of Anastasia's parents' names.

"How did I get here?"

"I brought you here."

"How?"

"How else?" she asked, amusement sparkling in her eyes.

Anastasia narrowed her gaze. “Magic?”

“There you go.” She smiled again.

“Why?”

“You need strength.”

Anastasia nodded. She knew that she was in over her head now. Honestly, she had been since the day she had been born.

“You sent Dakota away and stayed behind.”

“He would have died.”

“You could have gone with him.”

Anastasia shook her head. “I had to stay behind and try to take out Vincent.”

“There is no shame in surviving to fight another day, Anastasia.”

The words cut deep to her soul. She hadn’t gone with Dakota because she’d felt herself slipping away. What if she’d already been too far-gone?

“He is your light, my dear, and without light, we all will wander into the darkness.”

“Just as Vincent did?”

“Vincent is another story. There is a lot more at work here than light versus dark.”

She remembered what Vincent had said about there only being power and more power.

“Coffee?”

Anastasia’s eyes widened and Carmen laughed. “Your father once brought me quite the stash from his trip to your world. I have been saving a small amount for this day in particular."

"You knew him well?"

"I would say so." She laughed and went about grinding some beans. "Your parents came to me when you were but six months old. They urged me to help them defeat Vincent, but I warned them against it."

"Why?"

"Because it was not their duty to bear. It was yours."

Anastasia stared blankly, and she laughed softly. "I wouldn't have wished it on you either, child, but fate always finds a way of working itself out, and had they gone after him, they would have died quite a bit sooner."

She steeped the hot water through the beans and added some sugar.

"You're the Seer."

The woman laughed. "No. I just know that once something has been seen, it rarely can be changed." Carmen carried the mugs over and handed one to Anastasia. "I once delved into the depth of my power for revenge," she began. "You see, it is not the power that turns a soul black, but rather what that power is used for. Just like a person without magic may murder, but they were not *born* a murderer. We all make choices, and those choices have consequences."

Anastasia took a sip from her coffee, but she couldn't taste it. Was this a dream?

“I was about your age when it happened.”

“What happened?”

Carmen took a drink from her coffee and Anastasia noted the unshed tears in her eyes.

“One evening, a man from the local village came to my cottage. He said that there was an urgent matter and that they needed my help. It caught me by surprise because the villagers had always kept their distance from me, afraid of the power I possessed.

“Naturally, I jumped at the opportunity to show them I was not as they feared, so I kissed my husband goodbye and headed out the door. When I reached the village, I was surprised to see that there weren’t as many people in the streets as there usually were, but I assumed that it was because of the emergency the man had told me about.”

She paused, and Anastasia saw the difficulty she had with retelling the story. “It was when we got to the center of town that I realized I had been tricked. I turned to see that they were dragging my husband in as well and that he had been badly injured. The villagers began accusing me of being a dark sorceress. They offered a trade: my life willingly, or they would kill my husband. I agreed immediately, and they dropped him and came for me.

“I let them come, let them tie me up, and I awaited my sentence as I begged for mercy and pleaded my case to them. I had never hurt anyone—with my magic, or otherwise. I promised that we would leave, that they would never see us again. I promised them whatever I thought they might want to hear. But none of it worked.

"Then the man who came for me told me that he was disgusted with 'my kind' and that we were an 'abomination'. He pulled a knife from his waist and slit my husband's throat. I was forced to watch him die in front of me."

Carmen's wrinkled hands shook, and she set her mug on the small table in front of her. "I lost my mind, and before I knew it, I felt the depth of my power flowing through my veins. I decimated that town, killed every man who had stood in front of me, judging me for what I had not done. They were the *abominations*."

The anger in her voice had Anastasia balling her fists. How she wished she could go back and help this woman get vengeance for her husband, kill those assholes all over again.

"I knelt next to my husband and held him while blinding rage hummed in my veins. I wanted more blood, more power, and I was willing to do whatever was necessary to get it."

"What brought you back?"

Carmen smiled now. It was hollow, but Anastasia saw the light in her eyes as she thought back.

"My daughter."

"You had a child."

"Not yet. With the excess power in my blood I

began feeling something more—a life force, almost. It's the only way I can explain it. I felt her growing inside of me, her innocence, and she became my light. I pulled out from the power and promised my husband that I would raise her to make him proud, and that's what I did."

"Did she have magic?"

"Thankfully, no, she did not take after me in that aspect. Although, it seemed her heritage had her seeking out the power anyway."

"Seeking it? How so?"

"She married into it."

"Is she still alive?"

Carmen shook her head sadly. "Vincent killed her, and a woman by the name of Ophelia killed her husband. I think you know that name quite well."

"Wait—" Anastasia set her mug aside. "What are you saying?"

"That I know what you're going through, and that you aren't alone."

"Annabelle was your daughter?"

Carmen nodded sadly.

"But that would make you my—"

"Grandmother," she said strongly, her back straightening in her chair.

Anastasia didn't know what to feel. She was ecstatic that she had family that was still alive. She wasn't alone; there was someone here who understood what she was becoming and what she was capable of, yet a part of her was still confused as to how Carmen had found her in the first place.

"When your parents brought you here, and they asked me to help them defeat Vincent, I opened myself, and I felt the power within you, child. It is incredible what you are capable of, and I imagine you could spend an entire lifetime exploring it and still hardly scratch the surface."

"Why? How did I get so powerful?"

"Destiny is a funny thing. You were given the gifts you need in order to succeed in yours."

"But why me?"

"Why are any of us chosen for certain tasks? We may never know, but that doesn't take away from the fact that this is your destiny, child, and you are more than capable of achieving it. You only have to believe."

"How am I even talking to you now?" She searched for her last memory, and it was in the clearing when Vincent had slammed her in the dirt.

"You are trapped. I was able to free your mind temporarily, but my magic won't hold you much longer. I fear that Vincent has realized something is off."

Anastasia began to notice the strain Carmen was under. "We don't have much time. You have to fight, Anastasia. Do not give up. We will find you." She faded away, leaving nothing but darkness in her wake.

13

ANASTASIA

Her breath came out in puffs as the chill dug further into her body. Beating her wasn't working, so Vincent had resorted to freezing her to death.

Truth was, she missed the beatings. At least they were followed by some sort of numbness as her magic healed herself.

He had managed to keep her power from coming to the surface, but to his dismay it was still keeping her alive. Anastasia wasn't sure why the hell he hadn't just killed her, but as day after day passed, she wondered if for some reason he wasn't able to.

What other explanation was there?

The door to her prison opened and two men stepped

in. "Still alive!" one of them called back down the hall. "Man, you're a tough one, aren't you?" He knelt in front of her and ran a finger down her cheek. She growled, and he laughed. "What I wouldn't give to go a few rounds with you; I bet you're a hellcat in the sack."

"Touch her and I'll skin you where you stand," Vincent said from the doorway.

The man's eyes widened and he got to his feet. "Yes, Master, of course. I was only attempting to get in her head."

"Better yet, perhaps I let her magic loose and she can do the honors." Vincent stepped closer and the man crumpled to his knees. His hands flew to his tattooed throat as he gasped for air.

"You really going to kill him because of a *threat?* Please, you'd have no one left." Her teeth clattered as she spoke, and it pissed her off further. She hated the idea of him knowing one of his methods affected her.

"Fair point." Vincent released the man from whatever magic he was using, and the asshat scrambled to his feet.

"Thank you, Master. Your mercy is appreciated."

Vincent shrugged. "Don't expect it next time."

The man nodded and all but ran out the door.

"So, what's the plan for today? Beat me some more? Turn on the heat? Honestly, I could use a change." She stretched and forced herself to stand. She may have been bruised, but she was far from broken.

Vincent studied her. "Truthfully, I'm impressed, but there are certain things even you cannot withstand. It may take me some time, but I will find them."

Anastasia made a spectacle of rolling her eyes.

The door opened and Vincent turned. "Just in time."

A Brute walked in carrying a long whip, and Anastasia's eyes widened. *This was new.*

"Afraid?" the beast asked her.

"Of a glorified belt? I've had worse."

Vincent's temper flared and his eyes flashed amethyst. "You will break, child. I will see to it."

"Unlikely."

He raised his hand and Anastasia's arms shot above her head. A chain wrapped around them, holding her in a standing position that had every muscle in her body screaming in agony. "Do your worst," he instructed, and left the room.

"So, what do you have for me today?" She put on a brave face, terrified of letting the monster see the fear that had beat out the cold.

"Pain," it said with a smile.

14

ANASTASIA

Water dropped onto the floor somewhere in the room, a consistent sound that grated on every nerve in her body, each fucking drip like nails on a chalkboard to her now.

The sound was nearly as torturous as the pain they inflicted on her day after day. Blood ran down her arm, dripping into the puddle on the ground, and she closed her eyes. With her arms chained above her, there was no way to stop the noise, or to fight back. The whipping had truly been unlike anything she'd ever felt, and eventually the pain disappeared and her body went numb.

She was beginning to doubt how long she would be able to hold out. The pool of power beckoning to her was becoming more and more alluring with each passing day, but when she tried to reach it, the thought of Dakota pulled her back.

If she turned, there would be no future. If she died, there was no future.

Her situation was the epitome of a rock and a hard place.

The thudding of footsteps caught her attention, and Anastasia forced herself to get up from her knees, determined to appear strong even though she was anything but. They had nearly broken her, but they had not succeeded yet.

They would not succeed.

Even if they killed her.

"How's our esteemed guest doing?" Vincent stepped inside the tiny, damp room, a smug smile on his face.

"Just fucking peachy," Anastasia said through clenched teeth.

"Seems we haven't beaten that mouth off of you yet." He stepped closer and shook the chains holding her hands above her head. She bit down on the inside of her cheek to keep herself from crying out at the pain it caused. "Not to worry; I have something extra special planned for you today."

His eyes bore into hers, the black of his pupils nearly covering all of the silver.

"What's that? You going to talk me to death? Or send your blood hounds in here to beat me into submission some more?"

Vincent let out a laugh. "If you would only agree to join me, this wouldn't be necessary. Be glad I haven't just killed you." His eyes flashed blue for an instant, and then back to silver.

"What's with your weird ass eyes? Black soul doing that to you?"

He glared at her, and for a moment she wondered if he was going to hit her. As of now, he'd only ever sent his Brutes in to do the dirty work.

"Bring him in," he called over his shoulder.

Anastasia straightened. *Oh no, no, no, please don't let him have come for me.* Surely Dakota was still in Terrenia. How the hell would he have gotten here? Or had Vincent trapped him?

Two Brutes bearing giant bones through their noses, carried in a body between them. They each held an arm, and there was a hood on the person's head. Same build as Dakota, and he had tattoos peeking out from his bicep just like her love did.

Fuck, please no. She nearly screamed it, but bit back. She would not show fear, and when she got out of here, there would be no mercy for her captor.

The Brutes tossed their hostage to the ground at her feet and Vincent pulled the bag off his head.

"No!" she screamed, her earlier promise to not show fear forgotten.

"Ana," Dakota choked out. His face had been badly beaten—bruises and cuts marred the surface, and his eyes were nearly swollen shut. Vincent kicked his back, and he crumbled to the ground on his stomach.

"You bastard!" She yanked at her chains until fresh blood dripped down her arms from new gashes in her wrists.

"I told you that you would join me—willingly or otherwise. I *will* break you." He growled the last words and pulled out a blade from his waist.

Vincent gripped a handful of Dakota's hair and whipped his head back, exposing his throat.

"No, please don't," she cried. Pain gripped her chest, tightening a vise around her heart. "Dakota," she cried, willing him to fight back.

"You will obey me, Anastasia. Or this will be just the beginning." He pressed the edge of the blade against the skin of Dakota's neck and a drop of blood welled up on the surface.

"Stop!"

"Stop me, Anastasia! Use your power to save him!"

"I can't," she cried. She tried to access the power in her blood, but nothing came to the surface. Her body was too exhausted from trying to heal itself.

"Too bad," Vincent sneered, then drew the blade across Dakota's throat.

"No!" Anastasia screamed and yanked against her chains as she watched him bleed to death on the ground.

The shape below her began to shift, morphing from dark brown hair to ashy blond, from tanned skin to pale.

The body shifted from Dakota's strong build to a wiry, thinner frame until Dakota no longer lay dying in a puddle of his own blood.

Instead, a stranger lay dead at her feet.

Anastasia gasped, searching the room for Dakota.

"Oh, not yet, my dear." Vincent laughed. "Although that was fun."

"You fucking monster!" She lunged for him, but he was just out of reach. "I will kill you!"

"Unlikely." He gestured to the two Brutes waiting off to the side. "Get him out of here."

Anastasia watched in horror as they dragged the body from the room. Relief filled her chest with warmth even as guilt pushed her stomach to the floor. That man wasn't Dakota, but he hadn't deserved to die just so Vincent could torture her. His death was senseless and cruel.

But it wasn't Dakota, and she clung to that fact.

"You will use your power, Anastasia. Sooner or later, you will. Or I will kill hundreds of Dakotas in front of you before finally slaughtering the real one."

He stepped from the room and flipped off the light, leaving her alone in her prison.

15

TERRENIA

DAKOTA

"We have to find her, Tony." Dakota began to pace the small cottage. A week had passed since Anastasia sent him through the portal. He couldn't get the image of her standing in that clearing surrounded by Brutes out of his head. When she smiled at him, he'd seen her, but he could see she's only been hanging on by a thread.

"You think I don't know that? She is like a daughter to me. We will find her, but it has to be the right way. He will kill you; do you not understand that?" Tony shouted.

"What the fuck does it matter, Tony? Anastasia is gone!" Shane yelled from the counter. "None of this matters without her."

For once, Dakota agreed with the jealous bastard. “There has to be a way to get back to Seattle. Are there no more of those vials?”

Tony shook his head. “We’ve searched everywhere. There are no more.”

“Fuck.”

“We wouldn’t be in this predicament if I’d just gone,” Shane growled.

Dakota glared at him. “Excuse me?”

“You heard me.”

“Boys!” Elizabeth hollered.

Dakota continued to stare at Shane. “You have no fucking clue how much she means to me.”

“You think I don’t love her, too?”

“Then how about you stop attacking me, and we find a way to bring her home.”

Shane’s jaw twitched. “Fine.”

“So, first step, how do we get to Seattle?” Elizabeth asked.

A portal opened and they stared in surprise;. the familiar swirling blue light gave Dakota hope. Maybe she was coming back! The room filled with a bright light, but instead of Ana, an older woman stepped out, carrying a cat and a small bag.

“This must be where I come in handy,” she said as she surveyed the room.

“Who are you?” Shane asked.

"Carmen," Tony said, stepping forward to greet the old woman. He crossed the room quickly and wrapped his arms around her. "Been a long time."

"Too long, Tony." She smiled and hugged him warmly.

"I'm so sorry about—"

"It's okay, Tony." She patted him lightly on the arm. "I know that you did what you could."

Tony turned to face them. "Elizabeth, Dakota, Shane, this is Carmen. She is Annabelle's mother and Anastasia's grandmother." He turned, looking down at her. "And I do believe you showed up at the perfect time."

"You know what's happened, then?" Shane asked.

She nodded. "I spoke with Anastasia for a bit in a dream."

"You can talk to her?" Hope surged through Dakota again.

She shook her head, crushing Dakota's optimism. "Vincent has since blocked me."

"But you can open portals?"

She nodded. "That I can."

"Can you send me back to Seattle?"

"And me?" Shane stepped forward.

"It would be futile, as Anastasia is no longer being kept in Seattle."

"Where is she?"

"I'm not sure, but that was the first place I checked. I cannot sense her there."

"Sense her?" Shane asked.

"I've tried to get a read on her, but he's put up blocks against my magic." She said.

"Is it possible she is in Seattle, then?" Tony asked. "And that you just can't sense her?"

"No, she is not there. Honestly, I don't sense any magic there anymore. Whatever Vincent is doing, he is no longer using his power to do it."

Someone screamed outside, and they ran out into the hot sun. Villagers scattered, racing toward their houses, and Dakota bolted to Andrew who was leading a group of children inside a cottage.

"What's happening?"

"We're under attack." He spoke quickly and released the children to the woman who was inside before turning and running back to the gate.

Dakota looked toward the gate and swallowed hard. A handful of Brutes stomped through the trees toward them. "Let them fucking come." The need to take his rage out on something overwhelmed him and he drew his blade.

Shane and the other Fighters did the same, bracing for the attack.

Dakota lunged for the nearest beast. Using all his strength, he sliced across the beast's stomach, then swiftly brought the blade down on its neck. It crumpled to the ground, and he turned just in time to see a Brute sneaking up on Shane. He charged, driving his sword into flesh, then watched the beast fall to the ground.

Dakota and Shane fought side by side—two men who lost someone they loved—with a vengeance. As if somehow, the clashing of blades could bring Ana back.

"Agh!" Andrew yelled.

Dakota looked over as a Brute wrapped its fat hand around the Fighter's neck.

Shane reached Andrew first, throwing his body weight into the monster before driving his blade through the skull.

"Thanks," Andrew said.

Dakota pulled him to his feet. They looked around to see Fighters ready for another attack.

The Brutes lay dead on the ground, and yet Dakota felt no sense of satisfaction. "We need to get these bodies burned," he told them, and they went to work stacking the dead.

DAKOTA SAT ON THE SENTRY TOWER STARING OUT AT the darkening sky. The whiskey in his glass was doing little to dull the ache in his heart, but shit, he had to try.

What else was there?

Someone began the ascent on the ladder, and Dakota turned as Shane climbed over the ledge.

"Want some company?" he asked.

Dakota shrugged. The tower shifted slightly with the extra weight, then Shane stood beside him.

"You fought well today." The other man held up a bottle he'd carried, and Dakota held out his glass.

"Thanks. You too."

"I've been training my entire life with a blade. Is that what you use back in Seattle as well?"

"No, we use guns."

"Guns? Those things in the crates Vincent was bringing through?"

Dakota nodded.

"Fascinating." Shane paused, taking a sip of his drink. "Listen, I apologize for the way I've acted toward you." Shane took a drink from his cup.

"I get it; you are in love with Ana."

"I am. Have been for a long time. For about a year, I thought she loved me, too. As it turned out, she never did."

Dakota stayed silent, not wanting to interrupt.

"Every time we were together, I knew her mind was somewhere else. And it hurt. Then, seeing you here with her was another kind of pain. She looks at you the way I'd always wanted her to look at me."

"I'm sorry."

Shane drank deeply and shrugged. “The only thing that matters is getting her back.”

“Agreed.”

“Until then…” Shane held up his cup. “We kick the asses of as many Brutes as we can.”

“I’ll cheers to that.” The two men clinked cups, and went back to sitting in silence.

16

ONE MONTH LATER

ANASTASIA

Time no longer held meaning. Hours blended into days, and days into weeks, and nothing but unending darkness surrounded her. She couldn't even remember what it felt like to stand in the sunshine; what did a breeze feel like as it brushed her hair back?

The dampness of the room seeped into her bones, and the chill made it so she couldn't feel the warmth of her own blood. Anastasia wasn't even sure she was alive anymore. On some level, she hoped she wasn't.

But at least the fucking dripping had stopped.

They had stripped her clothing from her, allowing her only the bra and underwear she'd been wearing when they had taken her.

Her mouth was dry and her lips cracked from the lack of water. Her stomach burned with a hunger that she knew would never be sated. At least it was a *feeling,* something to indicate she was still alive; but was that a good thing?

The door to her prison scraped as it opened, and she bit back a scream, not willing to show any emotion. The Brutes had come for her again, just as she knew they would. Was it possible that this was the end?

They pulled her to her feet, the fingers on their large hands biting into her raw skin. They enjoyed causing her pain. So far, she had been able to push through the torture, but one question stood out in her mind as they pulled her down the hallway now: would she survive it this time?

"We have good plans for you, baby bird."

The large Brute to her left grunted. "Big plans," it repeated.

"Are you ready for some fun?" the other asked as it dragged her down the hall.

She tried searching for any clue as to where she was being held, but it was simply a concrete hall that could have been anywhere in the world.

They tossed her into a room and she fell to the ground, scraping wobbly knees that were already marred with cuts and bruises.

Vincent stared down at her, disgusted. "You look like shit." The edges of his irises turned an odd shade of blue. "Why are you making me do this?" he screamed. "I don't want to hurt her!"

Anastasia coughed, and eyed him suspiciously. *Her?* "Then stop and let me go."

He stared down at her and his eyes returned to silver. "Not a chance." He waved his hand and a portal appeared.

"Where are you taking me?" Would he take her back to Terrenia? Maybe she could finally escape!

He grinned down at her. "Don't get your hopes up. There are more worlds out there than this one and Terrenia." He looked up at the Brutes. "You know what to do."

They wrapped their large hands around her biceps.

"Vincent!" she screamed loudly as they carried her toward the light. "I will be back!"

The beasts stepped into the portal and Anastasia felt herself being carried away. To where—she had no idea.

But it wasn't like things could get any worse.

17

TERRENIA

DAKOTA

A month had passed since Ana sent him to Terrenia alone, and they still had no leads. Not one fucking shred of evidence as to what had happened to her. Where the hell was she?

Although they hadn't given up hope that they would locate her, some of the villagers didn't believe she could be rescued even if they did find her. Rumors that The Phoenix had gone dark floated throughout the village, driving Dakota insane.

Ana would never go dark.

"It's going to take time, Dakota," Carmen assured him as he continued pacing the floor in the small cottage.

"It's been almost a month," he snapped. "Why can't

we find her?"

"I told you, Vincent is blocking her. Although his magic is strong, it is not nearly as practiced as mine. He will slip up, and when he does, you will be the first to know." Carmen lightly touched his shoulder.

He looked down at the aging woman and smiled lightly. Ana looked so much like her grandmother. She was strong, and there was still hope lighting up her hazel eyes. There was no doubt in her mind that they would find and rescue her granddaughter, and Dakota allowed himself some hope. If Carmen was this confident, he could be too.

When they found Ana, they would put an end to this war, once and for all.

"Dakota, we need you." Tony opened the door to the small cottage and peered inside.

"Coming. Let me know if you find anything."

"You know I will," Carmen said as she took a seat at her table.

"How is the tracking going?" Tony asked as soon as they were outside. He was trying to be strong for his people, but Dakota knew that deep down he was just as scared that they may never find Anastasia.

"Nothing yet." He shook his head as they walked the short distance back to the village. "Why hasn't she opened another portal and come home?" he whispered loudly to Tony.

"Carmen said that Vincent is blocking her, correct?"

Dakota nodded.

"Then he may have her somewhere she can't use her magic. He could be blocking her powers just the same as he is keeping us from tracking her."

Tony's reply did little to soothe the growing fear in Dakota's chest. Deep in his bones, he knew they had to find her soon, or they may never get her back, and that was something he wouldn't survive. Hell, none of them would. Without Ana, they didn't stand a chance against the dark. Without her, no one else held the power that would be needed to end this war… not even Carmen.

Even now, the evidence of Vincent's destruction of this world was visible. Plants were not nearly as vibrant in color as they had been, dying off as if they were in the middle of a drought.

The last scouting mission had recovered a slew of dead animals, although their bodies showed no visible sign of injury.

Terrenia was dying, and soon there would be nothing left for them to save.

They walked into Tony's cottage, which had become the new headquarters for the war. Maps hung on the walls with markings and pins tracking where the Brutes were moving in this dimension, as well as where they had been in Seattle. Dakota's best guess was that they were continuing to bring more weapons through, and it seemed as though the more Brutes they took down, the more they just continued to pour into Terrenia.

"There's been an attack at one of our outposts." Brady came through the door directly behind them. He was covered in dirt and bruises, and Dakota gave him a quick once-over to make sure there were no severe wounds.

"Shit," Tony cursed, turning to the map of Terrenia. "Where?"

Brady stepped past him and pointed to a spot just east of the village. "The scouts must have not even seen it coming. When we arrived to get the activity report, there was no one left. We ran into a few Brutes on our way out, but none of our people were there."

"Shit," Dakota said, repeating Tony's response. "We have to develop some sort of advanced warning. Man, what I wouldn't give for an alarm system and some electricity right about now."

"Alarm system?" Tony asked.

"Back where I come from, people can install alarms in their houses, so if anyone enters who isn't supposed to be there, the alarm goes off, alerting anyone who might be inside. They can even be set up to notify the police."

"That would definitely be helpful," Tony agreed.

Terrenia had no power or running water, something that had taken some adjusting at first, but now Dakota found that he'd grown accustomed to and rather enjoyed the silence that surrounded the village. There were no bright lights to drown out the view of the stars, no traffic noise or horns blaring from the cars of angry drivers.

The door opened and they turned as Shane stepped inside. Over the last month, Dakota had grown to respect him, despite the fact they were both in love with the same woman.

"We've got a large grouping of Brutes making their way through the east side of the forest.

"Fuck," Tony cursed as he ran a hand through his hair. "They looking to head this way?"

"Not sure. They're carrying some large crates and have a few hostages they must've picked up on the way. Should we engage?"

"How many is a large grouping?" Tony wondered.

"Enough that we'll need triple the man power of my current team."

Tony considered. "Let's wait it out. If they head this way, we can take them out, but I'm worried removing that number of Fighters from the village will limit our options if we're attacked."

"You got it." Shane stepped back outside and Tony turned back to the map.

Over the last month, the Brutes had moved closer to Terrenia than ever before. It was making them all nervous, especially since they hadn't attacked yet. Dakota wondered just what in the hell they were waiting for.

18

ANASTASIA

Anastasia rolled over and opened her eyes. Sunlight shone through the windows, and she squinted as she sat up. She was surprised when her muscles didn't scream in protest. Last she remembered, she had been the owner of multiple broken bones, and yet she didn't feel any pain as she moved.

She was lying on a large bed in a bedroom she didn't recognize. A dark brown dresser was across from her, and as she sat up, she caught her reflection in the mirror. Her hair was mussed from sleep, but her eyes were clear, and no bruises or cuts marred her face.

She stood and made her way closer to the mirror to peer deeper at her reflection. Nothing. No sign of the torture she'd endured for countless days. Her eyes traveled down, and she lifted a pearl-adorned photo frame from the dresser.

"What in the hell?" Anastasia murmured as she looked down at the smiling faces staring back at her.

In the photo, she stood beside Dakota wearing a long, white wedding dress. Dakota was in a tux, smiling down at her. She searched the faces of the people surrounding them in the photograph and found his parents, then her eyes landed on the smiling faces of her own parents—Gregory and Annabelle.

She slammed the frame face down on the dresser and squeezed her eyes shut as emotion tightened her throat. *This is not real.* Was this some kind of game? A new type of torture? Dangle exactly what she'd always wanted right in front of her, only to rip it away?

Vincent was getting creative, she'd give him that.

Not wanting to see anymore false truths, Anastasia forced her eyes away from the other photographs, and moved to the window. She looked down and sucked in breath. She would have recognized this street anywhere.

She was in Dakota's parents' house, wearing her favorite pair of worn-out pajama pants. Pants that Dakota bought her for Christmas when they were in high school. Back before war had torn her away from this world and thrust her into another.

"Momma!"

Anastasia turned around as a little girl charged into

the room, flinging herself at her. The small child gripped her leg, and Anastasia knelt, more confused than ever.

Momma? Anastasia frowned. Surely this little girl wasn't talking to her.

"I'm so glad you're awake, Momma." She smiled, and Anastasia saw herself in the little girl's eyes, Dakota in her goofy grin. "Daddy said that we could have pancakes this morning! Come on, he is making them now!"

Slowly and disbelievingly, Anastasia followed the small girl down the stairs. The wall was lined with photographs of her and Dakota, as well as this mystery child. Was this it? Had she died, and this was her Heaven? Maybe she wasn't being punished after all—this seemed like a pretty great place so far.

"There are my girls." Dakota, wearing plaid pajama pants and a dark T-shirt, turned to face them. His face was clean shaven, his eyes the brightest shade of blue she'd ever seen. "I was wondering when you were going to get up, sleeping beauty." He crossed the floor and pulled her in for a quick kiss. The coolness of his lips against hers felt alien, though, not quite matching what she was used to. "Annabelle, go and make your bed. Breakfast will be done soon." He kissed the little girl on the cheek loudly, and she turned to run off to her room.

When he turned back to Anastasia, she wrapped her arms around him. Even if this wasn't real, and she really was dead, or Vincent had finally discovered the ultimate way to torture her, at least she got to hold Dakota again. He wrapped his strong arms around her, and kissed the top of her head. She breathed deeply; the pine-scented aftershave he wore filled her lungs.

After a moment, she pulled away.

"What is going on?" It was the first thing she had been able to say. Her heart ached, and her brain insisted that none of this was real.

"What do you mean? Are you all right?" Dakota's brows drew together, and he set down the mixing bowl he had picked up.

"This can't be real."

"Ana, what's not real?"

Her eyes filled with tears. "This, Dakota, all of this!" She gestured to the house and the pictures that hung on the walls in the kitchen.

"Honey, what's wrong?"

"I don't know. Last night I was in a dark, cold prison. I was injured and not even sure I was alive anymore, and then this morning, I wake up here. With you… and her." She gestured toward the hall where Annabelle had disappeared. "It can't be real."

Dakota shook his head slowly. "You had the nightmare again. Ana, I keep telling you, if they scare you, then don't write about them. Making them come to life like that is only going to make things worse for you." He wrapped his arms around her again and lightly kissed her forehead.

"Write about them? What are you talking about?" She pushed away and backed toward the wall.

"The monsters in your books—the Brutes, as you call them."

She shook her head frantically. "No, it all happened. It's real," Anastasia insisted.

"No, it didn't. Come here, baby, I'll show you." He reached for her, and she cautiously took his hand and followed him down a hall and into a small office.

Anastasia stepped into the room and turned. "Oh my God." The walls were littered with sketches of Brutes and Kaley. A timeline covered one whole wall, sticky notes with different events mapped out. She leaned in closer.

'MC sacrifices herself for 2nd MC. She is captured and tortured' was written on an orange sticky note next to a sketch of a woman who looked alarmingly like herself.

'Brute force attacks a small village and takes captives' was written on a blue sticky note next to a drawing of a Brute.

Dakota cleared his throat, interrupting her thoughts. "You've been writing about them for about a year now. Your first book was a bestseller, so you dove back in, ready for another." He spoke the words calmly, as if rehearsed. As if he'd said them to her before. "Every now and then, you have these episodes where your brain mistakes the events in your book for reality."

She turned to face him and could see the truth in his eyes. He believed everything he was telling her—didn't that make it true?

"Daddy, the pancakes are burning!" Annabelle yelled from the kitchen.

"Oh, crap!" He laughed. "Pancakes are your specialty, not mine." He grinned and turned for the kitchen.

Anastasia's brow furrowed. She didn't cook, did she?

Anastasia walked closer to the timeline board. She ran her fingers over the sticky note that read *'loses love to the Brutes and goes for revenge*'. Could all of that have just been a nightmare? Could what Dakota was saying be true? Her heart wanted desperately to believe it, but a voice inside her head screamed for her attention.

"Mommy?"

She turned toward Annabelle standing in the doorway. "Hi." She knelt in front of the girl and smiled softly. "What is it?"

"Do you remember me?"

Her words were a punch in the heart, so she lied. "Of course I remember you, Annabelle! How could I ever forget such a perfect little girl?"

Annabelle smiled and wrapped her arms around Anastasia's neck. "Just making sure."

She followed the little girl back into the kitchen and

sat next to her at a tall dining room table. Dakota set the platter of pancakes in the center of the table, and a plate with eggs over medium, just the way she liked them, in front of Anastasia.

"This is delicious, Daddy!" Annabelle grinned and scooped up a mouthful of scrambled eggs.

"Thank you, honey, now don't talk with your mouth full." He winked, and Annabelle giggled, small pieces of egg falling from her mouth.

Anastasia took her first bite of pancake, and the taste exploded on her tongue. Had she ever tasted anything so delicious? She ate quickly and cleaned her plate, even having thirds of the maple syrup covered pancakes. The fact that she could taste them was another checkmark in the 'this is real' box. If it were a dream, there would be no flavor.

Right?

LATER THAT MORNING, DAKOTA CAME DOWN THE STAIRS dressed in scrubs. Anastasia's mind fought against the image. He had never become a doctor. He was a detective. Hadn't he followed in his father's footsteps rather than his mother's?

"I should be home from work around five." He smiled and pulled Anastasia in for a kiss.

"Gross!" Annabelle laughed and made a silly face that had all three of them giggling.

"Okay, now, we get it." Dakota smiled at her. "Six and going on sixteen, huh?" he asked her, and then reached for her hand.

"Bye, Mommy! I'll see you after school. I love you so much!"

"I love you, too." It was her voice, but somehow felt like someone else's words. She reached down to accept a hug and then watched as they made their way down the driveway.

Anastasia walked back into the house and took a deep breath. The scent of jasmine and vanilla filled her lungs. It smelled like home to her, and yet she was almost positive it wasn't. Dishes filled the sink from breakfast and Anastasia headed over to wash them.

Once she'd loaded and started the dishwasher, she made her way back upstairs and walked down the hall into Annabelle's room. Pictures that the little girl had drawn covered the walls.

She lifted a small frame holding a photo of the three of them at the zoo, and caught herself smiling. If she focused hard enough—she could almost remember that day, but it was foggy. Like a dream that you couldn't quite recall.

Her brain shouted at her, telling her not to be fooled, that none of this was real, but she pushed the voice down.

She gently set the photo back where she'd found it, and turned to leave the room. A reflection in the dresser mirror caught her eye, and she jumped back.

Before her stood a warrior. Bloody, bruised, and dirty; a sword glinted in her hand. The Anastasia in the mirror reached for her, and she backed away. She closed her eyes and shook her head. Dakota told her it was only a dream based on the book she was writing. As long as she continued believing that, then maybe this horrible sinking feeling in her stomach would disappear, and everything would begin to feel normal.

Unless this was Vincent all over again.

When she slowly opened her eyes, she breathed a sigh of relief when a regular reflection looked back at her. Her face was clean and bruise-free, and she wore her pajama pants and a clean white T-shirt.

"Is this you, Vincent?" She screamed into the empty house. "Just another one of your fucking mind games?" Anastasia punched the mirror in front of her and the glass shattered.

"Fuck!" She pulled her hand back and looked down at the broken skin. Her knuckles throbbed. That certainly *felt* real. "Agh!" she screamed. Cradling her bleeding hand, she made her way downstairs.

If all of this was real, if everything she'd ever known as her reality was really fiction, then why did she still feel like everything was going to fall apart?

19

TERRENIA

DAKOTA

Dakota stared down at his hand-drawn map and nursed his cup of Terrenian whiskey. The Brutes had moved past them quickly and headed toward the mountains. What the hell were they doing? Gathering more weapons?

As far as he knew, no other villages had been attacked recently. Which, according to Tony, was the longest time between attacks this world had seen in recent years.

So, what was the game plan, exactly?

Dakota turned when a knock sounded against the wood of the door. “Come in.”

“Hey, honey.” His mom stepped into the living room

of his cottage and shut the door gently behind her. "How's it going?"

Dakota took another drink. "It's going. Just trying to figure out what game Vincent is playing."

She took a seat next to him at the table. "When was the last time you got some sleep?" Just as she had when he'd been young, she fussed with his hair.

"I'm fine, Mom."

She eyed him. "You and I both know that isn't true." She got to her feet and walked into the kitchen. "Tea?"

"Sure."

Dakota went back to staring at the map as his mom began heating water over the fire still burning from his dinner.

"Any news from Carmen?" she asked.

He shook his head. "She still can't sense Ana."

"We will find her, honey." His mother came to stand beside him.

"Let's just hope it's not another five years before we do."

After a few moments of silence, his mom set a steaming mug in front of him.

"Anastasia is one of the toughest, bravest people I have ever met, and I know that she is going to be just fine. You have to give it the time that is needed to formulate a good plan, and on top of that, you have got to get some rest. You will be no good if we find her unless you've slept."

Another knock at the door and Dakota called, “Come in.” Seemed his house was the popular place tonight.

“Can I come in?” Tony peeked through the door and Dakota’s mom smiled and waved him in.

“Of course. I was just making some tea, would you like some?”

“That would be wonderful, thank you.” Tony smiled, and his mom blushed.

Dakota laughed lightly and turned away. They had been flirting around each other ever since she and Dakota arrived in Terrenia, and although it bothered him at first, his mother deserved to be happy. She had suffered so much in the last four years, and if Tony could bring her peace, then who was he to stand in their way?

“How are you doing, Dakota?” Tony took a seat beside him at the small table.

“Just dandy,” Dakota said. Tony cocked an eyebrow and Dakota smiled softly. “I just miss her, Tony, and I’m more worried than I have ever been.”

“She is tough, Dakota; she will be fine.”

“That’s what Mom said.” Dakota laughed.

Tony watched Elizabeth as she worked in the kitchen. “She’s a wise woman.”

“She is,” Dakota agreed.

“Here we go, boys.” Elizabeth brought over another mug of tea, then sat next to Tony.

Dakota took his first sip, and the taste of chamomile and whiskey slid over his tongue like a blanket. Chamomile was always Dakota's favorite as a kid, perfect for those nights he'd have trouble sleeping, too worried about Ana next door.

"So, tell me of the Anastasia you grew up with," Tony said, setting his mug on the table. "I only know her from when she arrived, and I suspect she was a bit more guarded with us than she was with you."

"Well," Elizabeth started on a laugh, "Anastasia used to sneak into our house in the middle of the night, and the two of them would have sleepovers—the innocent kind," she added with a wink. "We would check, but we knew she didn't feel safe anywhere else, so we kept her where he couldn't get her. George tried to get her out of that house so many times, but she was so afraid."

"I wish I could strangle the bastard who hurt her." Tony clenched his fists. "I will get Vincent. He will pay for everything he has done to you all."

Elizabeth lightly touched his hand and smiled warmly. "Once they graduated, she and Dakota roomed together while going to school. Mitch and Monica had refused to pay for college, so Anastasia worked to afford classes."

"She was amazing," Dakota said, taking another drink. "Funny, smart, honest, and was the kindest person you'd ever met—or rather, *is*." He pinched the bridge of his nose. Even he was starting to refer to her in the past tense, as if she was never coming back. When he opened his eyes again, the room began to tilt, and he gripped the edge of the table to keep from falling.

"Dakota?" His mother asked, concerned.

Dakota's eyes began to lose focus, and the room continued spinning. He looked down at his hands which were nothing but a pigmented blur now.

"How much whiskey did you put in this tea?" he asked, and then passed out on the table.

20

ELIZABETH

"I'll get him." Tony lifted Dakota and carried him to his room. When he came back out, Elizabeth greeted him with a smile.

"There really wasn't that much whiskey in there."

"He's exhausted. I'm honestly surprised he was able to stay up as long as he did."

Tony reached forward and brushed a strand of hair from her face. Elizabeth's heart caught in her throat. Tony gave her butterflies in a way she hadn't felt since George had been killed.

"I enjoy being around you," he said softly.

"I enjoy being around you, too." She lifted their mugs and carried them toward the kitchen.

"I will wait," Tony said, and she turned to look at

him. His bright hazel eyes were wide but focused on her face.

"Wait for what?"

"Until you are ready."

She walked over to him and rose to her tiptoes to kiss him lightly on the cheek.

"I would like that."

"Goodnight, Elizabeth."

"Goodnight, Tony."

He turned and closed the door gently behind him. The silence of the small house settled over her. She took a deep breath and looked toward the room where Dakota slept. Ever since he was a boy, he had been head over heels for Anastasia. What must it be like to hold that much love in your heart? She wondered.

After Anastasia disappeared the first time, her son changed. He went from wanting to be a doctor to becoming a cop overnight, and she knew he had searched for Anastasia in every single victim he came across. It wasn't until they'd found each other again, and he'd come to terms with what had happened that night all those years ago, that she had finally seen him genuinely smile again.

Now, though, she worried she would never see his face light up again.

She wrapped her arms around herself. What were they going to do? It wasn't just the dying world that frightened her, but the son she was watching fade away to nothing right before her eyes.

Elizabeth knew he hurt more than he let on, and if they didn't find Anastasia soon, she feared that her son would never be the same.

If he survived it at all.

21

DAKOTA

Dakota stood on the edge of a tall cliff. He couldn't see the ground below, and the fog made it impossible to determine how high up he was. He turned to look behind him, but there was nothing but jagged, black rocks, and what appeared to be a tall building unlike anything he'd ever seen in the distance.

The wind picked up and he stumbled, nearly falling off the edge of the cliff. He took a step away from it, determined to discover where the hell he was. The sour stench of sulfur filled the air, and the wind whipped at him harder, as if pushing him toward the ground below.

When he turned back to the cliff, Ana appeared in front of him. Her face was bloody and bruised, and he took a step toward her. The wind ripped and pulled at her, and she stumbled.

"Ana!" he screamed, reaching for her. He caught her hand, and felt that her skin was ice cold. "Where are you?" he called over the sound that made it nearly impossible to hear anything but his own pulse pounding.

She smiled and pressed a hand to her heart.

"Tell me where you are!" he yelled again.

She released his hand and took another step back.

Dakota lunged for her and grabbed her hand again as she started to fall. His heart pounded, the adrenaline surging through his veins. "I've got you!"

Her blue eyes were wide with panic, her bruised face pale.

"Dakota! Save me... I need you," she cried out as she clutched his hand. "Please don't let me go!"

Her hand began to slip from his, and he reached for her with his other hand. "I won't let go!"

He tried to pull her back over the edge, but something below was pulling her down. When he looked, there was nothing there but fog.

"Dakota!" she screamed as she slipped from his grip.

"No!" He reached over the edge for her, but she was already gone, swallowed up by the thick fog below.

Dakota sat up in bed, his chest heavy. He rubbed his hands over the short beard on his face, and waited for his heart rate to slow. "Well, that was fan-fucking-tastic," he muttered and leaned back against the pillows.

A large furry head nudged his arm, and he looked down at Ana's lion-sized cat standing beside the bed.

"Hey, Kaley," he said as she rubbed her face against his arm. "I won't let her get away from us this time, girl. I promise I will find her."

Seemingly satisfied with his reaction, Kaley padded back over to the corner of the room and curled up to sleep. He glanced out the window; stars still glittered in the early morning sky.

He rubbed his hands over his face and climbed out of bed. It would be nice to get in a quick run around the perimeter of the village before the day actually began.

Dakota stepped into the modest living area and started the fire in the kitchen. How he wished he had some freaking coffee, but tea would have to do.

The door flew open and Brady burst in. His eyes were wide, and his chest rose and fell on heavy breaths.

"What is it?" Dakota asked quickly.

"We have Brutes coming!"

"Now? It's barely morning!" Dakota yelled as he threw on a shirt and grabbed his boots. Tea would have to wait. Fucking Brutes.

"They are coming up on the east wall," Brady informed as they ran toward the village's center.

"How many?"

"About three dozen."

"Fuck!" They didn't have the kind of manpower and weapons to hold off that large of an attack on such short notice. Even if they somehow managed to pull a win from the hat—they would lose dozens of their own.

He ran with Brady toward the scout platform on the east wall, where Tony waited. Elizabeth stood next to him, and they watched over the trees.

"Mom, what are you doing here?" he asked as he climbed up beside them.

"I was just heading to the cellar and wanted to see for myself." Her arms were folded across her chest and, had Dakota not been afraid for their near future, he would have smirked at the large knife that hung from her belt. It looked so out of place on the woman who had spent her life treating the sick and injured.

"Okay, make sure everyone stays quiet," he told her.

She nodded. "You guys be careful." She climbed down to run for the underground cellar they had built to hide the villagers from the Brutes. Even if they failed to keep the beasts out of the village, they'd at least taken steps to ensure the safety of the people.

He looked down at the Fighters assembled below him in front of the fence. They all stood firm, their faces unreadable, determined not to show fear to the enemy.

Dakota and Tony climbed down and made their way

toward the gate, joining the Fighters lined up outside the perimeter.

"No matter what happens, keep this closed," Dakota told Brady.

Brady nodded and sealed the gate behind them.

Dakota stood in front of the group beside Tony and swallowed hard as the Brutes grew closer. His people would not die today.

Heavy, rhythmic footfalls were the only sounds in the early morning, and the sunrise cast an orange glow on the otherwise pale beasts. The Brutes stopped ten feet from them.

Dakota's brow furrowed. What the hell were they stopping for?

"Who is Dakota?" one of them asked gruffly.

"I am," Dakota said, holding his ground.

"Our leader wishes to speak to you."

"Vincent?" Dakota asked, his fingers itching for his sword.

If Brutes could show disgust, this one certainly did. It's human-like mouth turned into a grimace. "That murderer is not our leader," it growled, pounding a fist against its chest.

Tony glanced at Dakota and gave a curt nod, a silent signal that they had his back if anything should go south.

Dakota turned back to the beast. "Then who is your leader?"

"We will not bring him forward until your Fighters sheathe their weapons."

"We will not stand down until we know there will be no attack from you."

The Brute shook its head. "We will not harm you." He lifted his massive arm and all but a small grouping of the Brutes stepped backward toward the trees until they were nearly half of a football field's length away.

Dakota turned to Tony, and he gave the signal for the Fighters to lower their weapons. Here's to hoping this wasn't a massive fucking mistake.

"Fine. Where's your leader?" Dakota asked, taking a step forward.

"I am here." The largest Brute Dakota had ever seen stepped toward him from the small grouping that had stayed put. The thing stood at least ten feet tall and, while he was covered in intricate designs like the others, his tattoos had colors woven in, whereas the others' markings were only black.

"I am Argento," the Brute said. It pressed a fist to its chest with a light bow. "The *true* leader of the Brutes."

22

DAKOTA

Dakota folded his arms. "What do you want to talk to me about?"

"This Vincent that you speak of, he is the sorcerer, correct? The one who is responsible for the spreading Darkness?"

"Yes, he is."

"He has been coming to my world and stealing my people, turning them against me in an effort to take over my world, much in the way he has done yours."

"He hasn't won yet."

The Brute inclined his head. "Just as he has not in my world. The captain of my force has been trying to overthrow my family for years, and Vincent promises him the throne if he helps him. But as long as I stand, he will not succeed."

"You are from a different dimension? Another world?" Dakota asked, slightly fascinated. "Legends said that the Brutes were once humans."

Argento scoffed, and the Brute next to him laughed.

"We are no puny humans underneath this." He pounded his fist to his chest again.

"We are no puny humans," Dakota growled through his teeth. "If Vincent has not been creating the Brutes from our people somehow, then where have our villagers gone?"

"We have some of your people, and we have brought them as a sign of goodwill."

"You have the other villagers? How?" Tony asked, stepping forward to stand beside Dakota.

"Who are you?" Argento cocked his head to the side, and puffed his chest up slightly.

Dakota nearly scoffed. He may have had Tony in size, but Dakota was willing to bet if it came down to a fight, his friend would rip this beast apart in a matter of seconds.

"Tony. I am the one who has gone through each and every village your Brutes have torn apart." Tony's body vibrated with barely leashed anger, and Dakota put his hand on his shoulder to calm him.

"You said you have our people," Dakota interrupted. "How?"

"Vincent," Argento began, returning his attention to Dakota, "has been sending them through a portal and into my world as a way to trade with my captain for more of my force. My captain has been using them to make weapons in an effort to kill me."

"Platinum-coated."

"Yes," he growled. "My people can't handle the platinum, and until Vincent started trading the humans, it did not even exist in my world."

"So what do you want from us?"

"We wish to work with you to bring down this Vincent. Those you see behind me are the only warriors I can trust to remain loyal to me. The rest of my soldiers can't be trusted."

"How do we know we can trust you? Or any of your warriors?" Dakota gestured to the Brutes behind Argento.

"I could tear you all apart before you could even blink," Argento said, folding his arms over his chest. "But I will not. You and your people are not those we are at war with. I am showing you goodwill by coming here, knowing that your blades are coated in poison and could strike me down. I have also brought your missing people here as an additional show of unity against our mutual enemy. You and yours will come to no harm by my hand or the hand of those I trust. We are not a violent race, Dakota. Vincent has made us this way.

Until he showed up in my world, we had no war with anyone."

"How did you know my name?"

"Word travels fast, Fighter. Rumors have spread about you, Dakota, the warrior from another world."

The Brute's words shocked him, but Dakota tried to not convey his shock. Why the hell were people talking about him?

"Give us a few minutes, please. We need to confer."

"As you wish." Argento stepped back with his people, and Dakota and Tony headed back inside the wall.

"Watch them," Tony whispered to Shane just before they stepped behind the gate.

Selena waited for them beside her son. "Did I hear that right?" she asked, her brows furrowed. "That they want an alliance?"

Dakota nodded.

"You can't be seriously considering this." Brady's hands tightened into fists at his sides. "They have been slaughtering our people for decades."

"According to Argento, he wasn't aware," Tony offered.

"Bullshit."

"Brady." Selena's tone left no room for argument from her son.

"Whatever." He turned and stalked off.

"What are you thinking?" Tony asked Selena.

She bit down on her bottom lip, contemplating their current scenario. Dakota could practically see the wheels turning as she decided the future of Terrenia. If they sought an alliance with these Brutes, and Argento spoke the truth, it could mean the difference between winning and losing this war.

But on the other hand, if Argento was lying, and this was just a way for Vincent to destroy them from the inside, they were screwed.

"What is your impression of these Brutes?" Selena asked.

"I think if they are truly returning our people," Tony responded, "it is worth going out on a limb."

"I agree," Dakota added.

Selena sighed. "Then let's do it."

Tony nodded and Dakota followed him back out through the gate. They stopped in front of Argento.

"Give us our people, and we will work together to bring this bastard down." Dakota took a step forward and reached his hand out. Argento took it, and they shook.

Argento smiled. "I like you, Dakota, even if you are a puny human." The humor in his deep voice caught Dakota off guard. "Bring them," he commanded the Brutes behind him.

Two broke off and headed back into the trees. Moments later, two rows of Brutes began marching out of the forest, a grouping of villagers between them.

Dakota's eyes widened. He had expected dirty, starving, tired, and beaten people, but—

"We fed them and allowed them to rest before we made the journey. Some were very near death when we found them, so we provided necessary aid."

"Thank you, Argento." Tony stepped forward.

Argento nodded. "If it were my people, I would have been angry as well. My captain will pay for what he has done. I am afraid to report that some of your people had perished before we could get there, but we brought the bodies of those who have passed with us so you may give them a proper burial. It is imperative in our culture to do so, and we wish to offer you the same respect."

"Thank you," Dakota said as Tony rushed to the villagers coming home, some for the first time in years.

"We will make camp out here until you trust us. I imagine your people would not take too kindly to those they perceive as their enemy sleeping inside the walls of your village."

"Do not set up camp out here just yet. I will speak to my people. I would prefer to keep you all hidden from view in case any of Vincent's scouts are lurking outside the walls."

Argento nodded in agreement and then showed his teeth in a frightening smile. "Yes, I would very much like to be a surprise to them as well."

"You are going to let them *in* here? To stay? Near our people?" Brady shouted. "Are you serious?"

"They are not our enemy, Brady," Tony said calmly.

"You have got to be kidding me! They have slaughtered and kidnapped our people, and you are just going to let them live in here with us?" Brady slammed his fists down on the wooden table.

"They aren't the ones we are at war with. Vincent and the rogue Brutes are the enemies," Dakota told him.

"So he says!" Brady gestured to the wall where Argento and his men waited.

"So all of the other villagers say as well, Brady," Tony added, a silent warning in his voice. "They all corroborated his story once they were back inside the walls. Three hundred people are back here, nearly too many to even house. They are sleeping a dozen to each cottage, and some are even setting up camp outside. They are back because of Argento."

"So now we are calling them by name," Brady spat. "Anastasia would have never allowed this."

Tony was in Brady's face so quickly Dakota didn't even have time to block him. "Anastasia would have done whatever was necessary to ensure the safety of our people. She would have welcomed Argento and his warriors with open arms if it meant defeating Vincent. Do not ever pretend that you know her better than I." He glanced at Dakota. "Or better than Dakota, for that matter. Don't you want your mother to be safe? Your sister? Because the only way that is going to happen is if we align with them to end this war."

Brady shot Dakota an angry glare and stomped out of the cabin.

"He will come around," Selena said, shaking her head. "We lost his father, and then Emma, to the Brutes."

"It's definitely going to be a tough sell, but I believe it is for the best." Tony leaned back against the counter.

"I do as well," Selena agreed. "Allow them inside and put them over in the empty field space near the training center. But I want them under constant guard, just in case."

Dakota nodded in agreement and went out to let Argento know.

He sure as hell hoped they weren't making a big ass mistake.

After meeting with the villagers, Dakota led the Brutes inside. They made up their camp near the training center, and Dakota assured the villagers that they would have Fighters guarding the Brutes the entire time they remained within the gates. He watched curiously as some of the villagers who had been prisoners walked toward their camp and spoke to the Brutes as if they had been friends for years. That showed him more than any words could have; Argento and his followers could be trusted.

Dakota smiled to himself. They had just been handed what they needed to get Ana back and win this war. Vincent wasn't going to know what hit him.

23

ANASTASIA

"Hey, honey, how was your day?" Dakota asked as he and Annabelle returned home that evening.

"It was good." Anastasia forced a smile.

"That's wonderful to hear." He kissed her loudly on the mouth, and she knelt to give Annabelle a hug.

"I love you, Momma! I missed you while I was at school."

"I missed you, too, baby. Guess what?"

"What?" Annabelle's eyes widened.

"I made cookies." She'd used a recipe Elizabeth taught her long ago, on one of the days she'd snuck over to Dakota's house.

Or had that all been a dream as well?

"Yay!" Annabelle giggled and ran toward the kitchen, but Dakota stopped her with a hand on her shoulder.

"Go get cleaned up for dinner and set your daily binder out."

With a groan, Annabelle changed direction and bounded up the stairs.

Dakota pulled Anastasia in for a hug. "I missed you, my love."

"I missed you, too."

Bringing his lips to her ear, he said, "I was thinking that maybe after dinner, we can pour a couple glasses of wine and give the new hot tub a try." His breath against her neck sent a shiver down her spine.

This was Dakota… she shouldn't feel so out of place with him.

"How does that sound?" He pulled away to look into her eyes.

She searched his blue eyes for the familiarity that should have been there. When he continued to stare at her, she responded quickly, "Great, except, I didn't cook dinner."

"No worries, Ana. You're not that great of a cook anyway." He winked and set his backpack down. "I'm going to get out of my scrubs, and then we will head out."

"Where are we going?"

"Dinner. We are meeting Max and his new girlfriend at that Italian place up the street today."

"Max?" she asked curiously.

Dakota playfully rolled his eyes. "We've only been friends with him since high school, Ana. Just because you based a character on him—a bad one, I might add—doesn't make him a bad person."

"A character? What?"

"Maximus?" Dakota raised an eyebrow.

She straightened. Surely he wasn't serious. "We're eating dinner with Maximus?"

"Ana, he is our friend. If you can't separate your book world from the real world, then you need to stop writing such shitty things about people we know." He narrowed his eyes.

The curtness of his tone caught her off guard. Had she ever heard that sternness from him before?

"Oh, okay," she responded, turning to finish folding the laundry she had washed.

"Be ready to leave in thirty," he called behind him as he headed up the stairs.

Anastasia finished folding the laundry and started up with her basket. As she reached the top of the stairs, the image of a bleeding Gregory caught her eye in the glass of the mirror. She dropped the basket and bit back a scream. His eyes were wide and wet with tears. He reached for her, and when she took a step back, he opened his mouth to cry out, but no sound followed.

She moved closer to the mirror, and when she touched the cold glass, she could have sworn she felt the warmness from his touch on the other side. Anastasia closed her eyes and shook her head. "It's not real," she whispered. "It's only in the story." When she slowly opened her eyes again, only her reflection stared back at her.

"DID YOU DO ANY WRITING TODAY?" DAKOTA ASKED AS they drove through Seattle.

"No, I just spent my time picking up and relaxing."

"Good."

"Why do you ask?"

"It's just been getting to you so much lately. Honey, you woke up this morning and didn't remember our daughter," he whispered quietly so only she could hear. "Maybe it's time you stop."

"Stop? It's all I've ever wanted to be. Why would I stop now that I finally have it?"

"I'm just worried about you, is all." He reached over and grabbed her hand. "Just think about it, okay?"

She nodded and looked out the window. She couldn't give up her writing. Her entire life, all she had ever wanted to do was write stories that would make people happy. Stories that had the power to pull the reader out of whatever was going on in their lives at that moment and submerge them into adventures that they would never be able to take on their own.

Nightmare or not, part of her believed that she had spent most of her life fighting beasts and not writing, so why would she let go of what she finally had? Still, his words rang with truth. Maybe she should change up her story. Erase what she had and start over again.

"Where have my parents been?" she asked him, curious as to why she didn't remember when she'd last seen them.

"They are in Africa on a safari this month, remember?"

"Oh yeah," she lied. "Must have slipped my mind."

They pulled into the parking lot of a small Italian restaurant. The car's headlights illuminated two people standing next to a silver sedan, and Anastasia's pulse pounded in her ears.

"Dakota, we have to go." She started to panic. Maximus and Ophelia stood hand in hand in front of their headlights, waving and smiling as if they were all best friends, as if they hadn't killed her father or been responsible for the death of hundreds of innocent villagers.

Anastasia reached to her back where her sword would generally sit, and she suddenly felt very empty without it. She dug down into her subconscious and tried to summon her magic, but nothing happened.

“Anastasia!” Dakota yelled, pulling her out of her trance.

Why did he use her full name?

“What?” she asked, hoping he didn’t notice how badly she was panicking inside.

“Do we need to leave?” he asked worriedly. “You look freaked out.”

“Just the remnants of my nightmare. Honestly, Dakota, I’m fine.” She smiled and turned to look at Annabelle. “Hungry?”

“Yes.” Annabelle smiled, and Anastasia swallowed her fear. In the back of her mind, though, a voice screamed for her attention. A voice that sounded suspiciously like her own.

24

ANASTASIA

Sitting at dinner, she did her best to focus on the conversation. Maximus and Ophelia were nothing but friendly, and both Dakota and Annabelle were at ease in their presence.

Anastasia smiled and nodded along with something Ophelia had said, although she had no actual clue as to what it was.

The Ophelia in front of her, wearing the white button-down blouse, with her hair falling loosely around her shoulders and the carefree smile on her face flashed in and out, morphing quickly into someone else. No, not *someone* else. Sitting in front of her now was the bloody, sadistic Ophelia who murdered Anastasia's father.

"You're going to die," she sneered, but before Anastasia could respond, she morphed back into the laughing, smiling Ophelia she'd been sitting across from all night.

Maximus was next, and in an instant, she was somewhere else.

"You think you are anything compared to me?" He slammed her to the ground. "You've been training for, what, two weeks? I've been training my entire life." He reared his fist back, but before it made contact, Anastasia was ripped back to the present.

"How is the book coming along?" Maximus asked sweetly.

"It—uh." She cleared her throat. "It's moving forward." She looked down at the napkin in her lap, wanting to avoid looking at him for too long. Her fingers trembled.

"You're writing a book? How exciting!" Ophelia exclaimed, clapping her hands together.

"She sure is. Made me a bad guy because I'm so devious." Maximus laughed, and Ophelia slapped him lightly on the arm.

"Devious, yeah, okay. If being devious means using all the hot water so I have to take a cold shower, then yes, you are as devious as they come."

They continued laughing, and Anastasia did her best to push her thoughts out of her mind, but they continued surfacing.

She saw Maximus standing over an unconscious boy —Brady, she remembered—and the anger rose in her chest as if it were happening right in front of her eyes. She looked to Dakota for some kind of reassurance that she wasn't going insane, but he appeared as happy as she had ever seen him, and Annabelle wasn't the least bit uncomfortable around Anastasia's enemies.

Because that's what they were, no matter what anyone told her.

Maximus and Ophelia were monsters.

She looked up at Ophelia and saw her cleaning her dirty fingernails with a blood-covered knife as Gregory lay bleeding on the ground. They fought until Anastasia threw a ball of light into Ophelia's chest.

Anastasia stood up so quickly that her chair fell back.

"Ana?" Dakota asked, and Anastasia flushed when she realized everyone's eyes were on her.

"I-I'm not feeling well. I'm sorry." She turned to leave, and Annabelle gripped her hand.

"I'll come with you, Momma."

"I think we are going to have to head out. She's been having some trouble today with getting out of writing mode." Dakota laughed lightly and shook hands with Maximus. "See you later, man. It was nice to meet you, Ophelia."

"Nice to meet you, as well. Hope you feel better, Ana."

"Anastasia," she corrected. "And thank you." Anastasia scolded herself for interrupting their evening. What was wrong with her?

"ANNABELLE IS TUCKED IN AND FALLING FAST ASLEEP." Dakota took a seat next to her on the couch.

"Good." Anastasia closed her eyes tightly, fictional images still clashing with her reality.

"How are you?" He brushed a strand of hair from her face.

"I don't know. I can't seem to get out of my head. I keep having these visions play out, and it's just not possible."

"I think you should talk to a coworker of mine." At her questioning look, he continued. "He's a therapist, a very good one, and he might be able to help you start separating. I want you to be able to do what you want with your life, Ana, but I don't like how it's affecting our family and your happiness."

Anastasia thought about it for a moment, then nodded in agreement. She had to do something to stop this assault on her emotions. Besides, if this was some sort of mind trick from Vincent, eventually it would play out. Right?

"I'll set you up an appointment for tomorrow."

Dakota smiled and rubbed his hands down her arms. “Everything is going to be okay, you’ll see.”

She did her best to offer him a warm smile.

“Now, how about a little of that wine?” He pulled her to her feet.

Ana frowned. Dakota didn’t like wine; he drank scotch. And so did she, didn’t she?

“Or, maybe we want to have something a little harder instead?” He glanced back at her, eyebrows raised in question. “How about a scotch?” He reached into the cabinet and pulled down a bottle. Strange.

When she hesitated, he set it down on the counter and stepped closely. “Or maybe we’ll skip that all together.” He kissed her, but something in it still felt wrong.

“Maybe we can just go to bed tonight? I’m really not feeling well.”

“Of course,” he said with a smile, releasing her. “Everything will be better tomorrow, you’ll see.”

Yeah, we’ll see.

25

TERRENIA

DAKOTA

"We need to find a way to mark you and your warriors so that our Fighters don't accidentally get one of you with the platinum blades," Dakota said to Argento as they looked over a map of the most recent Brute camps.

"Agreed." He nodded and rubbed his hand over his face. "So, this Anastasia, you say she is with Vincent now?"

"Yes." Dakota's jaw tightened.

"She is his niece?"

"Yes," Dakota said again, fearing he knew exactly where this conversation was going. The whispers of the Phoenix who'd gone dark were already spreading. "He kidnapped her as a baby and sent her to live with an abusive man and his wife. She hates Vincent."

"So you believe she can be trusted? You say this Phoenix, as some of the people call her, is the only one who can take him down?"

Dakota heard the grin in the way he spoke, a soft—almost amused tone. It pissed him the hell off. "Yes, she is. It was prophesized when she was a baby."

"By an old woman. Are you sure it still stands true today?"

"I wasn't an old woman when she was born," Carmen said from behind them, and both man and beast turned to face her.

"I did not mean any disrespect." Argento bowed his head, and she smiled.

"Oh, my feelings are not easily hurt." Carmen waved her hand as if to erase what he had said from her memory. "I'm not entirely sure where the vision came from, but I know it to be the truth. I saw her defeat him in a way that no one else will be able to."

"How?" Dakota asked.

She shrugged. "Wouldn't it be nice to have all the answers?" She chuckled. "I only know that her magic is the only thing that will take him down." Carmen turned to Dakota. "I've got something."

Hope surged within him. "You found her?"

"Not exactly." She sighed and folded her hands in front of her stomach. "But she is alive. I can't pinpoint whether she is here or in your Seattle, but she is alive."

"How can we figure out where she is?"

"That's just it, it doesn't feel like another world. It's as if he has her somewhere that exists, but isn't necessarily reality?" She shook her head. "I've been racking my brain but I can't figure it out. She's just a blip on the radar."

"What the hell does that mean?" Dakota asked.

"That is not good," Argento answered, and Dakota looked at him. "He must have her in a stasis."

"Stasis?" Dakota asked, confused.

"It's something we Brutes do when we are having difficulties with a decision, or if we need to deal with a complex emotion such as grief. We go to one of our healers, and they put us in a stasis where our minds can be manipulated to make a decision and see all possible outcomes for it. We can also see those who have passed, and it helps us to move forward."

"Is she aware of what is happening?" Dakota asked.

"It depends on how he is manipulating her. She could very well be aware, and he could be putting her through various tortures without the risk of killing her, or he could be weaving a scenario to help her to make an important decision." Argento must have seen the anger on Dakota's face, because he immediately continued, "I apologize for my candor, but I do not see the benefit in lying to you."

"I appreciate your honesty, Argento."

"That makes sense as to why I can't reach her mind again. Vincent must be using your tactic to hide her from me. How would he have learned this practice?"

"It's something that my captain would have been well versed on. His father was one of our greatest healers."

"Is there a way to find her?"

"I'm afraid not, Dakota." Argento touched Dakota's shoulder and looked at Carmen. "One of my warriors is a healer. I will send him to you and you can speak to him. He may know something I do not."

"Thank you, Argento." Carmen turned to leave the cottage, and Dakota slammed his fists on the table.

"Son of a bitch!"

"You love her," Argento said.

"Yes, I do."

"I am very familiar with love. It is a painful and frustrating emotion. One that can both lift you up and knock you down. Make you strong, and yet, can be your greatest weakness. I do not care for weakness." Argento smiled. "But time and time again I would choose weakness if it meant love."

Dakota nodded and took a deep breath. They would find her, he knew, and at least they had the comfort of knowing she was alive for now.

Tony stepped into the cottage, his face hard.

"What is it?" Dakota asked.

"We got word of a large camp set up about twelve miles from here."

Dakota crossed his arms over his chest. "How large?"

Tony ran a hand through his hair. "About half the size of our village here. It's heavily guarded, too, which tells me they have something there they really don't want us finding."

Dakota straightened. "Is it possible?"

Tony raised his hands. "I know you're thinking it may be Anastasia, but we need not get our hopes up on this. Either way, we should make a move while they aren't expecting it. It's a large enough force that they could do significant damage to us if they so choose."

"We should attack tonight," Argento offered. "It can be our first assault on Vincent."

Tony nodded. "I'll get the Fighters prepared." He turned to head back down the path, and Argento clasped Dakota's shoulder.

"We will find a way to differ ourselves from the enemy as you suggested."

"Good." Dakota responded half-heartedly. His mind was still on the idea that Anastasia might have been so close to him this entire time, and he hadn't even known it.

26

ANASTASIA

Anastasia stood nervously in front of the receptionist's desk in the psychologist's small office. "Hi, I have an appointment this afternoon," she began. "My husband made it for me."

"Name, please?" the woman asked without even looking up from her keyboard. There wasn't a single hair out of place in her red bun.

"Anastasia Parker."

The woman reset the black-rimmed glasses on her nose and pressed a few buttons on the keyboard.

"You're checked in. He will be with you shortly."

"Thank you."

"Uh-huh." The woman returned to whatever it was

she was doing, and Anastasia turned around slowly to get a closer look at the office.

Flowers danced in gold frames that were arranged neatly on the walls. Bright yellow couches sat on both sides, with a row of red chairs in the center. Throw pillows with green leaves embroidered on them decorated the couches, and magazines were placed neatly in a rack hanging on the wall.

Based on the decor, Anastasia should have been relaxed. But dread formed a heavy weight in her stomach, and it wasn't something she was able to shake off.

She stepped over to a thin, brown table to look at some of the brochures placed on the glass top, and she did her best to keep her eyes averted from the mirror hanging above it. She really wasn't having the best luck with reflective glass lately.

"Anastasia, so nice to finally meet you."

The voice sent ice up her spine, and she looked up and into the mirror. Vincent stood before her, clad in a dark robe, his silver eyes boring into her like twin daggers. He grinned and Anastasia jerked back.

Her body impacted with something hard, and she turned slowly to face Dakota's colleague. She backed up as far against the table as she could, and the receptionist huffed at her when the brochures spilled to the floor.

"Are you okay, Mrs. Parker?" Vincent asked worriedly as he took a step toward her.

"Yes, I'm sorry, I'm fine. I-I just need a moment."

The man smiled sadly, shaking his head. “Dakota warned me about your episodes. Come with me and we can talk about it.” He reached his hand out for her, and she pushed further back, knocking over a vase of fake flowers.

“Excuse me,” the receptionist said rudely.

“I'm so sorry.” Anastasia picked the vase back up and placed it on the table, then turned to face Vincent. “I’m sorry,” she repeated.

“There is nothing to be sorry about, Mrs. Parker. These things happen. Why don’t you come with me?” He gestured toward an open door and Anastasia followed.

It’s not real. Dakota said it wasn’t real.

“So.” He took a seat behind a large mahogany desk, and Anastasia sat on the edge of a chair facing him. “Dakota told me that you are having trouble discerning fiction from reality as of late.”

“It’s not real, it’s not real,” she muttered quietly as images of Vincent attacking her popped into her head.

“Mrs. Parker?”

Vincent kept flashing between the psychiatrist that sat before her and the hooded villain she knew him as. She squeezed her eyes shut and tears slid out. Her heart was pounding in her chest, and black spots began to swim in her vision. If she didn’t calm herself soon, she was going to pass out.

“Are you all right, Mrs. Parker?”

"Yes, I'm sorry." She took a deep breath and managed to gain some minor control.

"No need to apologize here. No judgment will be passed on you within these walls." He pulled out a notepad. "So, tell me what is going on."

Don't trust him! He's a murderer! Get up and run before he kills you! She closed her eyes and imagined Annabelle and Dakota. Their faces were the only things keeping her in this reality.

"I've been writing a book," she forced through clenched teeth, then opened her eyes.

He leaned back in his chair and folded his hands in front of him. "So I've been told. Tell me about it."

She took a deep breath. "I woke up two days ago and couldn't remember anything from my life. Instead, my memories had been replaced with those of the heroine in my story. I can't remember the day I married Dakota, or the birth of my daughter." Tears began streaming down her face. "Am I going crazy?"

"It is not unheard of for an author to be so entwined with their story that they begin to lose sight of their life. What you need to do is remove yourself from this story, and the rest will come back to you."

She looked up at him. "Remove myself?" His eyes flashed blue for a moment and she shook her head. *Just my imagination.*

"Yes."

She swallowed hard. "How am I supposed to do that?"

"Delete it, admit openly that you are not this heroine and that you do not possess magical powers." He laughed lightly and leaned forward in his chair. "I do think it speaks to your imaginative powers that you have placed yourself so far into the story, though. That's talent."

Anastasia straightened in her chair, her muscles tense. She narrowed her eyes. "I never said she had magical powers."

"I must have heard Dakota speaking about it." He dismissed her with a flick of his wrist and leaned back again.

The door opened and Dakota walked in, carrying Annabelle.

"She wanted to see you."

"Hi, Momma!" Annabelle waved.

"How is the session going?" Dakota asked as he sat down on the couch.

"It's going well, wouldn't you say, Anastasia?" Vincent looked at her, and she nodded slightly.

Why was her family allowed to interrupt her private session? Anastasia's gaze flicked back and forth between Dakota and the psychologist. This wasn't right. None of this was right.

Dakota cocked his head. "Ana? How is it going?"

She gave her head a quick shake. "Vincent was

telling me that I needed to remove myself from my story, and that if I did so, my memories would begin to come back."

"That sounds like a good thing." Dakota smiled widely.

"Yeah, it would be. If any of this was real." She spoke calmly even though inside her heart was tearing apart. Real or not, this life was what she wanted. What she'd always wanted. And it was about to be ripped away from her.

"What's that supposed to mean?" Dakota asked.

Anastasia narrowed her eyes at Vincent. "Whatever the fuck you're doing to me, stop!"

"Anastasia, you need to calm down," he stated calmly, rising to his feet.

She stood quickly and so did Dakota. She caught his reflection in the mirror and sucked in a breath. The blue scrubs he'd been wearing when he and Annabelle walked in were replaced with jeans and a long-sleeve shirt. He wore a shoulder holster with two handguns instead of a stethoscope.

There was no big-eyed little girl in his arms.

"Come back to me, Ana," he begged in her head. "I am what's real."

She closed her eyes tightly.

Hands gripped her shoulders and she opened her eyes.

Dakota stood before her, shaking her gently. "Anastasia, what's wrong?"

"The real Dakota never calls me Anastasia."

His brows drew together. "I am the real Dakota!"

"No, you aren't!" she screamed.

"Momma!" Annabelle yelled, then ran to the corner of the room.

"Anastasia, you are scaring her!" Dakota yelled.

Anastasia spun to face Vincent. He glared at her with all the hatred she felt toward him, shining back through silver eyes.

"You truly have lost yourself, haven't you, child?"

27

TERRENIA

DAKOTA

Dakota, Tony, Argento, and Andrew crept toward the front of the Brute camp. Dakota noted two sentries watching the front gate, and he motioned silently for Argento to take the one on the right while he and Tony attacked the one on the left.

As soon as the beasts had their backs turned, the trio attacked. Blood splattered Dakota as he drove his dagger down into the neck of the monster, while covering its mouth with his hand.

Once the beast had fallen, he looked over to Argento who had managed to remove the monster's head in complete silence.

Tony turned to wave the rest of their army forward, and they crept from the trees, silent as the breeze that danced through the air. Two of Argento's Brutes pulled open the gates, and they crept inside.

Most of the monsters were either asleep or gathered in the center of the camp near a large fire.

They started their attack in the tents that lined the makeshift fence. Tony, Dakota, and half the Fighters and Brutes took the tents to the left, while Argento, Andrew, and the other half of their armies split off to their right.

By the time they'd cleared the area, Dakota was slick with Brute blood. Killing the enemy while they slept was not an easy thing to swallow. Even though they were monsters, the idea that something didn't have the chance to fight back turned his stomach.

Still, they *were* monsters, and they had Ana. Somewhere. They managed to sneak up on the sentries and take them down swiftly, gaining the rest of their attacking army access to the camp.

Just as they exited the last tent, a booming horn split through the silence, and battle cries were sent up into the night.

"Shit!" Dakota yelled and they launched into battle.

Based on the number of beasts inside the tents, and those gathered at the center of the village, Dakota estimated there must have been a significant increase in enemy force even from the time their scout had reported back that afternoon.

It only gave him more hope that she was here. What

else could be so important it had to be so well protected?

"Duck!" Argento's booming voice ripped Dakota from his thoughts. He ducked quickly as a dagger sailed past his ear and buried in the forehead of a beast trying to sneak up on him.

"Thanks!" he called out, continuing to fight side by side with Tony. He couldn't help but be impressed by the older man's fighting skills. It was no wonder why he'd been chosen to lead the Terrenian Fighters; he was lethal.

After thirty minutes of bloodshed, most of which, Dakota was happy to see, had fallen on their enemy, they met back in the center of the village.

"How are your people?" Argento asked.

"No losses or serious injury. Yours?"

"We are fine as well, though I am disappointed in the number of traitors I had in my ranks." He looked around at the broken bodies, his mouth snarled up in disgust.

Before Dakota could respond, one of Argento's warriors approached, leaning over to whisper something to him.

The Brute king's eyes widened, and he looked straight at Dakota. "Come, now."

Dakota and Tony ran after Argento and the other Brute until they came upon a small trapdoor. It would have barely been noticeable in the daylight, and had it not been for the Brutes' extra sensitive vision, they may not have ever found it.

"What is it?" Dakota asked, studying Argento's face.

"I believe that we have found your Anastasia."

"What?" The adrenaline began pumping through his veins again as he reached for the door.

Argento grabbed his arm. "Be careful, Dakota, you do not know what she has been put through. It may be best to let my healer go in first."

"Absolutely not. No offense to you, but she's been fighting against Brutes for the last five years. She does not know anything about our friendship, so your warriors will only put her on the defense. It's best for everyone involved if I go in."

"Agreed," Tony folded his arms over his chest.

"Very well." Argento released him. "I am pleased to hear that you consider us friends. I do as well."

Dakota nodded and lifted the hatch. "Ana?" The cellar was dark, and Tony handed him a lantern. The light illuminated the small, damp space, and it was only a moment before his eyes fell on the small form in the corner.

"Ana!" He rushed to her. Her eyes were closed, and her battered body brought tears to his eyes. "Ana, wake up!"

She shook violently and lashed out at him.

"Dakota is a cop," she mumbled.

28

ANASTASIA

She folded her arms across her chest and tried to fight back the tears burning in the corners of her eyes.

"What?" The Dakota that sat before her laughed. "Anastasia, I really think we need to do what Vincent said. You need to erase that book and admit that you are not the heroine of this story."

"He never calls me Anastasia." She fisted her hands at her sides.

"Ana, come on."

Anastasia backed toward the door.

"Momma, what's wrong? You're scaring me." Annabelle watched her warily from the corner.

"Ana!" Dakota shouted, but the man in front of her had said nothing. "Ana, wake up!"

She looked at the little girl in the corner, and a sob escaped her lips. "I'm so sorry, Annabelle. I will have you one day." She closed her eyes and focused on the voice. *I'm coming.*

"What are you talking about? Daddy, what is Mommy doing?" Annabelle started crying. "Please just do what Vincent said! Just erase the book, Mommy! We will play!"

"This isn't real." But the pain certainly was. Her chest constricted, making it harder to breathe as she fought to gain control of whatever twisted game Vincent had been playing with her mind. "This isn't real," she repeated. "I am Anastasia Silvan, daughter of Gregory and Annabelle Silvan. I was kidnapped by my uncle, Vincent Silvan, and sent to live with Mitch and Monica Carter."

"Momma!" Annabelle yelled. "Stop lying!"

"Anastasia, don't do this!"

"You can stay with us, Momma!"

"Mitch was abusive," she continued, fighting to keep her voice steady, "but I lived next door to Dakota Carter and his parents, George and Elizabeth. My father came for me and brought me to Terrenia. I have magic. I am going to beat you." She opened her eyes and glared at Vincent, who smirked as the world began to spin around her.

Annabelle's sobbing was like a dagger to her heart, and somewhere, fictional Dakota screamed at her.

"You won't win," Vincent sneered. "No matter what you do, I will break you, sooner or later. I own you."

She shook her head. "No. You don't." The wind around her began to pick up, as piece by piece the fictional world Vincent had built for her fell away and she stared up into the familiar blue eyes of the only man she'd ever loved.

"Dakota?" she choked out, reaching for him.

"Ana!" He clutched her to his chest and she clung to him. "Shit, we need to get you out of here." Dakota turned his head and looked at the cellar door. "Tony! I need some help!"

"Tony?" she muttered through cracked, burning lips.

"I'm here." He stepped into the light of the lantern beside Dakota and Anastasia wept. His face was the only one Vincent hadn't tried to replicate, and seeing him standing here was the last shred of evidence that she'd managed to escape. His eyes were brimming with tears, his jaw tight as he looked down at her. "What did they do to you?" He knelt beside her and gently touched the cheek that wasn't pressed against Dakota's hard chest.

"We need to get these shackles off," Dakota told him.

Anastasia looked down at the weights around her ankles. Her skin was raw and bleeding, but the pain of all her injuries had blended together to make it impossible to determine where the agony stemmed from.

Tony pried at the manacles with his hands but shook his head. "We need someone with bigger hands," he growled. "Anastasia, do you trust us?"

She nodded.

"Remember that." Tony looked back over his shoulder and yelled, "Argento!"

Anastasia stared wide-eyed as the largest Brute she'd ever seen descended the stairs into the cellar. His large frame took up the entire space. Half his face was painted red, and he was covered in blood.

"Dakota!" She held her hand up, but Dakota gripped her wrist.

"It's okay, he's with us."

She watched in horror as the Brute knelt beside them. "This is Brute metal." He lifted one of her restraints, and with ease, snapped it off of her ankle. "Only a Brute can break it." He bent over the other restraint, and removed that manacle as well.

Dakota set her down for a moment and stripped his shirt off. He gently put it over her head, each movement causing pain to shoot through her broken body.

Tears streamed down her cheeks and she ground her teeth together as he lifted her. She burrowed her face against his skin.

"I got you, Ana." He kissed the top of her head.

Dakota carried Anastasia carefully as if she might break, and honestly, she was worried she would. The Fighters and Brutes that were with them surrounded her like a wall of protection as they made the journey back. She wasn't sure how these Brutes began working with her people, but she was grateful to them for helping free her.

Each step Dakota took jolted her slightly, even though she knew he was doing his best to keep her steady.

"We're almost there," he said softly and she nodded.

"Anastasia!" She heard Brady's voice before he ran to walk beside Dakota.

"Hey." She tried to smile, but knew it probably appeared more like a grimace.

"What happened?" he asked.

"The Brutes had her chained in a cellar."

Brady shot an angry glare at the large Brute who'd released her.

"Don't you dare disrespect Argento and his men," Tony snapped from her other side. "If it weren't for them, not only would we have not found her, but on the off chance we had, we wouldn't have been able to get her out of that cellar. She was chained with Brute metal."

Brady chewed on the inside of his cheek until his face softened slightly. "I am grateful to them for that."

"As we all are. Run ahead and have Elizabeth set up one of the beds in the medical cottage. Anastasia is injured badly."

Anastasia moved slightly, and Dakota shifted her so she was closer.

"We are almost there, Anastasia; it's okay now." Tony brushed some of the hair from her face. "You are safe now." She looked up at his face and saw the sadness that could only come from a father, blood or not.

"Oh, Anastasia!" Elizabeth's voice brought a small smile to her lips, and she turned her head to look at Dakota's mom. "Oh, honey, you must be in so much pain. Tilly, grab some pain-management herbs."

Tears welled up in Anastasia's eyes as Elizabeth placed a gentle kiss to her forehead.

Dakota laid her gently down on the bed and stepped back.

"Go," Elizabeth told him. "I need to remove her shirt to see the damage."

"I'll be right outside." Dakota turned and left the room.

"Okay, let's see what we've got here." Using a sharp knife, Elizabeth split the shirt down the middle and parted the sides. Anastasia craned her neck to look down, seeing splotches of blue, black, and purple, covered in a thin layer of dirt and dried blood.

"Shit," Elizabeth cursed. "Honey, I need help, and lots of it. Do you want Dakota or Tony?"

Both men would be furious, but since Dakota had helped her heal on more than one occasion, she hoped he would continue not looking at her like a victim. Tony, on the other hand, considered her a daughter. It was hard to look at someone you felt of as a child and not see a victim.

"Dakota."

"Okay. Tilly, can you please grab Dakota?" she asked when Tilly handed her a small container with a purple cream inside.

Moments later, Tilly returned with Dakota.

"I'm going to fucking kill him," Dakota growled.

Anastasia clenched her eyes shut. Other than what her undergarments covered, the entirety of her body was on display in the bright light of the cottage.

"Anastasia," Elizabeth said sadly.

"What is it?" she asked carefully, the words making her feel like daggers were stabbing into her chest.

"This is going to hurt, but I have to see how many are broken."

"How many of what?"

"Ribs."

Anastasia bit back a scream as Elizabeth started feeling on her side.

"Honey, I need you to stop moving. Dakota, hold her."

Dakota stepped up to Anastasia's head and looked down at her. His mouth was pulled into a tight line, and tears shone in his eyes. "I'm so fucking sorry, Ana."

Elizabeth snapped her fingers to get his attention. "I need you to focus. I have to see how many ribs are broken and make sure there is nothing going on internally, but I need you to hold her still. Can you do that?"

As carefully as he could, he gripped her arms and held on. "I'm so sorry," he whispered against her head.

Anastasia closed her eyes.

He felt so warm to her, so incredibly familiar, that some of her heartbreak began to smooth away. This was the Dakota she knew, the Dakota who called her Ana, and drank scotch, and would support her no matter what she chose to do with her life.

This man right here, the one holding onto her for dear life, was the man she loved more than her own life.

No fictional reality crafted by Vincent could create anyone as wonderful as Dakota Parker.

"Aghh!" Anastasia screamed in agony as Elizabeth resumed feeling her sides. She struggled to get away from the pain, but Dakota held on.

"I'm sorry," he whispered again, and he repeated the words as she tried to get away from the pain.

"There's one, two," Elizabeth muttered to Tilly, "three, four."

Ana sucked in a harsh breath.

"I'm so sorry, Anastasia, but I can't stop."

"Aghh!" she screamed again, then focused on Dakota until spots swam in her vision and, soon, the pain stopped.

29

TERRENIA

DAKOTA

Six hours, four broken ribs, some internal bleeding, a fractured arm, and multiple lacerations later, his mother and Tilly finally finished working on Ana.

Dakota stared down at her battered face. They'd wiped her clean of the dirt and dried blood, revealing the bruising and open cuts still marring her light skin. She'd passed out before his mom had finished checking for broken ribs, and it had been a damn good thing she did.

His mother had been forced to perform surgery in order to suture up a tear in her abdomen.

"I don't know how she is alive, Dakota." His mother wiped tears and sweat from her face, shaking her head.

"I'm glad she is, but I don't know how. The pain alone should have put her in shock."

"She's tough." The steady rise and fall of her chest were enough to put a bit of his fear to rest, but it did nothing to curb the bone-deep rage that had him wishing he could bring all those Brutes back from the dead just so he could kill them again.

There was a knock at the door, then Carmen and Argento came in with the Brute healer in tow.

"How is she?" Argento asked, approaching Ana's sleeping form.

"Alive," Dakota answered.

"I don't know how they kept her alive, even with her magic," his mother said, still shocked.

"The stasis would have helped." The healer moved to stand beside Ana.

"How so?" Dakota asked.

"We use the stasis for those who are injured beyond healing as well, as a way to help them pass peacefully."

"He was using it just so she wouldn't die?"

"I do not believe so." The healer placed his hand gently over her forehead and closed his eyes. "The stasis he used was much stronger than that. It wouldn't have worked long, though, with the amount of magic in her blood." He removed his hand. "I can feel it just by being here in her presence."

"She is very powerful," Carmen said proudly.

"That she is," the healer agreed.

"Why don't you all go and rest? I will sit with her until morning." Carmen took a seat next to the fireplace, a book in her hand and a cup of what smelled suspiciously like coffee.

"I'm fine," Dakota said, unmoving.

"Dakota George, let's go." Elizabeth squeezed his shoulder gently. "You need rest. We both do."

"You are just like some of the females in our world," Argento said. "They are strong and stubborn as well."

"I will take that as a compliment." Elizabeth smiled. "Let's go, son. Thank you, Carmen."

Dakota shook his head. "I'll sleep here tonight."

Elizabeth eyed him. "You and I both know you won't sleep if you stay in here. You'll do nothing but pace until she wakes up."

"I'll make sure he sleeps," Carmen offered. "I can knock him out with some magic if necessary."

Argento laughed again. "Just like the females in my world!"

Dakota shot him a glare that only made the Brute laugh harder.

"Okay." Elizabeth sighed. "But you'd better get some sleep."

"Scouts honor." He held up his middle and pointer finger.

"You were never a boy scout."

Dakota shrugged and watched as Elizabeth and Argento stepped out into the now bright day. He looked down at Ana and pressed a kiss to her forehead. She may not be out of the woods yet, but he had her back, and that was a huge relief.

"She will be fine if you sleep." Carmen took a seat in the chair he had vacated beside the bed. "But I won't tell on you if you choose not to." She winked and Dakota ran his hands over his face.

"I probably should get some sleep, I just—"

She held up her hand and said knowingly, "I understand."

"If she wakes up, please let me know."

"I will, get some sleep."

Dakota drug a cot over from the other side of the room and laid down. After being away for so long, even a matter of feet felt like too far. After one last look at Ana, he closed his eyes and let the sound of her steady breathing lull him into sleep.

30

TERRENIA

ANASTASIA

Anastasia opened her eyes and squinted at the light shining through the slats of the shuttered windows. The room was quiet, save for the crackling wood of the fire. She turned her head and nearly cried out when she saw Dakota sleeping beside her. His chest rose and fell gently with each breath, and her broken heart began to repair.

"How are you feeling?"

Anastasia turned her head to the familiar voice. The older woman set aside a book she'd been reading.

"Am I dreaming?" Anastasia asked.

"No, not this time." Carmen smiled and stood to walk toward her. "It is nice to finally meet you in person, Anastasia." She reached down and patted Anastasia's hand, and the gesture was so kind, so familial, that it brought tears to her eyes. She really was home.

"How did you get here?"

"Once I finished talking with you, I portaled here from where I was living."

"Which was?"

She shrugged. "A little here and a little there. I like to move around." Carmen took a seat near the bed. "How are you feeling?"

"My body aches in places I didn't even know existed." She laughed and winced when the movement sent a sharp pain through her ribs. "But I'll live."

There was a knock at the door, and Carmen stood to answer it. Anastasia leaned back against her pillow and tried to take a deep breath. The action was freeing, but sent a sharp pain through her chest.

"I'm not sure she's up for company just yet," Carmen said softly.

"I just want to see that she's all right."

Shane. "It's okay, Carmen." Anastasia pulled the sheet up higher on her body. She was wearing a large t-shirt, and it wasn't anything Shane hadn't seen before, but it still made her feel uncomfortable.

"Are you sure?" She glanced back at Anastasia, who nodded. "Come on in. Just for a moment, though." Carmen stepped aside and opened the door wide enough that light from outside shone into the cabin.

Shane stepped inside, his hands in tight fists at his

sides. His jaw was clean shaven, his brown hair pulled back at the nape of his neck just as he'd always worn it.

His brown eyes held hers as he made his way toward her and took a seat in the chair beside the bed that her grandmother had vacated. "How are you?" he whispered.

"I'm alive."

His eyes glistened with unshed tears. She knew he still loved her, but her heart belonged to the man lying on the cot beside her.

"I got in from a scout this morning and Tony told me about—" He ducked his head and pressed his fingers to his eyes. "I can't imagine everything you went through."

"I'm all right," she assured him, with what she hoped looked more like a smile and less like she was hiding pain.

"We looked for you."

"I know you did."

"Your face." He reached out to touch her, but when she leaned away just slightly, Shane dropped his hand. "I, uh, I just wanted to check in on you." He got to his feet.

"Thank you, Shane. I mean it."

His mouth turned up in a half smile, and he nodded. "Anytime. We're friends, Anastasia, and I hope we will always be at least that."

"Me too."

Shane left the room and Carmen returned to her seat beside Anastasia. "He seems nice.

She nodded absently. "I haven't thanked you yet."

Carmen raised an eyebrow. "For?"

"Saving my life. You told me not to give up. If it hadn't been for you, I don't think I would have been able to come back."

"All I did was let you know that you weren't alone. You brought yourself back."

Anastasia glanced down at Dakota's face. "He came for me."

"I told you he would."

She smiled softly and glanced back at him. "You did." She tried to sit, but the pain that shot through her body forced her to lie back down. "What did they do to me?"

"The list of your physical injuries is incredibly extensive. We aren't even sure how you survived."

"I was their favorite punching bag for a while," she commented dryly.

"It's the stasis he had you in that I'm most interested in hearing about. Do you feel like talking about it?"

"Stasis?"

"That's what Argento called it. He said the Brutes use a *stasis* state to heal their sick or help them pass on peacefully."

"I suppose it could work for that."

"But I imagine that's not what Vincent used it for."

It wasn't a question, but Anastasia still nodded in response.

"He crafted a fake life for me, one where just about every dream I'd ever had came true. I was a writer, married to Dakota." She reached down and placed her hand on his shoulder, reassuring herself he was real, then she glanced up at Carmen, her eyes starting to water. "We had a daughter, and she was… all of it was amazing."

"He must have used some of your memories to craft this alternate reality."

"Probably. It wasn't until the end that I realized anything I thought about or said was being used against me. Fake Dakota called me Anastasia, and when I said something about how the real Dakota never used my full name, things changed."

"What was the goal of it? Do you know?"

"He kept trying to get me to admit I didn't have power, and that I needed to press the 'delete' button on my book to remove myself from the fake memories."

"Your book?"

"Yes. In this fake world, I was a writer who only wrote about Terrenia and magic and Brutes."

Carmen's brow furrowed. "That's strange. If you were fighting the stasis, it's possible he wanted you to give into it so you would no longer be a threat. But I don't understand why he'd leave you alive in the first place. It's not like he could have used your power or turned you to his side."

"He's fucking crazy." She managed to raise an arm and pinch the bridge of her nose in an attempt to ease the new blooming pain spreading in her head.

"Undoubtedly."

For the first time, Anastasia noticed the silence that surrounded them. It was the middle of the day—shouldn't there have been some noise? Children playing? Fighters training?

"Where is everyone?"

Carmen nodded. "They were getting fairly noisy out there while they waited for you to wake up, so I shielded us from the noise."

Anastasia gaped at her. "How did you do that?"

The other woman shrugged. "I'll teach you one day."

"Where did you come from? How did you get here?"

"We'll talk another day, and I promise I will fill you in on everything. For now, you need rest." Carmen pressed a hand to Anastasia's forehead. The warmth of her touch eased some of the pain, and her eyelids grew heavy. "Sleep now," Carmen whispered.

Anastasia closed her eyes.

31

DAKOTA

Dakota sat up and stretched. His body was cramped from the small cot, but overall, he felt energized. It was the best sleep he'd had in weeks. He looked over at Ana, who slept soundly.

After pressing a kiss to her forehead, he rose to his feet and stepped out onto the porch.

Carmen greeted him with a smile. "Morning."

"How long was I out?"

"Since yesterday morning."

"Damn." Dakota yawned and stretched again. "I suppose I was tired."

Carmen nodded and held out a thermos. "Coffee?"

"You been holding out on me, Carmen?"

"Perhaps I just don't want my secret getting out."

"It's safe with me." He took the thermos from her, and poured some of the steaming liquid into the lid that doubled as a cup.

"Gregory used to bring me some from time to time. He spent so many years searching your world for her." She gestured to Anastasia.

"Why did Vincent choose Seattle?" Dakota set the thermos down on the table beside her chair.

"Truthfully, I'm not sure. My guess would be that Seattle has something he needs, although I wouldn't even know where to begin figuring that out."

Dakota nodded and took a drink. "This is phenomenal."

"Fan of instant coffee?"

"Not usually, but after not having it for weeks? It's even better than a cup of Seattle's finest."

Carmen let out a laugh. "Good."

"So, any change?" he asked, breaking the silence that had surrounded them.

"She woke up briefly, but I put her back to sleep with a mild spell. She needs to heal, regenerate her magic."

Dakota nodded. "I can't believe what he did to her."

"I fear there's more to the story, too. We won't know everything until she wakes up."

"How could he do this to her? His own family?"

"Another mystery. I only met Vincent a handful of

times, but I never would have thought him capable of this."

"But you saw him in the vision?"

"I saw darkness in the vision, a man with no face destroying worlds and laughing while the occupants fell at his feet. When Vincent began his quest for power, we discovered he was the man. He had to be, after all."

"But you saw her beat him?"

"I saw her win. Don't give up hope, Dakota."

He nodded and continued drinking. The village was just starting to stir, and a group of Fighters made their way toward the gate to take over for the night shift.

Was there ever going to be a day when they didn't have to worry about an attack sneaking up on them in the night?

"Morning." Tony greeted them with a wave and stepped up onto the porch. The older man's greying hair was pulled back today and secured at the base of his neck with a cord. His eyes were hard this morning. *Guess we're all a little on edge.*

"Morning," Dakota said.

"How is she?" Tony leaned against a beam holding the roof of the porch up.

"Sleeping soundly." Dakota took another drink. "She'll be fine."

He nodded. "Shane said he spoke with her yesterday."

Dakota glanced at Carmen, who raised her hands in

surrender. "She told me to let him in and he was only here for a few minutes."

He swallowed the bite of jealousy that stabbed at him. He had never been a jealous person before, but the idea that Shane had spent the last five years getting to know the woman Ana was now irritated him.

"Green is not a good color on you… doesn't match your eyes." Carmen winked, and Dakota's irritation deflated. It was impossible to feel anything but happiness in the woman's presence.

"I'm going to get started on this morning's training." Tony's voice was deeper than usual, and grated with a thick layer of pain.

"I'll come by in a bit if that's all right?" Dakota asked.

"Sure." Tony stepped from the porch without another word.

Kaley rounded the corner and made her way over to him. She climbed up the stairs, her intelligent eyes focusing on him as she moved. "Hey, girl. I bet I know who you're looking for." He patted her head and opened the door so she could go inside.

Dakota and Carmen sat in silence for a few more minutes, enjoying the quiet of the morning.

Thirty minutes later, Dakota made his way toward the training cottage. When he turned the corner, he saw Tony already had Brady pinned to the ground. Dakota moved to stand beside his mom and Shane, who watched from the porch of the center.

Brady tapped and Tony stood, pulling him to his feet.

"Hey, Mom." Dakota wrapped an arm around her shoulders. "Shane," he said to the other Fighter.

Elizabeth leaned against him. "Hey, honey, get some sleep?"

"I did, actually."

"Good." Her voice was distant, and her eyes never left Tony.

"What's wrong?"

"I'm worried about him," she whispered, gesturing to Tony.

"What about him?"

"He's bottling up all his anger and taking it out on the other Fighters. Not that he's *trying* to hurt them, but he nearly dislocated Andrew's shoulder. The only reason Shane is over here is because Tony separated his and I had to put it back in place."

"He's only been here for half an hour."

His mom eyed him. "Exactly. He's been on a war path since he made his way over here."

"Shit." Dakota studied Tony closer. The man's jaw was set, his body tense. He was looking for a fight, but these guys weren't right for that.

"Why don't you go check on Ana?" he told his

mom. "Maybe relieve Carmen so she can get some sleep."

Elizabeth nodded warily and turned to leave. "Be careful, Dakota," she said over her shoulder.

"Anyone else?" Tony asked, studying the circle of Fighters.

"I'll take a run at you," Dakota offered.

Accepting the challenge, Tony moved to the edge of the circle and Dakota removed his shirt.

"You sure you're up to this?" Tony asked.

"Better me than these guys."

"What's that supposed to mean?"

"You're angry," Dakota said as they began to circle each other. "I'm pissed the fuck off too."

Tony charged and Dakota barely dodged him in time. In skill and size, Tony had him beat, so his best bet was to evade.

"I don't fight with anger."

Dakota managed to catch him off guard, and threw him to the ground. Tony rolled him around and pinned him, but not well enough, and Dakota threw him off.

"That's a load of bullshit." Dakota jumped to his feet.

"Fighting with an angry heart only causes you to lose focus."

"You can say that all you want, but you're still human, Tony." Dakota dodged him again, but Tony caught him with a kick to the leg. He fell to the ground and they rolled around for a few moments before Dakota managed to get him into a headlock.

Pure luck on his part—not that he'd admit that anytime soon.

"They nearly killed her," Tony growled. "She was damn near naked when we found her. He stripped her of her strength and her dignity!"

"I know." Dakota released him and they got back to their feet. "Let that fire burn. Shit, let that damn angry beast rage inside you, but don't take it out on your people. On your Fighters."

Tony studied the circle of exhausted men around him and nodded. "Training is over." He headed back toward his cottage.

"Tony." Dakota caught up to him, and when the man turned around, tears welled in his eyes. "We have her back and he won't get his hands on her again."

Tony nodded and walked away without a word.

Dakota watched him leave, then turned back toward the circle.

Shane held out his shirt. "Those were some impressive moves."

"Yeah, well he's not focused."

"True. Still, though. I'd love to spar with you once your mom lifts my ban."

Dakota snorted. "If she has her way, you'll be down for a month."

Brady walked past them and Dakota called out to him. “Hey, Brady!”

The boy stopped and turned to face Dakota. His eyes were darker, nearly black, and his jaw was set from what Dakota guessed was humiliation from Tony pinning him.

“You okay?”

“Fine.” The clipped, one-word response was so unlike Brady that it surprised Dakota.

“Your mom? Sister?”

“They are fine,” he snapped. As he walked away, he eyed the Brutes in their camp. How could Brady still hate them? Even after everything that they’d done for them?

Dakota spotted Selena walking toward her house and broke into a jog to catch up. “Morning, Selena.”

“Morning.” She greeted him with a smile. “What can I do for you?”

“I just ran into Brady and—”

She raised her hand. “Let me guess, he was short with you?”

“Yeah, actually.”

“He’s been acting strange since last night. I’m guessing he’s just worried about Anastasia, but he’s refusing to talk about it.”

“Nothing else is going on?”

“Not that I know of. I know he’s been stressed since the Brutes moved in, but no more than the rest of us.”

He nodded. “It was necessary.”

“I know that. But it doesn’t make it any easier for those of us who lost family and friends to them. We’ve spent years afraid of those beasts, and now they live within our village.”

“Can you let me know if he gets any worse?”

“I will.” She played with the edge of her shirt. “Listen, if you’re up for it, you can come over for dinner. I know with everything going on you could probably use a break.”

He smiled awkwardly. “I appreciate it, but I’m going to stick by Ana, just in case she needs me.”

“I completely understand. She’s a lucky woman, Dakota.”

“Thanks.” He turned headed back toward the medical cottage.

32

ANASTASIA

Anastasia opened her eyes, slowly assessing her body from the neck down. She wiggled her fingers, her toes, twisted gently to test her ribs—she sucked in air through her teeth as pain throbbed through her abdomen. Her body still ached, but as long as she didn't twist her torso again, it was a dull pain that only reminded her of why she needed to keep fighting: to save those she loved from suffering anymore at the hands of Vincent.

She sat up and put her feet on the floor. The wood felt warm beneath them, and she stood. The simple act of standing without help brought a smile to her face. Vincent probably hadn't believed she'd ever stand again. In fact, she'd be willing to bet that he'd counted on her remaining broken.

She looked down to see she was wearing a pair of sweats and a t-shirt. Desperate to feel the sun on her skin, she didn't worry about trying to change first, she just stepped out onto the porch.

The sight of the village bustling around her was nearly enough to bring tears to her eyes. People that were out and about stopped and stared at her, surprised to see her standing before them.

"Anastasia!" Sarah called with a smile and rushed toward her.

She accepted the hug, smiling at the other villagers who greeted her and welcomed her back. Dakota came into view and Anastasia's heart leapt. His dark hair was messy and had grown a decent amount since she'd last seen him. A short beard covered his face, and when his blue eyes landed on hers, Anastasia felt a jolt of lust break through the pain.

She nearly ran to him, aching to feel his arms around her, but the harsh setting of his jaw had her resisting. Instead, she continued greeting those she passed, enjoying the way the dirt felt beneath her bare feet.

The crowd faded away, and soon it was just Anastasia and Dakota staring at each other. The space between them was too much to take, so she stepped forward.

"Hey."

"Hey," he said tightly. "Want to get changed?"

She nodded and they headed away from the medical cottage and the village, toward the home where she'd learned who she truly was.

When the familiar site of the cabin she'd shared with Gregory came into view, Anastasia had to force herself not to break into a run.

They stepped inside and she smiled. She'd never thought she would see this place again. The last time she'd been here, she'd cried over Gregory's journals, but now she felt nothing but peace and a sense of belonging.

She still grieved her father, but it felt lighter somehow, and she knew that he was somewhere watching over her. She stepped forward and trailed her fingers across the back of the couch.

Everything was so much the same, but parts of Dakota had made their way in as well. Little things like the mug on the counter, the whiskey glass on the table next to the couch, and his scent that clung to the air.

She turned to face him, alone at last, and saw the questions in his eyes before he even opened his mouth to say them.

"What happened in that clearing?"

Just starting with the hard hitters, huh? Anastasia took a deep breath. "I knew only one of us was getting out of that clearing, and I chose you."

"But why? Why not come through with me? You could have closed the portal from the other side."

"I didn't trust myself. I felt that power, Dakota, the humming in my blood, and I wanted it." She stared down at her hands. "I changed that night, and had I come through the portal with you, I worry I would have hurt someone."

"I could have brought you back."

She stepped forward and cupped his face. "You did. In more ways than one."

When he leaned into her touch but didn't press her further, she dropped her hand and continued. "I killed Mitch."

His eyes widened but he didn't pull away. "Can't say I'm super bummed about that one."

"He didn't fight back. Vincent offered him to me and I reached into his chest and ripped his heart out." She studied his face for any sign of horror at her words.

"If you think I'm going to be angry or upset, you're wrong. That asshole shot me and spent your entire childhood beating you. If I'd had the chance, I would have done the same."

"But after feeling that rush of"—she searched for a word—"power, I lost myself for a time. I don't really remember what happened, just that, for a brief moment, I wanted more." She sighed. "Then your face popped into my head, and Vincent was so angry, he hit me with a blast that knocked me out. Carmen came to see me and told me to hang on, that you all were coming for me."

Tears burned in her eyes and a lump formed in her throat as memories from her captivity came back. "He killed you, Dakota. In front of me, so many different times, in so many different ways. I watched you die every single day for what felt like eternity. Even though I knew it wasn't you, it felt like a part of me died each time you did." She closed her eyes tightly.

"But I'm here, Ana." He gripped her shoulders.

"I know you are." She smiled through the tears and he rested his forehead against hers.

"I know you are," she whispered again. "When that didn't work, he sent Brutes in to beat me, thinking I would use my magic to stop them. I didn't, afraid that if I did I wouldn't come back again. I fought the beasts off without weapons for nearly two weeks. I lost count after that."

Anastasia stepped back.

"We know he had you in a stasis for a while; is that what he did to you in there?"

"No, I think the stasis was how he manipulated my reality."

"What do you mean?"

"The son of a bitch put me into a new world and made me feel like I was going crazy. It was probably the worst of the torture methods he *tested* on me."

Dakota leaned against the counter. "What happened?"

"I woke up in your parents' house in Seattle. We were married, and we had a beautiful little girl together. She was so perfect, and we were all so happy." She smiled softly. "I was a writer. You were a doctor, just as you had always wanted, and none of this had ever happened." She opened her eyes and looked at him, afraid to stop talking.

"The book I had been working on was about all of this, a work of fiction—if you can believe that crap. You —or rather, fake Dakota— told me that I had episodes where I would forget my real life and believe that my story was my life. In fact, I was nearly convinced of this. So much so that he talked me into seeing a psychiatrist who just so happened to be Vincent," she growled. "That bastard told me that to have the life I always wanted, I had to delete the book I was working on and admit that I had no magic. To erase everything I believed was reality. I almost did it, even though on some level I knew all along that it was an illusion. I wanted that life so badly that I nearly gave everything up to have it until I saw you—the real you."

"Me?"

"You appeared in a mirror in his office, and you asked me to come back to you." She shut her eyes and wiped the tears from her cheeks.

"Our daughter was screaming at me, crying and

begging me to stay with her, and I left, forced myself out of the illusion, and when I woke up in that cellar again, a part of me was so angry at myself." She clenched her jaw and shook her head. "So angry for leaving all of that behind."

"It wasn't real, Ana." He walked back over to her and touched her face gently, tucking a strand of hair behind her ear.

"It could have been… for you. Had you never met me, you could have gone on to be a doctor and have a beautiful daughter. You could have had a normal, happy life, Dakota."

He cupped her face in his hands. "Ana, I wouldn't have wanted any of that unless it was with you." His thumbs brushed away the tears on her cheeks. "You hear me? You are it for me. I don't want anyone else, and I never would have wanted my life to turn out any other way. Everything has happened the way it was meant to. We will have that life one day, and you will hold a daughter in your arms, I swear it. But I don't want any of that unless it's with you." He wrapped his arms around her and held on tight.

"It hurts so bad, Dakota." She cried into his chest. "It all felt so real, and I wanted it so badly." Her fists balled in the front of his shirt. Emotional pain she hadn't realized she'd been carrying poured from her as they stood there.

"I know, baby." He stroked his hand down her hair.

"I thought I'd never see you again." She stepped back and looked into his bright blue eyes.

"I never would have stopped looking." Dakota leaned down and pressed his lips to hers, gently at first, and she savored the way they felt. This was reality, and this felt right.

33

ANASTASIA

Anastasia stepped out into the sun for the second time that day, feeling refreshed and rejuvenated. It was amazing what fresh clothes and the first actual bath in weeks could do to one's mood.

"So, what's been going on?" she asked Dakota as they made their way back to the village.

"We've been doing what we can to take out the Brute camps popping up all over the damn place."

"So, before they stayed hidden, and now they're setting up shop in the open?"

Dakota nodded.

"That's worrisome." She paused as a group of Brutes chased some younger kids in a game of tag. Her hand itched for her sword even though she knew there was no danger; Dakota had told her of Argento and his followers, but it was hard to break the habit.

"It's obvious they're planning something, but we don't know what that is just yet," he said, pulling her from her thoughts.

"Anything else?"

He shook his head.

"Brady!" Anastasia called, but he barely looked up at her, and when he did, his eyes were darker than before.

And a hell of a lot colder. She'd never seen anything but warmth reflected in those brown depths before. "What happened to him?"

"No damn clue. He's been like that since we let the Brutes in. Selena thinks he's just having trouble adjusting."

Anastasia bit the inside of her cheek "All right." She'd go check on him in a bit.

They continued walking until they reached the medical cottage. Elizabeth sat on the porch, and when she saw them, she smiled. "Anastasia, it's so good to see you."

"You, too." Anastasia grinned and wrapped her arms around Elizabeth.

"How are you feeling?"

"I feel great, surprisingly."

"Carmen said your body would begin to heal itself."

"Why?" she asked.

"Your magic."

Anastasia's brow furrowed. "But I never had that capability before."

"It grows as you use it, like any muscle does," Carmen said from behind them. She smiled as she made her way up the steps and into a chair next to Elizabeth. "I'm so happy to see you out and about."

"It's nice to be out and about."

"I can imagine," her grandmother said. "I'd like to start working with you soon."

"Working with me on what?"

"Your magic. We need to get you trained up."

Anastasia shook her head. "I don't think that's such a good idea."

"Anastasia, you can't beat Vincent without it."

"I'm strong, and if I can get close enough to him, I can take him out with a sword rather than power."

Carmen opened her mouth to argue, but stopped.

The truth was, Anastasia was terrified of what was inside her. What if she reached down for it, and it drug her back into the void? What if next time Dakota couldn't bring her back?

The emptiness she'd felt the night she'd embraced her magic still chilled her. and just the memory of it made her feel like shivering. She remembered how it had felt to have the power surging through her, how she had wanted nothing more than to gain more at any cost.

"When you're ready, we can talk," Carmen finally said.

"Anastasia."

She turned toward the sound of Tony's voice. His bottom lip quivered, and his eyes shone with unshed tears. Not caring who saw, she ran to him and wrapped her arms around the man who was so much like a father to her.

His arms held her tightly, her muscles aching from the contact, but she didn't care. She looked up at him, smiling brightly. "It's so good to see you Tony."

"You have no idea how wonderful it is to see you." He grinned, and Anastasia hugged him again.

"It seems you guys have been up to a lot lately," she said as she released him.

He ran a hand through his black and silver hair. "We've been doing what we can."

"Anastasia!"

She turned, surprised to hear a voice she hadn't heard in years. "Leo?" She stared dumbfounded at him, then back at Tony, as he crossed the space between them. When he got close enough, she hugged him hard. "It's so great to see you! What happened? Where have you been? Is Patrick okay, too?" She studied the man who'd been missing since that night four years ago when Maximus had kidnapped Brady. While he was quite a bit thinner than before, and his blonde hair was shorter, he looked roughly the same.

Leo shook his head sadly. "Argento brought me back with the rest of the people the Brutes kidnapped. Patrick died a few years ago."

Her heart dropped. "Leo, I'm so sorry."

He shrugged. "He went down with a fight, and that's how he would have wanted to go."

"I'm so happy you're back."

He beamed. "You too."

Anastasia caught movement out of the corner of her eye, and turned her head. Brady scoffed at a group of villagers laughing with a couple Brutes.

"What is he up to?" Tony asked as they watched him leave through the gate. "No one is supposed to leave unaccompanied. It's not safe."

"Shall we find out?" Dakota asked, rising from the bench.

Tony, Dakota, Anastasia, and Leo exited the gate after Brady, heading toward the woods. A scream split through the silence, sending birds fleeing from the trees. They pushed into a run, and Anastasia winced as she tried to keep up.

She was much better than she had been, but her body still ached. *Come on.* She groaned and pushed forward. They burst into a clearing, ready for a fight.

Brady stood over a Brute, the blade in his hand dripping with blood.

"Brady!" A woman knelt beside the injured Brute,

applying pressure to a wound in his side. "Why the hell did you do that? He hadn't done anything wrong!"

"He was going to kill you, Noelle!" Brady screamed, his hand still gripping the blade.

"He was not!" Noelle yelled back. "We were out here together. It was consensual!" Her cheeks were flushed, and Anastasia realized she had been so caught off guard by the attack that she failed to notice the other signs. Her dress was wrinkled, one of the shoulders down on her arm.

"I confided in you, Brady!" she yelled.

"You're an abomination," he whispered. "He is a monster!"

"Brady, you had better shut your mouth, or I will shut it for you," Tony warned.

"So you're sticking up for them, too? What's next? Half-beast babies running around? Disgusting!"

"Brady! This isn't you," Anastasia insisted.

He sneered at her. "Yeah, because you know me so well. You've been running around either chasing him" —he gestured to Dakota—"or trying not to die yourself. Some fucking protector you are."

"Brady," Dakota warned.

"Save it. You've been here for, what, a month? And everyone thinks you somehow know best. Dakota is Anastasia's boyfriend so he must know everything," he mocked. "You bring these beasts into our home and think you can get away with it?" He took a step toward

Dakota but Tony stopped him by grabbing his shoulder.

"Brady, watch what you're saying," Tony warned.

"No," he growled, quickly turning and thrusting his dagger into Tony's side.

"Tony!" Dakota shouted, lunging for him.

Brady ran, dodging Dakota as he disappeared into the woods.

"Son of a bitch!" Tony yelled as he fell to his knees.

Anastasia ignored the pain in her body and broke into a run after Brady. Her lungs burned and the muscles in her legs ached as she moved. When she tripped, Anastasia stopped and fought to catch her breath.

"Dammit!" she screamed into the empty air.

"What the hell, Ana?" Dakota and Leo raced to her side. "You aren't strong enough yet!"

"What is his deal?" Leo asked when he came to a stop beside her.

Anastasia's blood iced. "Surely it's not possible."

"What's not possible?" Dakota asked.

She straightened. "I don't think he's Brady anymore. Vincent must be controlling him somehow." Why the hell had she not seen it before? Deep down, she'd never even considered he would be capable of mind control.

"How do you know?" Dakota asked.

"I just do. What other explanation is there? Brady would never hurt anyone, he's not him." She moved and the pain that sliced through her side had her wincing.

"Fuck," Dakota cursed. "We need to get you back."

"I'm fine. We need to get to Brady… maybe we can bring him back."

"Ana, you can't push yourself like this. I get that you heal fast, but dammit, you nearly died three days ago. We will find him, but let's do it without dying ourselves."

She stared at the tree line where Brady vanished and nodded sadly. Dakota was right; she was no use to Brady, or anyone for that matter, if she were confined to a bed. They made their way back to the village, each step another nail in Vincent's coffin when she found him.

Elizabeth sat on the porch of the medical cottage, her face pale. Hands folded in her lap, she stared absently at the darkening sky.

"How is Tony?" Anastasia asked, taking a seat next to her.

"He lost a lot of blood." Her voice was empty. "The blade nicked an artery. He passed out before Tilly started working on him."

Panic surged through her, sending her stomach into a sickening flip. "Is he going to be okay?"

She nodded. "I think so. I hope so." She buried her face in her hands. "I'm so tired of losing people I love."

Anastasia's eyes widened, but when she looked to Dakota he didn't seem surprised. Was she missing something? Had something happened between Elizabeth and Tony while she'd been gone?

Elizabeth wiped her face and straightened. "Are you okay?" she asked, turning to Anastasia.

"Just tired, but I'm all right."

"Okay. I am going to try and help with Griffith."

"Griffith?" Anastasia asked.

Elizabeth nodded. "Yes, the Brute Brady stabbed."

"How is he?"

"Argento got him to their healer, who was able to eliminate the poison somehow. He should be fine."

"What are we going to do about Brady?" Leo asked in a whisper.

"We will send out a group to look for him," Dakota answered.

"If I had to guess, he's going to come to us," Anastasia said softly. Unless she was wrong, and Brady was just a pissed off teenage boy with a grudge.

But she very much doubted that.

34

TWO WEEKS LATER

ANASTASIA

"Anastasia, watch your stance." Tony held his sword out, and she tapped hers against it.

"I remember." She smiled lightly and got her footing. He stepped toward her and she dodged, swinging her sword and knocking his out of his hand.

"I see I don't need to go easy on you."

"Let's be serious, Tony, you weren't going easy on me." She laughed lightly, and Tony grinned.

"It was a minor flesh wound," he insisted.

"That nearly had you bleeding to death."

He shrugged. "I'm too tough to die."

Anastasia rolled her eyes and Tony charged her. She dodged, as she'd been doing all afternoon. This time he spun around her and knocked her weapon to the ground. “Not quick enough.” He grinned down at her.

“Maybe I’m taking it easy on you, old man.”

Tony let out a laugh and helped her to her feet.

They’d been sparring for the better part of an hour, and while her body no longer ached with every move, her stamina was down. Apparently being locked in a cold cellar for over a month had done a number on her in more ways than one.

“I feel useless,” she muttered, then drank from a canteen of water.

“You are many things, Anastasia, but useless is not one of them.”

“Hey, girl.” Anastasia smiled and pet Kaley’s soft coat as she rubbed against her. “I see you made time for me today.” Even now that Anastasia was back, Kaley spent most of her time tailing Dakota.

“Seems she does have a bit of a crush on our Dakota, doesn’t she?” Tony laughed, but when he looked at Anastasia, his smile vanished. “What is it?”

Her thoughts drifted back to the real reason she was so tired. She couldn’t seem to catch a full night of sleep, no matter what she tried.

“Nothing,” she assured him with a slight smile. “I’m still having some trouble, is all.”

“The nightmare again?”

She nodded. Tony had been the only one she confided in about the nightmares she’d been having.

The horrible repetition of waking up back in the house from Vincent's illusion. This time Brutes came and destroyed it. She had watched them kill Dakota and kidnap Annabelle every single night for a week.

She was beginning to have trouble coming out of the nightmare, even after she woke up. It was much like it had been in her illusion, where she was having difficulty distinguishing real from fake, only this time there were no images of reality to pull her out. It was a trap for her mind, and she kept falling right into it.

"Still haven't told Dakota?" he asked, his voice stern.

She shook her head. "He knows I'm having night-mares—let's be honest, it's not like that's a new devel-opment—but I haven't told him about the actual content. We have enough to worry about. With Brady missing, and the daily searches for him, Dakota has plenty on his plate."

"Don't you think he deserves to know?"

"They're just nightmares. If I tell him, he's going to panic and think Vincent is getting to me again. I need him to stay focused so he can stay alive. And I need to get some damn sleep so I can get back in the fight."

He patted her on the back. "Maybe talk to Elizabeth; she has some tea that might do the trick."

"Speaking of Elizabeth." Anastasia smiled and turned to face him. "What is going on there?"

"Nothing. Yet," he added, laughing. "I have fallen

head over heels for that woman, but she is taking her time. It's okay, I will wait. I'm very patient." He winked.

"I've noticed." Anastasia laughed, and Tony wrapped his arm around her.

"Your father would be so proud of you, Anastasia. You have come a long way."

"Thank you, Tony."

"Anytime. I am going to head to town and check on my woman." He winked again as he stood. "You know where to find me if you need me."

"See you, Tony." Anastasia sat on the porch of her home and stared out at the sky that was fading into night. The calm of Terrenia settled over her and she breathed in the scent of her world.

Her dying world, she thought with disgust as she caught a grouping of trees that were turning black, their leaves falling to the ground. She needed to get back to a hundred percent so she could get back into the fight, and yet here she was, out of breath after only an hour of light sparring. It was pathetic.

Damn nightmares.

"Hey." Dakota's voice pulled her from her thoughts.

"Hey, you." She smiled brightly.

"I was wondering where you went off to," he said to Kaley as he took his seat next to Anastasia.

"Any luck today?"

Dakota shook his head sadly. "No sign of him."

She nodded absently, and continued to stare out at the trees.

"How are you?" Dakota asked.

"Good."

"Ana, it's me." He lifted her face with his hand and kissed her forehead. "Please tell me the truth."

"Dakota, I'm fine. Not perfect yet, but a whole lot closer than I was." She took another drink from the canteen in her hand.

"You have to stop lying to me. I know something is bothering you. What you went through, it was awful. No one is expecting you to be back to normal overnight."

"It's not overnight, though, Dakota. It's been two weeks. Do you see what's happening?" She gestured to the trees. "Vincent's darkness is spreading and it's going to destroy everything. I have to get back into the fight."

"You will, soon." Thunder roared above them, and they looked to the sky as rain began to fall. It hammered down on Terrenia, and the loud roaring of it on the porch above them drowned out all other noise.

Dakota reached over and threaded his fingers through hers. She looked down at their joined hands and wished like hell things were different. That he was just another man and she were just another woman, and they weren't face first in a giant volcano just waiting to erupt.

The rain washed away some of the dirt from the path

in front of her, trailing down toward the rotting trees she'd studied only moments ago.

If only it could wash away the darkness, too.

If only the drops could cleanse her soul.

35

ANASTASIA

"Good morning, my loves!" Dakota greeted Anastasia and Annabelle with a smile as they came down the stairs.

"Daddy is making waffles!" Annabelle yelled in delight as she smelled the cooking food.

Anastasia took a moment to take the scene in, knowing it wouldn't last long.

"Honey, what's wrong?" he asked, narrowing his eyes.

"Nothing, I'm just having a bad dream, is all." Tears streamed down her face.

"You're awake now, Momma. It will all clear up soon." Annabelle grinned up at her.

"I hope so." She smiled and kissed Annabelle's cheek. "Let's go somewhere," she said to them.

"Where would you like to go?" Dakota asked, amused.

"Anywhere, let's just get out of the house," she pleaded, hoping to hang on to the happiness for a little longer. "Now, let's go now."

"Well, hang on, Ana," Dakota said on a laugh. "I just made breakfast."

"Yeah, Momma! I love Daddy's waffles!"

"Me too, but please, let's just go. Please," she begged, but the splintering of the door told her it was too late. "Dakota, move!" she screamed as the Brutes barreled through the door. She grabbed Annabelle and reached for Dakota. He turned toward her and, just as he started to move toward them, a dagger buried hilt deep in his chest.

His eyes went wide and he stared at her as he crumpled to his knees.

"Daddy!" Annabelle screamed in horror.

Anastasia gripped Annabelle to her chest. She tried to run up the stairs, but was slammed in the back with a blast of magic. The pain sent white spots swimming in her vision and she fell forward, still cradling her daughter.

Four Brutes surrounded them. Anastasia shoved Annabelle behind her.

"Mommy!" she screamed.

"No! Get away from us!" Anastasia cried. A Brute latched its large hand around her throat and lifted her from the stairs. Her lungs burned as they fought for oxygen, and she kicked out as hard as she could.

Nothing happened.

"Mommy!" Annabelle screamed again, and Anastasia watched in complete hopeless horror as her daughter was ripped away from her and carried from the house.

"You will die," the Brute still holding her by the throat growled in her face. His breath was hot against her skin.

The glint of a blade caught her eye, and she thrashed as he drove it into her abdomen.

Pain seared through her body, and Anastasia crumpled to the floor.

ANASTASIA WOKE ON A SCREAM, TEARS STREAMING down her face. She gripped her pillow and screamed into it again. When she looked up, Dakota stood in her room. She took a deep breath, only briefly wondering why he was fully dressed in the middle of the night. His arms were crossed over his chest, and he watched her intently, his lips in a tight line.

"Want to tell me what's going on now?" he asked.

"I'm sorry, it was just a nightmare."

"Was it?"

Her gaze fell to Dakota's chest where a dark stain spread over the front of his white shirt.

"Ana," he whispered as he fell to the floor.

"No!" she screamed and tried to lunge for him, but it felt as though hands were pressing her back against the bed instead. "Let me go!" She thrashed, but whatever held her down didn't budge.

"I'm in your head, Anastasia." Vincent's voice flooded her mind. *"And I'm never going away."*

Anastasia shot up in bed, covered in a layer of sweat. She pressed the palm of her hand against her hammering heart, and took slow, deliberate breaths to calm the panic.

It was just a nightmare. A long, grueling, horrific, nightmare.

After her heart rate started to slow, Anastasia got to her feet and made her way out to the living room. Wanting to see that he was all right, she peeked in Dakota's room, but his bed was empty.

She clenched her fists at her sides as images of the nightmare still plagued her.

She searched the house quickly, her pulse racing, then swung the front door open. He sat on the porch, staring out at the dark sky, and she let out a breath of relief.

He was here with her, and he wasn't going anywhere.

She made her way over to him and sat beside him.

"Couldn't sleep?"

Anastasia shook her head. "You?"

"Nah. Too much on my mind."

"Like what?" She folded her hands in her lap. The pajama pants and t-shirt she wore weren't doing much to fend off the chill from the storm. Dakota wrapped an arm around her and she leaned against him. The warmth of his body seeped into hers, and her stomach flipped.

"Brady, for one. I don't like the idea of him being out there. Selena is going out of her mind with worry, and I don't want to have to tell a mother her son may never come home."

"We'll find him," she said, hoping like hell she was right. "I want to go out tomorrow and see if we can't find some trace of him. He has to be somewhere."

"Unless Vincent has him hidden away."

"Which, unfortunately, is entirely possible."

They sat in silence for a few minutes, just listening to the soothing sound of the rain as it fell. They must have gotten quite a bit because even in the dim light from the moon that managed to sneak through the clouds, she could see that the pond beside the cabin was full.

"So, what's the next thing?"

"Hmm?"

"You said 'for one', so I'm guessing there's more."

"It's stupid," he said with a laugh.

"Let me be the judge of that. I promise I won't lie."

Dakota grinned and removed his arm, leaving her feeling like a part of her was missing.

"I'm wondering where we stand."

"What do you mean?"

"You and me. We haven't really talked about it since you got back."

"I didn't think anything had changed."

"Me either, I just…" He sighed. "I want to make sure we're on the same page."

"Which is?"

"That I want to be with you, that we want to be with each other."

"Isn't that apparent?"

"You've been distant with me since you got back. I know Vincent put you in that stasis, and it messed with you, but it has just felt like we took huge steps back toward the friend zone." He rubbed his hands over his face. "I'm not trying to pressure you into making a decision, I just want to make sure I know where we stand."

Anastasia studied the lines of his face. His mouth was firm and pulled down at the sides, and his eyes were heavy. How could he ever think she'd want to take a step back? She'd never wanted anything as badly as she wanted to be with him.

Hell, ever since she'd been old enough to know what a crush was, she'd had one on her best friend. Dakota was everything to her. So what the hell was she waiting for? Anastasia rose to her feet and reached down for Dakota. He gripped her hand and stood. Butterflies danced in her stomach, and she took a step closer to him. They were a breath apart, and she looked up into the dazzling blue eyes of the one man she loved.

"I want to be with you, Dakota." She swallowed hard when his pupils dilated and his nostrils flared. Desire pooled in her belly and she tipped her face up.

Dakota leaned down and pressed his lips to hers. Anastasia opened beneath him, begging him to take everything she had to offer.

He lifted her up and she fisted her hands in his hair, wrapping her legs around his waist. He began walking, but between her thundering pulse and the feel of his hard body against hers, she couldn't have cared less where he was taking her.

The entire world could be crumbling apart at the seams and there was not a damn thing she'd want to do about it. Irresponsible? Possibly. But didn't they deserve a break? Didn't she deserve to be happy for once?

Dakota pulled away, breathless, and looked into her eyes. His were lust-filled and heavy, and she imagined hers reflected much of the same.

"Ana," he whispered.

"Please don't stop, Dakota."

"Are you sure?" He tilted her head up with his fingertip. "Because while I've wanted this for a long damn time, I don't ever want to pressure you."

Her response was to pull his mouth back to hers. The kiss was frenzied, and she wrapped more tightly around him as he carried her away from the door. The softness of the mattress was at her back within moments, and Dakota's hard body pressed against hers.

While she was still afraid, still broken on the inside, this was where she belonged.

Her arms wound their way around his neck and he pulled her closer to him still. The kiss deepened, and she gripped the hem of his shirt, breaking the kiss only long enough to lift it over his head.

His lips found the pulse pounding in her throat, and she leaned her head back, aching for his touch.

"Ana, you need time," he whispered against her mouth.

"I need you." She pulled him tighter against her. She tried to not see the scars on his chest from Mitch's belt, and focused only on the now. The way he stared down at her with hunger in his eyes.

His fingers played with the waistband of her pants until he eased them from her body, slowly torturing her as he allowed his fingers to heat her skin.

"When you're gone, it feels like I'm bleeding to death. You're a piece of me, Ana." He pressed his lips to the inside of her thigh. "You're my reason, the breath in my chest." He trailed his lips up her body, and lifted the shirt over her head.

"You're mine, too," she responded, breathless. He

was tearing the pain away from her, piece by piece, until there was nothing but a sore spot left.

He stepped away and she watched as he removed the rest of his clothes, then covered her body with his.

The feel of him above her, against her, deep within her body, was something she needed more than anything else. He was her sustenance, her entire world, and without him, she would fade away into the black.

Lying beside him, Anastasia traced the lines of the scars on Dakota's chest, pink and raised, still fresh on his taut skin. Candlelight flickered as the storm still raged outside the safety of their walls.

The belt marks from the night she'd found him in that warehouse were etched in harsh lines now, and the sight of it brought tears to her eyes. "I can't believe he did this to you." She traced the line of the largest mark down the center of his chest with her index finger before leaning forward and placing a gentle kiss to it.

"It wasn't anything worse than what he did to you." He toyed with the ends of her hair.

She trailed her fingertips down his abdomen to a round scar. "Gunshot?"

He nodded.

Anastasia sat up and the blanket fell away from her bare body. The flickering light of the candles danced across Dakota's skin, and she took a moment to soak the sight in.

His body was hard, and she splayed her fingers over the muscles of his abdomen. She reached forward and traced the intricate tribal tattoo that started on the top of his shoulder and wound down over his heart and to his elbow. A police badge was tattooed over his heart, and she traced the lines of it gently.

"For my dad." He watched her intently as she continued surveying the design. Halfway down his arm, the tattoo exploded in color and circled around a compass that pointed north.

"What's this for?"

"I thought it looked cool."

She snorted out a laugh, quickly covering her face with her hands. "I cannot believe I just snorted."

Laughing Dakota pulled her back down onto his body. "I can, you used to do it all the time."

"Still, its mortifying now."

"Why? We're still best friends."

"Yeah, but now you've seen me naked."

"That's true." He eyed her, a devious smile playing at the corner of his mouth. "So, you've gotten quite a look at my ink, can I see yours?"

She rolled onto her stomach so he could see the phoenix tattoo on her back.

"Damn, this is amazing."

"Zarina did an awesome job."

"Zarina?"

"She tends to stay hidden in her area," Anastasia answered with a laugh. "She's a major introvert."

"She does kickass work, though."

Dakota trailed his fingers over the lines of the bird, and the sensation of his calloused hands on her skin nearly lulled her to sleep.

"What are you thinking about?" he asked as he lay back on his side.

"How wonderful this is. Being here with you."

He leaned forward and kissed her gently before pulling her against him. "I was just thinking the same thing."

36

ANASTASIA

"Anastasia."

She shot out of bed at the sound of the voice, her hand already gripping the dagger she kept at her bedside.

"There is no need for that," Vincent said, amusement in his tone.

"I don't believe that for a second."

"You know I'm not truly there. Your Dakota still lives, doesn't he?"

She looked down at Dakota sleeping soundlessly on her bed. "What the hell do you want?" she asked the empty room in a hushed whisper.

"You. All I've ever wanted is to have a relationship with my niece." His voice was only inside her head, and

Anastasia clenched the dagger she wanted so badly to drive down into his heart.

"You are no family to me, you bastard," she said through gritted teeth.

"Watch your tongue, girl. I have been patient with you—"

"You call torturing me for nearly two months patience? You are a coward and a monster."

"I did what I believed was necessary in order to show you the depth of your capabilities."

"You wanted to use me to destroy everything so you could have more power."

"I will have your magic."

"You will not have anything. I will destroy you. Even if it takes every breath from my body, I will see you take your last."

"You think you have the power to destroy me?" His laughter filled her head, causing her to wince from the pain. *"Please, child, you don't possess even an ounce of what is necessary to destroy me. I will kill him and every single person you care about unless you succumb to me. If you continue to fight against me, I will show you just what I am capable of."*

"I'm not afraid of you."

"Then you are just as stupid as Mitch claimed you to be."

"Show yourself, you coward," she growled into the darkness, but sensed the second he vacated her mind.

Anastasia crept slowly through the house, confirming they were still alone.

Once she was sure they were, she leaned against the counter, the adrenaline leaving her shivering. What if Vincent was right? What if she didn't possess what she needed to destroy him? What if it was too late?

So much sat on her shoulders; so many people relied on her for a future she couldn't promise them. What if she failed?

37

ANASTASIA

Anastasia entered her grandmother's cottage the next morning.

"Shall we?" Carmen asked as soon as she entered.

"Where are we headed?"

"Just out for a bit. It's much easier to focus without all these distractions." Carmen pointed to the wall behind her, where floor-to-ceiling bookcases held hundreds of hardback books. "If I am here, I will want to read one, or three, and then there goes the day." She smiled, and Anastasia followed her out into the crisp morning air.

"How did you move past the fear?" Anastasia inquired as they walked.

“The fear?”

“Of the dark.”

“Ah, yes.” Carmen shook her head. “That was a tough one for me to move past as well. Fortunately for me, I had much more time to gather myself before I had to use magic again.”

“I don’t know if I can do it,” Anastasia said, voicing her fears.

“Of course you can.” Carmen laughed lightly. “You have already done the hardest part.” At Anastasia’s silence, she continued, “You came back. You tasted the absoluteness of your lineage, and you returned. My dear, you not only have your father’s magic in your blood, but mine as well. It is very rare that someone has two magical lines in their heritage.”

“Is that why I am so powerful?”

“That is one theory.”

“What is the other?”

“I believe that you were blessed with what you needed to complete your purpose.”

“My purpose.”

“You are meant for much more, my dear. Defeating Vincent is only a portion of your destiny, or purpose, if you will.”

Anastasia looked up at the sky as they walked. Birds chirped, and a light breeze carried the scents of the fires the villagers had built to keep warm. So lost in the beauty of the early morning sky, she nearly ran into

Carmen when the woman stopped near the edge of the fence.

They sat on a bench and Carmen took a deep breath. "It is sure lovely here, isn't it?"

"It is the most beautiful place I have ever seen," Anastasia agreed.

"Do you have any questions for me?"

"A few," Anastasia admitted. "Mostly I want to know about my—"

"Mother?"

Anastasia nodded and Carmen let out a sigh. "Annabelle was the light of my life, in so many ways. I tried to shield her from magic for years, but as soon as I saw the way she looked at your father I knew it had only been a temporary separation."

"But she didn't have any power?"

She shook her head. "Not active anyways. I believe hers were in the salves she made."

"I wish I would have gotten more of a chance to know her. To know them both, actually."

Carmen patted Anastasia's hand. "I wish you would have too."

"Why did you stay away? I was here for five years and I never heard anything about you."

"I was hard to reach. As you know, your father wasn't big on using his magic. He was only comfortable using portals to travel, and when you use a vial, you have to know exactly where you're going; there is no room for error."

"But conjuring one isn't the same?"

"No, you only need to have an idea of where you wish to travel when you conjure one, as the power is much stronger that way."

"So he never sought you out?"

"I saw him a time or two over the years when he'd been looking for you. But I didn't know he'd found you until I heard about Annabelle, and by then I was afraid of getting too close. I felt guilty for not being there for her." Carmen wiped a tear from her wrinkled cheek. "There is no way to go back, but if I could, I never would have left."

Anastasia touched Carmen's hand and they watched as a bird the color of eggplant, landed on a nearby branch.

"So do you have any questions for me about magic?" Carmen asked after a moment in silence.

"Is there a way to shield your mind?"

"What do you mean?"

Anastasia swallowed hard; how much to tell her? "I don't want Vincent to ever be able to manipulate me again. I want to protect myself from him."

"There is a way to shield yourself from him, but it wouldn't help against a Brute stasis, if that's what you're referring to."

Anastasia thought back to Vincent's appearance in

her bedroom. "Not just that. I know he can project his voice into people's minds, and I want to make sure he can't do that to me." *Ever again.*

"Has he done that to you? Recently?"

"Once," she admitted.

Carmen nodded. "I see. It is strong magic, and as I told you before, magic is like a muscle. It grows the more you use it, so it may take some time for you to get where you need to be with it."

Time we probably don't have. Anastasia watched as the purple bird flew past a dead tree, and she grimaced at the dark stain around the base of it.

"Why don't you try something now?" Carmen wondered. "Something small, just to stretch that muscle, so to speak."

"Okay." Anastasia straightened, hesitant at the thought of using her magic again. If she focused hard enough, she felt the power calling to her, beckoning her to dive in and lose herself in it.

She shook her head and closed her eyes. The first thing her father had taught her was to conjure light, so that's what she did. She pictured the small orb of light in her palm, and when she opened her eyes, there it sat. Bright and beautiful, just as she imagined it.

"How do you feel?"

"I feel fine." Anastasia smiled. She felt no deep thirst for power or bloodlust; only happiness in her heart.

“Your father told Tony that you have the power to freeze time.”

Anastasia nodded. “Yes, but I have only used it once, and I didn’t even know I was doing it.”

“I want you to try again. It won’t work against Vincent, as he has the same power, but it could help in a Brute assault.”

“I don’t know how I did it.”

“Just close your eyes and focus. You need to be able to sense everything that is around you, or you could end up focusing your power on the wrong target. Use all of your senses and reach out.”

38

ANASTASIA

Anastasia did as she was instructed, but she couldn't clear her mind. When she opened her eyes, she was staring directly into a smiling Vincent. His silver eyes bore into hers with all the ferocity of a lion awaiting an attack.

She flung herself back off the bench and felt against the fence behind her. He faded away, and Carmen's voice broke through her fear.

"Anastasia!" she yelled.

Eyes wide, Anastasia focused on her grandmother.

"Close your palm, Anastasia."

She looked down and saw that she held a ball of flames in her palm; she had conjured it without even realizing what she was doing. She closed her hand, and the fire fizzled out, leaving a small red mark behind.

"What did you see?" Carmen narrowed her eyes, searching her face.

"Vincent. He was here."

"He was not here, not even projected, or I would have felt him."

"He was here! I saw him!" she insisted.

"I think that is enough for today. We need to pace you." Carmen smiled and reached for Anastasia.

"What is going on?" Tony and two Fighters came down the path toward them.

"I think Anastasia is just tired."

"I'll walk her home." Tony held out his arm, and Anastasia took it. "You two make sure Carmen gets back okay."

"It's not that far of a walk, Tony, I can see to it myself."

"I know you can." He smiled kindly. "I would just feel better if they went with you."

"Well, all right," she replied reluctantly, "if it will make you feel better. I suppose it has been a while since I've been escorted home by two handsome men." Carmen winked at Anastasia. "Come on, boys," she said with a laugh.

"Where's Dakota?" Anastasia asked as they walked.

"Out on a scouting run with Argento and some of the others."

"He's out there? On the other side of the fence?" She stopped and her heart began to pound in her chest. *Why was he out there?*

"Kaley is with him as well, Anastasia. He will be fine. They should be back shortly." They began walking again, and when they reached the steps of her cottage, he sat, and she followed. "Want to tell me what happened out there? I heard Carmen scream your name."

"I saw Vincent."

"He was here?" Tony's jaw clenched, and he looked around them.

"Carmen didn't see him."

Tony's brow furrowed. "I don't understand… did he project himself? Like he did to you in Seattle?"

"I don't know. Carmen said she would have felt him, but she didn't." She covered her face with her hands. "I think I'm losing my mind."

"Why do you say that?"

"Things have just been different since I've been back. My nightmares are getting more real." She pressed the heels of her hands to her eyes.

"Anastasia, what you went through was horrific. No one expects you to be a hundred percent overnight."

"We don't have time for me not to be."

"I know the prophecy says you will be the one to stop Vincent's dark magic, but that doesn't mean you have to do it alone." He rested his large hands on her shoulders. "You are not alone."

"I know I'm not." But that wasn't how she felt. No matter how many people were on her side, no matter how many times she tried to remind herself that she had a family and a home, Anastasia felt more alone than ever.

The nightmares were only making that fact even more concrete.

"You coming down for the party tonight?" Tony asked.

Kline, one of the Fighters who'd been held captive by Vincent, was marrying a woman who'd come over from one of the smaller villages Tony had brought back with him the night Anastasia went to Seattle.

It seemed strange to her to have a wedding in the middle of a war, but it had been nearly all anyone wanted to talk about recently. There would be music, dancing, and food, and truth be told, she was looking forward to the distraction.

Hell, she'd bet they all were.

"Of course. I want to grab some sleep first, though. I'm exhausted."

Tony wrapped his arms around her. "I'll see you later then."

He released her and she watched until he disappeared around the bend in the path. Anastasia headed inside and removed the daggers from her waist, before heading into her bedroom.

A slow smile spread across her face as she remembered waking up beside Dakota that morning. Even now, when he was nowhere in sight, just the simple memory of what they shared sent heat pooling low in her stomach.

She pulled back the heavy quilt and climbed beneath the blanket. Just as she closed her eyes, the door opened and she sat up quickly. Maybe rest wasn't something she needed after all.

"Dakota?" Anastasia crept into the living room, a smile on her face. A smile that quickly disappeared when she saw who was standing on the other side of the room. "What the hell are you doing here?"

"I told you I would come for you," Vincent sneered. He stood in black pants and a grey long sleeve shirt, and was flanked by four Brutes and—

"Brady," she whispered.

"Don't look so surprised." The hatred in his eyes was so unlike the boy she knew, it drove a dagger into her heart. His eyes were completely black now, no shred of the chocolate brown.

"Why are you with him?" She tried to inch closer to her daggers in case the Brutes attacked, but they moved with her. Shit. She reached down for the power in her blood, and felt the familiar humming. Now she only needed to make sure Brady didn't get caught in the crosshairs.

"You left," Brady sneered. "And they brought those monsters here."

"Vincent is working with Brutes too, Brady. The Brutes he works with are the ones who killed Emma, not Argento and his men."

"They are all the same!" he screamed, and his face turned red. "Vincent is only using them, he doesn't actually like them!"

"Get her." Vincent instructed the Brutes behind him, "By whatever means necessary."

They attacked, and she rolled out of the way. A large fist connected with her side and she cried out, her body still not fully healed from her time in captivity.

Anastasia flung out a ball of light, but the closest Brute dodged it and spun around to knock her to the floor.

Vincent laughed as the remaining Brutes wrapped their large hands around her wrists and ankles, pinning her to the floor. "I'm not going to have to kill everyone, Anastasia. Because you will."

"No!" She screamed and thrashed against her attackers, but they held strong.

"Anastasia!" Someone screamed her name, but she focused on fighting off the Brutes. She flung her arms out and kicked her legs, using all the strength she had.

The buzzing in her blood began to grow, and she looked down to see her skin glowing. The Brutes released her, and she jumped to her feet, feeling nothing but the power in her veins.

39

DAKOTA

Dakota made his way down the path toward home. The scout had gone well—there were no new Brute camps to report—but they still hadn't found Brady. Selena had been avoiding Dakota, probably hoping that no news was good news—which, typically, he would agree with.

Except with this. There was no telling where Vincent was keeping Brady or, shit, if he was even forcing him to do his bidding. No one wanted to think about the idea that maybe Brady had *chosen* to switch sides.

He shook his head, he didn't honestly believe that. Brady may have had a grudge against the Brutes, but it would make no sense to form an alliance with the man in charge of bringing them here in the first place.

His and Ana's cottage came into view and a scream tore through the air. Even in the daylight, the light shooting through the windows was near blinding. He broke into a run and closed the distance in a matter of seconds.

Dakota pushed the door open and raced inside, skidding to a stop in the living room. His breath flew out of him in a *whoosh.*

Ana was on her back in the middle of the room, thrashing and screaming against some unseen force. Her eyes were open and she stared wide-eyed at something above her, but there was nothing there.

"Ana!" He rushed to her side, but she kicked out and he blocked it just before her bare foot contacted with his chest. "Ana!" he screamed again, but she continued to thrash.

"What the hell is going on?" Tony shouted.

Dakota looked over his shoulder. Tony, Shane, Argento, and Elizabeth stood in the doorway, breathing hard like they'd been running. Tony's eyes flicked all over, quickly scanning the room for threats.

"I don't know," Dakota said, panic gripping his chest. "She screamed and I can't get her attention."

"Anastasia?" his mother called, trying to get her attention.

Ana thrashed again and this time her fist contacted with the side of his head.

"Fuck!" Dakota shouted.

Elizabeth stepped beside him, placing her hand firmly on his shoulder. "I need you to hold her down."

Shane, Tony, Argento, and Dakota each grabbed an arm or leg and pinned her to the floor. She continued thrashing, her body bucking uncontrollably, and Dakota held firmly. Her pupils were tiny pinpricks in the center of eyes blazing blue. "Look at her pupils," he whispered. "What the fuck is happening to her?"

"I have no idea." Elizabeth sat back on her heels. "Let me see if I can get some herbs, maybe we can sedate her until we figure it out."

"Anastasia!" Shane yelled. "Come on! You're tougher than this!"

Ana's skin began to glow. "What the hell?" Tony murmured. They released her and stepped back. She jumped to her feet and grinned menacingly at them. There was no trace of the Ana he knew on her face. This woman was powerful and dangerous.

"You better run." She grinned at them. She opened her palm, and flames danced on the skin.

"Anastasia, come back!" Shane yelled.

They backed away from her as she moved closer. Tony tucked Dakota's mom behind his body as they moved. Ana continued stalking toward them, and Dakota took a step forward.

"Ana!" he screamed.

She shook her head as if trying to clear it, and her skin dimmed back to normal. Her eyes faded back to their normal blue, and widened.

He took a step toward her, but Argento gripped his shoulder. "Stay away from her."

"Get off me." Dakota pushed away from him and reached for her.

"Don't touch me." Ana stared at them, her mouth open and tears shimmering in her eyes.

Shane took a step forward. "Ana—"

"Get out!" she yelled. "It's not safe! Get out!" Her skin started glowing again, and everyone but Dakota began backing away.

"I'm not leaving you!" He told her.

"Go, Dakota! Tony, please make him leave. It's not safe! Get away from me!" she screamed, tears trailing down her red cheeks. "I don't know what's real!"

"I am real!" Dakota shouted.

She backed away from him and fell to the ground in the corner. Dakota moved toward her but she flung a hand out, and they were thrown against the wall of the cottage.

"Get out of here!" Ana screamed, and the others scrambled out while he got to his feet. Dakota's head rang from the impact with the wall.

"Ana," he said and took a step toward her. She lifted her hand again and he was slammed outside. He was dazed, but wasted no time getting back to his feet and racing for the door.

"Ana!" He slammed his shoulder into the wood, but it wouldn't budge. "What the hell is happening?" he yelled, turning to face the others.

"It is the effects of the stasis," Argento said. "She unable to discern reality from illusion."

"I thought that this would clear up; why is it getting worse?" Elizabeth asked him.

"I honestly am not sure. I have never seen a human put into stasis, let alone ripped from one as abruptly as she was. Normally, when we pull a Brute from stasis, we do it gradually by adding doses of reality back in until everything is back to normal."

"She thought she saw Vincent today, while she was with Carmen," Tony told them. "And she's been having trouble distinguishing reality from nightmares."

Dakota clenched his fists at his sides. He knew she'd been having nightmares, but that wasn't anything new. She'd had them all growing up. Why the hell hadn't she told him they'd gotten so bad? "Care to explain why you're only just now telling me about this?" Dakota stepped toward Tony and Elizabeth moved in between them.

"Dakota, calm down," she urged.

Dakota saw the look of guilt on her face and felt his anger spike. "You knew?" he accused her. "Why wouldn't you tell me? I understand Tony keeping her secret, to some extent," he added with a glare at Tony, "but you should have told me."

"Dakota, I—"

"It doesn't matter now." He turned abruptly toward Argento. "What can we do?"

"I do not know. As I said before, we have never used stasis on a human. If we try to reinsert her, then her mind could break, and we may not ever recover her. I think the best course of action is to leave her be until she comes around."

Dakota pointed to the cottage. "Does that look like she is going to come around?" he spat.

"We need to place guards outside so someone can sound an alarm if need be," Argento suggested.

"Guards? Are you kidding me? She is not the enemy!"

Tony stepped beside Argento. "He's right, Dakota."

"You agree? How can you, of all people, agree to this?"

"She is dangerous right now, Dakota. Think about it from her side… how do you think Anastasia would feel if she tore this village apart?" He stepped closer to him until they stood nearly chest to chest. "Do you think this does not tear me apart inside? She is like a daughter to me! I will not risk her hurting any one of our people. Not just for their sake, but for hers." He turned to face Argento. "I'm going to get Carmen. She might be able to keep her inside until either Anastasia comes around or we find a way to drag her ass back to reality."

"Dakota," his mother began, but when he refused to look at her, she turned and headed back toward the village with Tony.

"I am sorry, Dakota." Argento touched his shoulder. "I will see to it the guards stay hidden and do not harm her." He began his way down the path leading to the village.

Dakota slumped against the door. Her crying was deafening, and the screams as she fought her battle inside tore him apart.

"I'm here, Ana," he said quietly. "I'm not leaving until you come back."

40

DAKOTA

"Anything?" Tilly walked down the narrow path to the cottage, carrying a plate of food.

Dakota shook his head and continued staring at his hands. He had never felt so helpless in his life. Even when Anastasia was taken from him, he'd been able to do something to bring her back. Now, everyone kept telling him that if he went in there, she might kill him by accident, which would only cause her to spiral further.

"She will come around, Dakota."

"Thanks, Tilly."

She smiled and gently patted his cheek.

"That for me?" he asked.

"Unfortunately, no." Tilly laughed and set the plate

by the door. “Your mother is still angry with you, so I am under strict orders to not bring you any food until you go talk to her. But just in case she asks”—Tilly gestured toward the door to the cottage—“there’s an extra helping of stew on the plate.” She winked and headed back toward the village.

“Ana?” he asked, pressing his hand to the door. “There is food out here.”

The silence began to worry him, but she screamed and threw something at the door. He reached for the knob and then pulled away. She was fighting her own war in there, and he would only be in the way, at least until Carmen and Rayden, the Brute healer, came up with something to snap her out of it.

“How is she?” Argento asked.

Dakota turned to face him. “The same.”

“Rayden is working with Carmen. They will find something.”

“I hope so.” Dakota sat back on the steps and Argento took a seat next to him.

“It is hard to feel useless when you are so used to being strong.”

Dakota nodded in agreement and stared out at the trees in the direction of the village.

“My wife is so strong that sometimes I feel useless.”

His words shocked Dakota. “You are married?”

“Of course.” Argento scoffed. “It is how I am king.”

At Dakota’s curious look, Argento smiled. “We

Brutes are a matriarchal race. Therefore, the royal line is passed down through females."

"Seriously?"

"You seem surprised."

"Well, honestly, yes."

"Most who learn of it are. We may seem tough, but it's mainly on the outside. We are very family-oriented, and honor is incredibly important to us." His jaw set. "It is why these traitors must be brought to justice."

"They will be."

"Your Anastasia will come back, Dakota, you must have faith. She has a strong mind, and when she comes back to you, it will be with a fire that will propel her forward into victory."

"Thank you, Argento." Dakota smiled lightly.

"You should go and talk to your mother. Time is not on our side right now, and you don't want to miss an opportunity."

"You're right. I just can't believe she didn't tell me."

"Perhaps it's because she was being faithful to Tony."

"Tony?" At Argento's awkward silence, it hit him. He'd been too wrapped up in An's recovery to notice the new relationship. "So she finally took that step. Good for her." Dakota smiled, glad that his mom had finally gone for what she wanted.

"You are not angry?" Argento asked, confused.

"Does it not bother you that she is with someone when you lost your father?"

"Honestly, no. My dad would have wanted her to be happy and to not be alone for the rest of her life. Tony is a great man, and I know he will be good to her."

"He is very honorable," Argento agreed. "I will wait here while you go speak with her."

Dakota eyed him warily. "I appreciate the offer, but maybe wait out of view? If she does come out, I don't want her to mistake you for the enemy."

"Good idea." Argento moved to the side of the porch, out of sight from the front door. "Go. I will be here."

DURING THE SHORT WALK BACK TO THE VILLAGE, DAKOTA almost turned around three times. He was still pissed off. Could this have all been avoided had they just told him about her dreams? Maybe he could have talked to her, and they could have figured out what was going on sooner.

They wouldn't know now, he supposed, so there was no need to focus on the past when there was already such an uncertain future ahead of them.

He turned the corner to his mom's cabin and paused. She and Tony sat cozied up together on the front porch. Tony kissed her lightly, and she smiled.

Dakota cleared his throat and walked closer, his eyes trained to the ground.

"Dakota." His mom's stern voice immediately took him back to his teenage years and he looked up at her.

"I'll leave for a bit and let you two talk." Tony started to turn away, but Dakota waved his hand.

"Tony, please stay. What I have to say I need to say to both of you, so it will save me some time."

"Go on." His mom crossed her arms over her chest and looked at him down her nose just as she had done when he got in trouble as a kid.

"I'm sorry, I shouldn't have gotten so angry at the two of you. Mom, I know you were only keeping Tony's trust, and Tony, you were keeping Anastasia's."

"I would have told you, had I believed this was ever a possibility," Tony said, sitting on the steps. "This is my fault."

"It's not your fault, Tony. It's that bastard Vincent who is to blame." His mom ran a hand down Tony's arm.

"Have Carmen and Rayden found anything out?"

"Not yet." Tony rubbed his hands over his face. "Carmen is feeling the magic, too. The protection she has placed on the house has nearly drained the woman. I worry that if we don't figure something out, we may lose her as well."

"Can she stop? We can take other precautions."

"That's what I said, but she is stubborn and says she can handle it."

"Now we know where Anastasia gets her hard head from," Dakota's mother said lightly, turning to go back into the house. "Dakota, would you like to stay for dinner?"

"Thanks, Mom, but I'm going to head back."

"You should really get some sleep. I can take tonight's watch," Tony said, gripping his shoulder.

"No thanks, Tony, I want to be there."

"I will have Tilly bring you some food," Elizabeth said, closing the door behind her.

Dakota smiled and headed back toward the cottage. After sending Argento back to his camp, he took his seat against the door and fell asleep looking at the stars. In his dreams, he imagined life the way it could be once all of this was over, and he prayed he got a chance to see that future become a reality.

41

DAKOTA

When Dakota woke, it was still dark. His heart was pounding, and it took him a moment to shake the sleep and figure out where the feeling of panic was coming from. The scent of smoke filled the night air, but it was far too early to be coming from anywhere inside their village walls.

Kaley stood on the porch, staring out into the night, and when he got to his feet, she broke into a run. Dakota followed, making his way to the nearest sentry tower and climbing up the ladder.

Large flames leapt into the sky about a mile outside the village. He heard the crackling from the burning trees and his pulse pounded as adrenaline surged through him.

"Shit!" He jumped down and sprinted to Argento's camp.

"Argento!" he called.

Someone rustled inside the tent, then Argento peeked out. "Dakota, what is it?"

"You need to see this." He turned and ran for the tower again, but this time Argento was on his heels.

"This is not good. Even if we manage to hold off whatever attack is headed our way, we will not be able to put those fires out."

"This whole fucking thing was a trap," Dakota growled. "He knew we'd use Carmen to protect Ana, so she'd be too drained to protect the village or even sense him coming. Son of a bitch!"

Argento watched the fire, his brow creased.

"How much time do you think we have?" Dakota asked.

"Not long. They will attack before dawn."

"We need to gather everyone and get them ready to evacuate. I bet those fuckers are out there waiting for us to leave."

"Do you think Vincent is out there?"

"I think he is the one pulling strings, but I don't think he's here, fucking coward."

"We need to prepare for war." Argento climbed down the ladder and Dakota followed. "I will rally my warriors. You get Tony and the Fighters."

"We will not cower!" Tilly shouted as Tony addressed the villagers. The center of the village was packed with its occupants. They stared back at Dakota and Tony, wide-eyed and afraid. How the hell was he supposed to tell them what might be waiting for them beyond the flames?

"It's not cowering, Tilly, it's called being cautious. What will you do when they come in here? Would you put Robbie at risk?" Tony asked.

"I can help!" she insisted.

Robbie stepped forward. "Tilly, I can't focus unless I know you are safe."

"We are staying," Elizabeth said. "If it makes you big bad men feel better, then we can stay inside the medical cottage. That way, if there are any injuries, we can tend to them." Elizabeth folded her arms and jutted her chin out.

Dakota recognized that stance; she wasn't going anywhere.

"Fine." They didn't have time to argue. Not when they had an entire village about to go up in flames.

Robbie shot Dakota a glare that could cut glass, but Dakota shrugged. "It's going to do us no good to argue with them, Robbie. They have made up their minds, and as of now, we are wasting time."

"I'm afraid I won't be much help." Carmen staggered over to them. "I am fairly worn out." She stumbled, and Tony caught her.

"Drop the barrier," Dakota said.

"Now is not the time, Dakota," she warned. "If Vincent is close and I drop Anastasia's protection, he will be able to get to her."

"Drop it," Dakota told her again. "He won't be able to get to her. Get into the bunker and seal the door. Keep everyone quiet. We need to stay inside the walls until we know for sure what's waiting for us. They haven't made a move yet, which makes me think they're waiting for us to leave."

"Where are you going?" Elizabeth called after him.

"I'm going to drag Ana back to reality whether she likes it or not," he said over his shoulder. Let them try to stop him.

As he walked away, Argento began commanding his warriors. "You form a line inside the gate. They want a fight? We will give them one. I know that you know them, and at one point, they were your neighbors and very possibly your friends, but they have chosen a side, and it's the wrong side. We will show them just how wrong they are."

DAKOTA PUSHED THE DOOR OPEN TO THE TRAINING cottage and stepped into the dark. "Ana?" He shut the door behind him, quickly locking it. She was not going to push him away anymore. He was either leaving with her or not at all.

"Leave now," she demanded from the corner of the living area.

"I'm not leaving."

Her body began glowing and she stood. The Anastasia he knew was in there somewhere, and he was going to show her the way back.

"You are making a mistake." She showed her teeth to him. "Vincent, you will not win. I've had enough of your mind games."

"I'm not Vincent," he said, swallowing a bit of fear as she stepped closer.

"Of course not," she spat. "This time you're real, right?" Sarcasm dripped from her voice as she circled him, predator and prey.

"It's me, Ana. The same Dakota you grew up with, who has been in love with you since we were kids."

"You shut up!" she yelled, lunging for him. "You don't know anything about Dakota!"

"I know everything about myself and damn near everything about you."

"Lies!"

"I know that when you were eight, you fell and skinned your knee climbing a tree with me."

He saw the flash of recognition in her eyes and knew that she was in there somewhere.

"I know that you used to climb over to my house almost every night to sleep because you said it was the only place you felt safe."

Anastasia circled him, her body providing enough light to illuminate the inside of the cabin. Bright flames danced on her palms, and Dakota briefly wondered if she was going to kill him. At least if he went out he wouldn't have to live without her.

"The Brutes are here, Ana, the ones who have been responsible for all those deaths of the ones you love. Annabelle," he said, and pain flashed on her face.

"You know nothing about Annabelle!"

"Gregory."

She lunged for him and made contact, knocking them both to the ground. Her palms were hot on his chest as she straddled him. One hand burned against the skin above his heart, but instead of pushing it away, he gripped it. "You feel my heart? It's real. Those scars on your back are real, as is all of the pain, both physical and mental, you grew up with. Losing your parents, that was real, and those people out there, your people who are going to die without you tonight, are real, Ana. Pull yourself out of whatever hole you are in and start seeing what is around you. I love you, and that love will last until my very last breath leaves my lungs and probably even after that because how I feel about you is the damned most real thing in this entire world. *Feel* it." He gripped her hair and dragged her mouth down to his.

The kiss was harsh, and he poured all the anger he felt into it.

When she ripped her head back from him, he could see that he was getting to her. The blazing blue of her eyes was dimming back down, and her hands fisted in his shirt.

"Kill me or come back, Ana, because death would be preferable to the pain I feel knowing I can't help you."

The cabin went dark as the light faded from her skin. The only sounds were their breathing, and he waited until she spoke, afraid he might set her off again.

"Dakota?" she whispered.

"Yes." He pulled her down against his body and buried his face in her hair. "We need you, Ana."

"What's happening?" She climbed off him and pulled him to his feet.

"We're under attack."

"He used me again," she growled. "He fucking used me."

"Easy, Ana," Dakota warned when her fingers sparked. "There is plenty for you to demolish outside. But you're going to want to put shoes on first."

42

ANASTASIA

Anastasia followed Dakota back into town. Fighters raced to their posts, but the rest of the villagers had disappeared into the bunkers. Not that the underground space would protect them from the fires, but she hoped she could.

She climbed up to the top of the sentry tower and stared out at the burning forest beyond. The flames had devoured dozens of trees on their way toward Terrenia. Closing her eyes, Anastasia focused on the power in her veins and a blast of magic rocked through her.

She jolted, and when she opened her eyes, the leaping flames had turned to smoldering ash. *Take that, asshole.* Vincent had tried to break her, again. He'd used her as a distraction so he could get to her people.

No more.

Brute calls erupted from the trees as dozens poured out toward her village. Anastasia climbed down from the tower and walked to the other side of the gate. Fighters launched into attack and Anastasia unsheathed her sword.

She could feel the drain from the power it took to put out the fires, so she would have to use her physical strength to fight.

For a moment it seemed as if time slowed to merely a crawl as she watched the battle that raged before her eyes. Dakota had immediately thrown himself at a Brute who was trying to get through the gate. His forehead creased as he plunged his sword into the beast's chest. Argento dispatched two of the enemy Brutes and was working toward a group who had attacked a Fighter who was much too young to be beyond the gate.

Her heartbeat quickened and the excitement of the war pounded in her blood. These bastards were going to pay.

Anastasia lunged at a Brute who took an interest in her, and time sped back up. She sliced through him as if he were nothing more than a nuisance, leaving a smoldering corpse behind her. She lunged and dodged, seeing nothing but what was in front of her. Blades clashed together, filling the night air with the sound of war. Blood splattered her as she fought, the movements blurring together.

Brutes fell at her feet, and the satisfaction she felt at not being a victim filled her. Mitch had been the first to victimize her, and even though Gregory brought her back and she became something more, Vincent managed to return her to the weak, shell of a person she'd promised to never become again.

A Brute struck his arm out, sliding his massive hand around her throat. She reached down and grabbed the dagger at her waist, driving it down into the beast's throat. Anastasia tumbled to the ground, and when she stood, Brady faced her. His eyes were black, and she could all but see Vincent above him pulling strings.

"Brady."

"Anastasia."

"I know you are still in there, Brady." She lowered her sword and stepped toward him.

"You are truly foolish."

"Brady, remember all the times we ran through the woods together? With Kaley? Remember when you asked for my advice about Emma?"

His face twitched, but his eyes remained soulless.

"Oh, but Emma is dead, isn't she, Brady?" Vincent's voice filled her head, and by the pained look on Brady's face, he heard the words too. "The Brutes slaughtered her before your very eyes."

"You mean the Brutes that you are working with, Vincent? The monsters you are forcing Brady to work with? Why don't you show yourself and we can end this now?" She warily stepped to the side to check behind her.

"I am needed elsewhere at the moment. Besides, it will all be over soon enough."

She felt his presence leave her mind, and she turned her attention back to Brady.

"Brady, I know you are in there. Please come back," she pleaded, tears filling her eyes. Next to Dakota, Brady had been her best friend, the only other person she had confided in.

She watched the war on his face as he fought, the lines creasing and his pupils dilating and retracting. When he finally looked up at her, she sighed with relief at the sight of his kind brown eyes. She watched them widen with fear just as he lunged for her.

"Anastasia!"

He shoved her out of the way, and she watched in horror as a Brute buried its sword in Brady's chest.

"No!" she screamed. She threw her palm up, striking the beast with flames. He fell to the ground, and she ran to Brady.

His body shook, and his hands clutched at the front of his shirt. "I'm. Sorry. I—I – I don't want to die." Blood pooled in the corner of his mouth and tears slipped down his cheeks. She cradled his head in her lap and brushed the hair from his face.

"Shh, Brady. It's okay, you aren't going to die." Tears filled her eyes as she stared down at him.

"Please tell my mom and Sarah that I…" His breath came in spurts. He coughed, splattering her face with blood. She reached down to cover his wound with her hands and apply pressure, but the blood continued to seep through her fingers. "Someone *help*!" she screamed, but the sound was drowned out by the battle around them.

"Brady, I'm so sorry, this is all my fault. I should have been here."

"Not your fault. You're my best friend." Tears fell down his face.

"Hang on, Brady! I will get help." She gently set his head on the ground and stood. "Help!" she screamed again, trying to lift him.

"No. Use," he muttered.

"Brady, please, I need you." She didn't have the strength to carry him, and everyone around her was too occupied trying to fight off the enemy.

"Thank you, Anastasia."

"Brady, please."

His body stopped moving as he drew his last breath. Empty eyes stared up at her and she turned her head to the sky and screamed.

43

DAKOTA

The scream ripped through the sound of the battle and one by one Brutes fell to the ground turning into smoldering piles of ash before their very eyes. Dakota searched frantically for the origin of the noise, and his eyes landed on Ana who knelt next to a body.

Dakota raced for her, pushing past the Fighters who stared dumfounded at their now dead opponents. His arm stung from where the blade had torn it open just before his opponent spontaneously combusted, but he ignored the pain now, focusing only on the woman in front of him.

Her face and hands were slick with blood, but she

otherwise looked uninjured. She cradled Brady's body in her arms, tears streaming down pale cheeks.

"Oh, Ana." He fell to the ground beside her.

"He saved me." She cried and kissed his forehead. "He saved me and he died for it." She buried her face in Brady's chest and her shoulders shook.

"Ana, this isn't your fault." Dakota rubbed a hand on her back and swallowed his own pain. Brady had been his responsibility while she'd been gone. He'd promised himself he'd keep Ana's friend safe, and he failed—miserably.

"I should have been here, I should have done something!" She screamed up to the sky.

The agony in her voice ripped Dakota's heart from his chest.

"You *were* here; there was nothing you could have done."

"You can't possibly know that." She stared at him, her bloodshot eyes glaring straight through him.

"Ana—"

"Oh no, Brady."

Dakota looked up at Shane who stood just behind him. The Fighter knelt on the other side of Ana, and reached forward to close Brady's eyes. "I'm so sorry, Anastasia." He placed a hand on her shoulder and her bottom lip quivered. "Let's get him home." Shane reached down and lifted Brady's body.

If Shane felt the strain, he didn't show it, and he carried Brady's body like it was light as a feather.

Dakota helped Ana to her feet and wrapped an arm around her waist. Her shoulders shook as she cried, and he rubbed a hand on her arm in an effort to soothe her. Nothing he was going to do would fix the pain, and he knew that, but he didn't know how not to offer her comfort.

They followed Shane as he carried Brady through the grouping of Fighters gathering the rest of their dead. Brady's hadn't been the only life that was lost tonight. They had lost dozens of good Fighters—human and Brute alike—and the pain of it would be something Terrenia would feel deep in its heart.

They reached the entrance to the village and Dakota heard Selena's horrified scream before he saw her. She and Sarah rushed to Shane as he set Brady's body down on the ground.

They fell to their knees and Dakota watched helplessly as she wrapped her arms around Sarah and pulled Brady into her lap. She cradled him as she grieved, and as Dakota turned to survey the rest, he felt the agonizing pain of each family member grieving the ones they'd lost.

He wanted to cry right along with them, scream in anger, or just *do something*, anything that might help lessen the blow for them.

Ana pulled away from him and walked toward the

sentry tower. He started to follow, but changed his mind, opting instead to finish helping the Fighters collect the dead.

They needed him right now, and Ana needed time.

He joined Shane and Tony, and together they stepped back onto the battlefield.

44

ANASTASIA

Sixty-eight Fighters died. Sixty-eight men and women who had families and loved ones who expected them to come home. She'd counted each blanketed body from where she still stood on the sentry tower and watched from afar as Selena covered Brady.

Anastasia closed her eyes and let the tears fall down her cheeks. The pain of losing another family member—because that's what Brady was to her—was nearly too much for her to bear.

This was the bloodiest battle she had ever seen, and somehow, she knew it was only going to get worse.

The ground on the other side of the fence was coated in blood, and the stench of sulfur still clung to the air.

"We will end him," Argento said, startling Ana. She turned as he climbed the last rung of the ladder.

"He will pay for what he has done."

She nodded into the darkness. "I am going to kill him."

"That boy did not deserve to die. I feel great sadness that his mother must now bury him."

"I know you do, Argento. You are a good man."

He snorted. "Not much of a man, though, am I?"

She turned her head up to look at him. "I disagree. Being a man is more than being human. Vincent is human, and I don't consider him a man." She ground her teeth together. "You are more of a man than most."

He grunted at the compliment. "Do you have a plan?"

"Working on it."

"Whatever you decide on, know that my people and I will stand with you. I trust you with my life, Phoenix."

"Thank you, Argento."

He nodded and turned to leave. He said something to someone below, but it was muffled, and seconds later boots scuffed on the ladder again.

She turned her head just as Dakota stepped onto the platform.

"Hey." He shoved his hands into the pockets of his pants and moved to stand beside her.

His bicep was bandaged, his face coated in dirt and

dried blood. She reached for him, needing the physical contact to keep her grounded. "You okay?"

"Yeah, caught the business end of a blade. I'm fine though."

"Good."

"How are you?"

She looked up at him and the sting of tears returned. Dakota wrapped an arm around her shoulders and she buried her face in his chest. "He shouldn't have died."

"I know, baby." He cradled her.

"I don't know how I'm supposed to even face Selena now. She probably hates me."

"She doesn't. Not even a little."

Anastasia took a shaky breath, and looked out as the sun began to rise over her home.

"What are we supposed to do now? We aren't any closer to finding him then we were yesterday."

"We keep fighting, and eventually we'll find a way to bring this war to that bastard's doorstep."

45

ONE WEEK LATER

ANASTASIA

Anastasia stared at her reflection in the mirror. She looked the same on the outside; her hair still curled and fell to her waist, and her eyes were the same shade of blue that they had always been. She looked just as she had every single day since she arrived in Terrenia, and yet… she felt nothing like who she'd been.

Dakota was off on a scout with Tony and Shane. There had been no other attacks since the horrible night a week ago, but they'd scouted daily just the same.

The lack of an attack was making her nervous; what the hell were they waiting for? It wasn't like Vincent didn't have the power to come in and take them out; he'd proved that much in the last attack.

So why the radio silence?

There was a knock at the front door, and Anastasia finished strapping on her weapons, then pulled the door open.

Shane stood on the other side, his mouth pulled into a tight line. "We need you."

"What is it?"

"Dakota and Tony found a new camp."

She nodded and followed him down the path to the village. The people were quiet today, still reeling from burying their loved ones over the past week. She hadn't even seen Selena or Sarah since Brady's death. Not that she could blame them; she hated herself, too. No matter how she tried to spin it, Anastasia couldn't erase the blame from her shoulders.

Had she been strong enough to take Vincent out that night in the clearing, Brady would never have been taken.

Dakota, Tony, Argento, Andrew, and Leo stood in Tony's cottage. Argento spoke to Dakota in a low voice, but when she stepped in, Dakota's eyes found hers. She stared into their blue depths. Just how long could they keep this fight up before it claimed one of them—or both?

"We will need to make a move sooner rather than later." Tony said. "The camp is large, about twice the size of the one we found Anastasia in a few months back."

"If we wait for them to attack, we can fortify," Shane argued.

"Yes, but if we do that, we put our people at risk," Leo said.

"They're at risk no matter what," Shane insisted.

"We have to keep the fight as far from here as possible," Argento added, turning to Anastasia. "What do you think, Phoenix?"

"I think taking the fight to them is our best bet. We might be able to catch them off guard."

"Agreed," Dakota said.

Shane huffed. "I'll do whatever you guys want, but we need to make sure we don't leave Terrenia unprotected." He folded his arms across his chest.

"Very well." Argento's voice filled the room again. "We shall head out at nightfall."

Anastasia couldn't keep the smile off her face. It was well past time to spill some of Vincent's blood. And even if he wasn't there in person, the idea of hurting something that was his filled her with anticipation.

"Anastasia." Tony's voice pulled her from her thoughts and she looked up. Only he and Dakota remained in the room.

"What?"

"You all right?" he asked.

"Fine, why?"

"You're smiling."

"Because we might be able to hit Vincent where it hurts. You damn well bet that makes me smile."

"You can't be out for blood," he told her.

"Aren't we all?"

"You fight with anger in your heart, and we will lose."

"I don't think there is anything but anger in my heart right now, Tony. So if that means I need to use it as motivation to keep myself from giving up, I will."

THEY MOVED QUIETLY THROUGH THE TREES ON FOOT. Horses would have been faster, but there was more risk for noise, so they'd made the five mile journey without them. The Brute camp was nestled in the base of the mountains, in a valley that made it easy for them to gain a vantage point. Tony, Argento, Anastasia, and Dakota crept to the top of a small hill and looked down at the camp.

"I count fifteen," Argento said quietly.

"Same," Anastasia agreed.

"There's more." Dakota pointed to the north.

"What do you mean?" Argento asked.

"Look at those tents, there are more than fifteen in this camp."

"Some may be out," Anastasia argued.

"Unlikely, look at the fires. There are at least ten,

and they are all lit. What reason would they have for being that spread out unless there were more? And why light them all if they weren't all there? It would be stupid to attract more attention with the smoke than necessary."

"He's right," Tony replied.

"Send me in first," Dakota said.

"No," Anastasia said simply. "I should go in first."

"Absolutely not." Dakota scoffed. "What possible reason would we have to show you first? You are the only one who can handle things if they get bad; we send you in first, and we show our hand early."

"And what reason would we have for sending you in?" she argued.

"I can draw them out, then we can see exactly what we are dealing with."

"That's ridiculous." She turned and shook her head.

"It is actually quite wise," Argento offered.

Anastasia whipped her head around. "Excuse me?"

"I agree," Tony chimed in.

Anastasia threw her hands up. "Are you serious? You will be sending him into a camp with possibly dozens of Brutes, and you are okay with that?" She all but yelled it, fear gripping her heart.

"Ana," Dakota pleaded. "It's the best plan."

She gaped at him. "Do whatever the hell you want. You're going to anyways." She stomped off to the side, her blood running hot.

"You be careful, Dakota. You will be going in with your group, and you need to wait for us before you attack. You will be significantly outnumbered, it's important that you play this smart."

"I will." Dakota made his way over to where Anastasia stood. "Ana."

"What?" She rounded on him. "Final goodbyes before you get yourself killed?"

"I'll be fine."

She glared at him. "You damn well better be, or I swear I will find a way to bring you back and kill you all over again."

Dakota pulled her into his arms and pressed a kiss to her lips. "I love you," he whispered.

Anastasia closed her eyes and leaned into him. "I love you, too."

Dakota broke their embrace and stepped back toward the others.

"May all the strength follow you, Dakota. We will be right in when we get a better look at what is in there."

"Thank you, Argento. See you guys in a few."

Anastasia watched, heart in her throat, as he walked away.

Watching Dakota walk into the Brute camp was the most difficult thing she had ever done. He appeared so arrogant, as if he wasn't afraid at all, and although she knew it to be a front, she was still concerned that he didn't understand how much danger he was actually in.

A black shape caught her eye when it took form directly in front of Dakota. It hovered in front of him, a stain against the landscape. He didn't seem to see it, and that worried her even more. "What the hell is that?"

She looked at Argento, whose eyes were wide, his mouth open slightly in a dumfounded look she would have otherwise laughed at. Now, though, it chilled her to see the Brute king so shocked.

"It can't be," he whispered worriedly.

"What is it?"

"It's a Trepido. A horrific monster who brings your worst fears to life. I believe your world knows them as the boogeyman."

Tony's eyes widened. "I thought they were a myth."

"Far from it." Argento motioned for his Brutes. "They are loathsome creatures and live on a planet that is separated from ours by only a thin veil. I do not know how Vincent would have gotten them to come here. He must have offered them something in return, as they don't work for anyone but their creator."

"We have to get them out of there."

"You can't go down there, Anastasia." Argento put his hand up.

"Get out of my way, Argento," she growled. She started to push past him, but he gripped her arm. "We can't just leave him there!"

"We aren't going to, but you are incredibly powerful. If they get into your head, there is no telling the damage you could do." Argento's men moved to stand behind him.

"He is right, Anastasia. We will get them out, but you have to stay here," Tony insisted.

"You expect me to sit here and do nothing?"

"Do you not remember the cabin? The way you nearly killed us all because of the effects of the stasis? Those monsters can make you see, hear, and feel things as if they're happening. You cannot possibly understand the damage they could do simply by getting to you."

She knew in her heart they were right, and yet she still wanted to argue. When someone screamed in the valley below, she ran to the hill and watched in horror as each Fighter began running in separate directions while the enemy Brutes watched, amused.

"Go!" she yelled at Tony and Argento.

46

DAKOTA

Dakota, Andrew, and the other three Fighters headed for the gate to the camp.

"Well, isn't this a sight?" One of the enemy Brutes scoffed when he saw them come from the trees. "Fools."

Four more Brutes surrounded them from behind, pushing them toward the gate.

"What's up, assholes?" Dakota taunted.

Confused, the Brutes looked from one another.

"Come on, I find it hard to believe you've never been called an asshole before." At their confusion, he laughed. "Anyway, where's this big bad Vincent? He around? Because, you see, I have a bone to pick with him."

"You annoy me." The Brute who had spotted them first waved his hand, and the gate opened. "He annoys me."

The Brutes pushed them forward into the camp, and Dakota swallowed a bit of fear. His heart stammered in his chest, and his hand clenched around the hilt of his sword.

"Dakota!" The familiar voice sent ice through his veins.

"Mom?" How the hell had they gotten her? Hadn't she been back in the village when they left? He raced toward the gates, not paying attention to the fact the Brutes weren't attacking.

He caught sight of her being drug by two Brutes, bleeding from a deep gash in her head.

Dakota raised his sword to attack. "Mom!"

"Dakota, save me! Dakota, help!"

"Mom, I'm coming!" he yelled after her.

Her screams ripped straight to his soul, and he pushed through a circle of Brutes. One had his mother by the throat, holding her up as if she were a trophy for the others.

"Let her go!"

"No. I think we will keep her." The Brute raised her higher and laughed.

Dakota lifted his sword and charged.

The Brute holding his mom threw her to the side and braced for the impact. He spun easily and avoided

Dakota's blade, while kicking out with a foot and knocking Dakota to the ground.

He fell and his head slammed into the ground. "Dakota, save me!" his mom cried, and Dakota pushed back up to his feet.

A Brute charged, and Dakota drove his blade into its abdomen. It fell to the ground, but three more charged. Dakota was grabbed from behind and his blood iced as the gripping fingers of fear dug their way into his stomach.

"Now we have the baby bird's plaything." One grinned in his face. "What shall we do with it?"

47

ANASTASIA

"Focus, men!" Argento yelled. "Stay rooted in reality. Focus only on the task at hand!"

Anastasia watched in agonized terror as the enemy Brutes took the Fighters out one by one with ease. They laughed at the fear on each man's face as the Trepidos toyed with them. Fighters scattered throughout the village chasing invisible ghosts until the Brutes grew bored and struck them down with their blades. She looked down at her shaking hands and wasn't the least surprised to see that her skin was glowing. How long was she supposed to stand here and watch this massacre? She could end this now if only she could get close enough!

Her focus turned back to Dakota, who stood in a group

of a dozen Brutes. He charged and managed to take one down, but when three more flanked him, Anastasia focused on her mind and did her best to put up walls around herself. She would keep the Trepidos out of her head, and she would stop the monsters from causing any more death.

When she reached the camp, Tony and Argento were trying to calm a frantic Andrew.

"Melanie!" he screamed for his wife, lunging at an empty space. "Let me go, they have her! They are going to kill her!"

"Andrew, it isn't real! Melanie is perfectly safe!"

Anastasia searched for the source of his panic, and noticed one of the shadows hovering near him, so she walked toward it. She called on light and threw the energy at the form. When it hit the creature, the shadow disappeared, and a monster took its place. The thing formed in black smoke, and stood at least ten feet tall. It grinned, revealing razor-sharp teeth, and its inky black eyes focused on her face. Something poked at her mind, trying to push past the walls she'd erected, but she pushed back at it using the magic in her blood.

When she didn't give in, it hissed, and Anastasia shoved her blade into its chest. It crumpled to the ground, and the shadows that had been following the other Fighters near her disappeared with it.

"You better run," she muttered and ran toward Dakota.

"Mom, hang on!" he yelled as he fought the Brutes. He had only taken two down, and the others just watched him.

"Dakota!" Anastasia cried as she jumped into the fight. The shadow that had been following him was still there, keeping him stuck in whatever nightmare it projected into his mind.

"Dakota, it's not real!" She ducked, using her sword to keep a blade from taking her head off. She dodged the attack and blasted out with her palm, knocking the Brute back.

The Brute slashed out with its blade, slicing into her palm. "Fuck!" she cried out. The pain stung but she ignored it, focusing entirely on the battle. She flung magic at the beasts until she began to feel exhaustion from the drain and, realizing she needed Dakota back in reality to win, she used one last blast to knock the monster from its shadow.

It took form in front of her, and she blasted it one last time for good measure. It screamed—a nightmarish squeal—and disappeared.

Confused, Dakota turned to look at her a moment too late.

"Dakota!" She screamed as a blade pushed through his chest just below his ribs. He stared down at it and then looked back at her as he crumbled to his knees

"No!" she screamed and ran to him.

"Anastasia? Where's my mom?" he whispered as he fell to the ground.

"She's fine, Dakota, it wasn't real. None of it was real."

At least a dozen more Brutes ran toward her, and she lit her blade again and bared her teeth.

"Bring it on, assholes, I can't wait to get a piece of you."

"What is an asshole?" she heard one of the Brutes ask the other before they charged.

Let's play a game you, bastards. She threw up her hands and watched as they all stopped in place, frozen and unable to move. She focused her magic and released their consciousness. Anger polluted her mind, spurring thoughts that only belonged in the darkest places. She wanted nothing more than for them to feel the pain she was going to inflict, but be helpless to stop it.

"You like to watch people face their worst fears? How about we make you face yours?" She shoved her blade into the stomach of one of the beasts and laughed when the others felt his pain. "That fun for you guys?" she yelled and spun to see the pain reflected on their faces. "How about this?" She brought her blade down on the Brute's arm, and it cried out. Anastasia laughed and brought her sword up again.

"Anastasia." Tony's voice cut through, and she turned to face him. "This isn't you. You need to come back."

"They hurt him!" she gestured to Dakota. "They need to pay for what they've done."

"Ana," Dakota choked out.

His voice brought her back. She went to him, leaving the monsters frozen for Tony and the others.

"Dakota, I need you." Dakota couldn't die today. She wouldn't survive it.

"I've had worse." He tried to smile, but coughed, and blood came up.

"Remember what I said?" she whispered. "I will bring you back and kill you myself."

Anastasia pressed her hands against the wound in his chest, and pushed down to apply pressure.

He stared up at her and tried to smile. "You don't scare me."

The world seemed to stop around them, and a tingle started in her hand. It ran up her arm, like a jolt of electricity, climbing until it reached her chest.

The power was unfamiliar, something she'd never felt before, but she grasped at it. Threads of magic snapped in the air around them like lightening, and Anastasia poured everything she had into Dakota.

All of the light inside her, and even some of the dark.

She closed her eyes, feeling the drain on her power, but she kept going. She had no idea what she was doing to him, but the wholeness she experienced within the power gave her hope.

"Ana."

Anastasia opened her eyes and looked into Dakota's familiar blues.

"What the hell just happened?" Tony asked.

Anastasia looked up to see all the Fighters, Argento, and his Brutes staring down at them. She looked back down at Dakota who looked just as confused as everyone else.

"I have no damn clue," he said.

Anastasia lifted her hands. Dakota's wound was still there, but it had stopped bleeding, in fact, it looked partially healed. Had she done that? She stared down at her hands. The cut on her palm was still open and bleeding, so how had she healed Dakota's wound?

Tony knelt beside her. "We need to get him out of here."

She nodded and got to her feet. One of Argento's Brutes, Griffith, reached down and lifted Dakota from the ground.

"I can try to walk." He winced when Griffith settled him against his chest.

"Let's not risk making your injury worse," Argento said and nodded to Griffith who headed toward the gate.

Anastasia still stared down at her hands.

"Anastasia, we need to go." Argento touched her shoulder gently.

"What else is out there?" She turned to face him.

"What do you mean?"

"There are you guys, and now these boogeymen… what else is out there?" she repeated. "What other monsters should we worry about?"

"We are hardly monsters, Anastasia. The Brutes were once peaceful. It was your uncle who changed that."

"I know that. I'm sorry." She shook her head as her anger dissipated. "That was rude of me. What about these shadow monsters?"

"Trepidos. They were never peaceful."

"Are there more like them?"

"No. Not like them."

"So what else is out there?"

"There are so many different races, it would be easier for me to explain them if we see them."

A loud bang pulled them from their conversation, and they ran around a corner just as one of Vincent's Brutes dragged a body-shaped bag toward the forest.

Argento bolted for the Brute. He shoved him away from the covered body and dispatched him quickly.

He knelt and gently uncovered the body of the most beautiful woman Anastasia had ever seen.

Blonde—nearly white hair fell to her shoulders in soft waves. Her eyes were frozen open, twin baby blues that would never behold the sunrise again.

"No, no," Argento cried out, cradling her to his chest. "Calista, I'm so sorry." He held her tightly, rocking her as a mother would an infant.

"Argento?" Anastasia started to kneel beside him, but she caught movement from the corner of her eye and turned, ready to defend the grieving Brute king.

One of Argento's warriors cradled an infant in his arms, and she lowered her sword.

"My king." The Brute knelt beside him on the ground.

Argento looked to him, and his eyes widened when he saw the small bundle in the Brute's arms. "It is her, my king," he told him, gently placing the baby in his arms.

Argento stood and began walking toward the gate, his eyes never leaving the face of the infant.

"Who is that?" Anastasia asked, pointing to the woman lying on the ground.

"That is Calista, our queen." The Brute knelt and closed her eyes. "She is Argento's wife."

Anastasia stared down at the battered woman and her heart shattered. Her hands clenched into fists at her sides. Why would the Brutes do this to their own queen?

"The baby is his daughter. Calista went missing right after they discovered she was with child. It had been such a happy time for my people, as it is tough for our women to become pregnant." The Brute knelt and covered her face. "We need to follow to ensure he is not attacked."

Anastasia nodded, and the Brute lifted the queen's body.

48

ANASTASIA

The village was grim as they entered. The bodies had been laid out and covered with sheets. The sight was becoming an all too familiar one.

People knelt next to the bodies of their loved ones and cried. The Brute she'd walked back with carried Calista's body to the Brute camp, and Argento carried his new child into the cottage he had made his own.

"Anastasia!"

She looked over as Shane approached. "What is it?"

"Dakota. The wound, it started bleeding again."

Her stomach flipped and she ran on shaky legs to the medical cottage. He'd been fine, though, hadn't he? The bleeding had stopped!

Elizabeth sat in the corner, Tony's arms around her, and she stared at Tilly as the woman worked on Dakota. His face was pale and he was unconscious.

"No, he was fine. What happened?" She rushed to him.

"He needs blood," Tilly told her while she worked. "Even if I can get him closed up, he isn't going to survive. We don't have the supplies here to do a transfer, and if he doesn't get one soon, he is going to die."

The door opened and Anastasia didn't bother turning to see who it was. She placed her hands on Dakota's face and willed him to open his eyes. Maybe if she touched him again?

"Dammit! I can't get his wound to close. It seems as if it just keeps reopening," Tilly muttered, frustrated.

"Oh, my." Rayden, who came in moments before stepped forward. He stood and watched silently as Tilly worked. "They must have coated the blade in poison."

"What?" Tilly asked as she re-stitched the same place she'd stitched only moments before.

"It is eating at your stitches." He gestured to the thread as it dissolved. "I'm not sure what would cause that, as I don't know of any poison that would continue to reopen the wound, so I am not sure how to fight it."

Anastasia squeezed Dakota's hand and willed his injury to heal. Where was the power she'd felt before? She couldn't lose him.

"Whatever you are doing, Anastasia, keep it up."

"Huh?" Anastasia opened her eyes. Her skin glowed. She watched with hope as Tilly was able to close the hole in Dakota's stomach and then held her breath, making sure it stayed closed.

"How did you do that?" Tilly asked.

"I'm not sure I even did anything."

"You are a healer," Rayden said proudly. "That is magnificent."

"She did that earlier, after the attack," Shane said.

But she hadn't done that earlier, at least not exactly what she was doing now. The power was different, more familiar now. Was it because she'd already accessed it?

"Why isn't he waking up?" Elizabeth asked, joining them at the bedside.

"He needs blood, and soon," Tilly said.

"What if we go back to Seattle? We can take him to the hospital," Anastasia said.

"I will go with you." Tony stood. "I can carry him, and fight if necessary."

Anastasia nodded, and Tony lifted the unconscious Dakota.

"I am going, too." Elizabeth wiped her face. "Tilly can handle things here."

Not wasting any time, Anastasia closed her eyes and called to her power. A wind began to pick up in the cottage, and when the swirling light appeared, they all stepped through with no hesitation.

They appeared moments later in the alleyway beside Elizabeth's hospital.

"Let's get him inside. We are running out of time." Tony headed for the emergency entrance and the doors opened before them.

An older man with glasses looked up from behind the counter. His eyes widened and he gaped at them. "Elizabeth? Where have you been? We have been worried about you."

"Hi, Richard. I'm sorry, I've been very ill. My son, he fell, and I was able to get the bleeding stopped, but he needs a transfusion." Tears filled her eyes again.

"Let's get him inside, then. Nurse! We have a trauma victim!" Richard yelled behind him. He looked back, eyeing the weapons that Tony and Anastasia had strapped to their waists and slung over their shoulders.

At his glance, Anastasia faked a smile. "We were going to a Renaissance festival."

He seemed to buy her explanation, but held up a hand. "Still, you will need to leave those in your car, so you don't scare security. We can get him in, just come to find us when you're done."

Two nurses pushed a gurney toward them, both of them glancing nervously at Tony as they approached.

"It's okay, Tony." Elizabeth touched his arm, and he gently set Dakota down. "I will be fine. You guys go and change out of your costumes."

"Come on, Tony." Anastasia gripped his arm. "We don't want to scare security," she said, adding Richard's earlier warning.

"I will be right back." Tony kissed Elizabeth, then turned to follow Anastasia. "We can go to Dakota's apartment and change. I think it's this way." She headed up the street, then turned around when Tony didn't follow.

Eyes wide, he slowly surveyed the area. "What is that?" Tony asked, eyeing the cars that drove by.

"Those are cars. They take you from one place to another."

"By themselves?" He looked at her, shocked.

"No, you drive them."

He watched everything with fascination. She couldn't imagine what it would feel like to see this for the first time. Terrenia had been an adjustment for her, but at least she had studied time periods that had similar attributes. This was all new for Tony.

She breathed a sigh of relief when Dakota's building came into view and raced up the stairs. "I promise I will show you everything, but I want to get back to the hospital as soon as possible."

They reached Dakota's door and Anastasia gripped the handle. "Dammit, its locked."

"Here."

"If we break Dakota's door, he's going to be pissed."

Anastasia looked around the hall, grateful no one was outside their apartments. Using what was left of her energy, Anastasia conjured another portal she hoped would lead inside the apartment.

"Wait here." She stepped through the portal and into Dakota's living room.

After opening the door, she let Tony inside, then secured the lock again. Spots swam in her vision and she swayed on her feet.

"Woah." Tony steadied her. "You okay?"

"I think I've used a bit too much magic recently." She straightened. "I'm okay now."

"Let's take it easy," he said as he studied the room. "So this is an apartment?"

"Yes." Anastasia removed her weapons and set them on the kitchen table, then she went into Dakota's room to find them both some clothes that weren't covered in blood.

She found some sweats and a large t-shirt she hoped would fit Tony, and one of Dakota's button-up long sleeves for her. She put it on over her shirt and kept her leather pants and boots on.

"Try these on." She handed Tony a pair of Dakota's tennis shoes. He tried to squeeze his large feet into them, but his heel wouldn't go in.

"Dammit," he cursed and tossed the shoes.

"Just wear your boots." She headed for the door as Tony pulled his boots back on.

"I look ridiculous." Tony scoffed as he looked down at himself.

"Yes, you do," she agreed with a slight smile. "But, surprisingly, you will fit in a lot more this way."

"Strange world," he said as he followed her out into the hall.

49

SEATTLE

DAKOTA

When Dakota woke, a wave of pain hit him like a ton of bricks. He winced, and he pressed a hand to his stomach. It stung as if it had been split in half, which it had, he supposed, remembering the earlier battle. He did his best to sit up when he felt the weight of someone lying next to him. He looked over to Ana, who was curled into his side. Seeing her visibly relaxed him, and he settled back down into the pillows.

"She hasn't moved since we got here," Tony whispered from the corner. He stood from his seat on the floor and moved to stand next to the bed.

"My mom?" Dakota asked cautiously.

"She's fine." Tony pointed to a chair in the corner where Elizabeth slept soundly.

Dakota took a deep breath. "What happened? The Brutes had her, is she hurt?"

"It was all an illusion. They never had her."

"But how?"

"A Trepido got to you."

"Trepido?"

Tony's brows drew together. "Nasty monsters, they force you to see your worst fears play out. They take joy from the pain they cause others to inflict on themselves. Had Anastasia not gotten to you, you would have killed yourself or been killed by a Brute who was taking in the show."

"Shit. So it was a trap."

Tony nodded.

Dakota looked around, taking in his surroundings. "Where are we?"

"You're in Seattle."

"Andrew? The others?"

"Andrew is fine, we got to him in time, but the others were gone before we could get to them."

"Shit," Dakota muttered, closing his eyes. "How many did we lose?"

"Three of the men that went in with you, and two more that went in with Argento and me, There's more news as well, I'm afraid."

Dakota opened his eyes.

"Argento found his wife, but she was already gone when we got there. She'd been pregnant when she was kidnapped and gave birth to the baby while captive."

"The baby?"

"A girl; she's fine. Argento has her now."

Dakota nodded. There was no replacement for the loss of his wife, but at least Argento wasn't completely alone.

"How long until I'm out of here?" Dakota asked, looking up at the machines.

"I think I can get you out later today," Elizabeth answered from her post in the corner. "But only so that you can be put on bed rest at home."

Dakota groaned quietly. "Bed rest?"

"Nonnegotiable. You almost died, Dakota."

"How did I survive?"

"Anastasia closed the wound enough to slow the bleeding. It was the strangest thing I've ever seen. The entire air pulsed with the magic… you could *feel* it," Tony told him. "Rayden said she was a healer. The Brutes had coated the blade in poison that kept eating the stitches."

"That's awesome," Dakota said dryly. "Any word on Vincent?"

"He's all over the news," his mom said. "Apparently he's being revered as some sort of hero."

"It was like that when we left, too. He set it up to look like he fixed everything."

“Other than that, we haven’t seen him.”

Dakota looked down at Ana as she slept. Her face was relaxed, and she looked peaceful. The magic must’ve drained her. He pulled her closer against him and pressed a kiss to the top of her head.

He could still see the way she had stared down at him, the absolute agony on her face when she’d thought he was going to die. The way she’d looked as magic snapped in the air around them. He’d felt it too—the strange bond they’d shared in that moment.

The threading of power that surged through him had been the most intense thing he’d ever experienced.

He closed his eyes and drifted back to sleep to the steady sound of Ana’s breathing.

50

SEATTLE

DAKOTA

"Mom, I'm fine," Dakota assured her as she tucked yet another pillow behind him on his couch. She'd managed to break him free of the hospital with the promise to be on bed rest. She refused to let Ana take them back to Terrenia until he'd had more time to heal, just in case something went wrong.

"Can I please have some coffee?" he begged, folding his hands together in a plea.

She fought back a grin and he knew he'd won. "Fine, but only one cup and then you sleep. How's your pain level?"

"Can't feel a thing." He smiled and pinched his arm for good measure.

"Good." She turned and headed to grab his coffee.

"Hey, Mom?" He craned his neck around to look at her.

"Yes?"

"I love you."

"I love you, too, Dakota. Now sit still."

"Hey, Tony, can you hand me the remote?" When Tony just stared at him, he added, "The thin black rectangle with the round symbols on it."

"Oh." Tony handed it to him and Dakota clicked the power button. A commercial about toilet paper came on and Tony was immediately sucked in to the images of a cartoon bear family in the forest.

"It's called a cartoon." Ana smiled and stepped from his bedroom, wearing a pair of his sweats and a t-shirt. How she managed to look mouth-watering wearing his gym clothes he had no damn clue, but she did, and unfortunately, there was nothing he could do about it at the moment.

She finished towel drying her hair and walked into the kitchen to help his mom with the coffee.

"So how long are we stuck here?" he asked.

"Just until we make sure you aren't going to come down with any kind of secondary infection," Tony answered, his eyes still glued to the television screen.

"Tony and I are going to head back to Terrenia in the morning, just to check in. We'll be back as quickly as possible. I just want to make sure everything is fine and let them know you lived." Ana handed him a cup of coffee and sat on the chair next to the couch.

She looked so perfect sitting in his space, so incredibly beautiful, that it tied his stomach in knots. He blamed the pain meds.

"Probably a good idea." He took a drink of the coffee and groaned. "You have to make sure you take some of this back for your grandmother."

"I will." Ana tipped her mug and took a drink.

"It feels like we've been gone forever," Dakota commented. "Damn good thing my bills were on auto-pay, otherwise we wouldn't have had anywhere to come back to."

His mom glared at him. She'd told him auto-pay was lazy and he should handle things 'like a grown ass man', as she so eloquently put it.

"You better watch your tone, or I'll withhold the coffee," she retorted.

"Just saying, Mom, how many late bills do you have stored up?"

When she didn't answer, Dakota turned to her. "You did it too, didn't you?"

Her cheeks flushed. "I looked into it, yes."

"Ah-ha!" He winced. "Ouch."

"You had better sit still," his mom scolded, and Ana snorted.

"I'm having childhood flash backs over here."

"How did they get inside of it?" Tony asked in awe as another commercial came on.

"They aren't inside of it." Dakota laughed. "It's happening somewhere else and then gets broadcast to the television."

"Broadcast?"

"The images are sent through cables, and they appear on the TV."

"This makes no sense to me," Tony said as he stared at the screen.

"I'm not explaining it very well either. I am honestly not even sure how exactly it works."

When Vincent's face filled the screen, Tony jumped from the chair, grabbing his sword from the table beside him.

"Wait!" Dakota yelled.

"He is here!"

"No, it's a broadcast, remember? Don't skewer my TV, Tony."

Vincent's voice came through the speakers, and at the sound of it, Dakota's stomach churned.

"I'm so happy to have been working side by side with Mayor Roberts in an effort to curb the recent violence caused by the horrific Brutes. Rest assured, we are working diligently to make sure you are safe."

"Lying asshat," Dakota's mom said. "I can't believe everyone is buying this crap."

"Fear is a great motivator," Dakota muttered.

"But why? Why not destroy this world as he's done Terrenia? I haven't seen any evidence of death in this world—at least not like back home. We have plants and animals dying every day because of him, so why not here?" Tony asked.

"Maybe he likes this world," Ana responded angrily. "Maybe he has bigger plans for it."

"We need to stop playing defense and find his ass." Dakota said.

"Agreed." Ana answered. Mood killed, they sat and watched commercials and sitcoms until the day turned into night.

51

ANASTASIA

Anastasia rolled over and checked the readout on Dakota's clock. *Four fifteen am, great.* She and Tony were traveling back to Terrenia today, and the last thing she needed was to be short on sleep.

How was it she slept better on a handmade mattress than Dakota's plush pillow-top? Probably all the damn noises. As if on que, someone honked a horn in the street below. Dakota folded an arm behind his head and she stared down at him.

She reached out and gently stroked a finger over the scar next to his left eye, one he'd gotten climbing over to her window when they were twelve. He'd slipped and smacked his head on the windowsill and Anastasia had panicked. Both for her best friend, and for whatever Mitch's retaliation was going to be.

To her surprise, though, Monica had bandaged him up and sent him on his way and, to her knowledge, had never mentioned the incident to Mitch. It had been the first—and last—shred of hope that both the people she thought were her parents didn't hate her.

Anastasia placed her feet on Dakota's soft carpet and stood. No sense in living in the past. *What's done is done.*

She made her way to the bathroom for a shower—her third one since they'd been back. Hot showers were the one thing she missed that she couldn't get back home.

FORTY-FIVE MINUTES AND ALL THE HOT WATER LATER, Anastasia walked back into the bedroom. She turned to head out to the living room and realized she and Dakota weren't alone.

Not having a weapon, Anastasia placed herself in between Dakota's bed and Vincent.

He threw his hands up. "Easy, I come in peace."

His eyes were bluer than she'd ever seen them, the silver barely threading around the edges of his iris's. Vincent's face was clean-shaven, revealing an angled nose and sharp jaw, and he wore a suit with a tie. He looked so out of place in this world, even though he was trying to blend in. The resemblance to Gregory was a stab to her heart.

"What the hell are you doing here?" she growled.

"Come on, Anastasia, if I wanted him dead, I could have killed him while you were in the shower."

Anastasia rolled her eyes. "What do you want, Vincent?"

"A truce."

"Excuse me?"

"My plans are going really well for me, and I've realized that I don't actually need your help." He laughed. "Wish I would have realized it sooner, as it would have saved me a ton of trouble, and I could have just killed you to start." At her glare, he waved his hand in the air. "But that's beside the point and in the past, so let's move on. What I want now is a truce: I'll go my way, you go yours, and neither one bothers the other."

"A truce."

"Yes."

"How can we have a truce when you want to destroy my world?"

"Oh, I'm leaving this one alone. I am finding that I quite like it here. Magic is not well known, so I am both feared and revered here. I love it." He brushed his hands over his suit.

"You're leaving this one alone, but what are you doing to Terrenia?"

"That's part of the truce; *you* leave Terrenia alone."

"*I* leave it alone?"

"Yes, you stay here, in Seattle. I will make sure you never want for anything, dear niece. You will have money, food, Dakota, and he and Elizabeth can both have their jobs back." He shrugged. "Hey, even Tony can do whatever he wants. You can all live out your lives in peace, together, rather than continuing with this silly feud we have going on. I can even bring your grandmother here—as long she follows the rules, as well, of course."

Anastasia's jaw dropped. "Feud? You think we are in a feud? We are at *war*, Vincent. You have murdered hundreds of people I care about, and you want me just to walk away? To leave my people at your mercy?"

"Look, I don't even have any interest in Terrenia anymore, but old debts have to be paid. I personally will not harm a single Terrenian ever again. I promise." He held his hands up in surrender.

"I don't believe you even for a second," she spat.

"If you don't believe that, then believe this." He stepped closer to her. "If you continue with this 'war', as you call it, you will lose everything. He almost died." He paused, motioning toward Dakota. "Are you prepared for that *almost* to become *fact*? Are you so set in your vengeance that you would allow him to suffer? You'd allow Elizabeth to lose her son?" He shook his head, clicking his tongue in disproval.

"I won't walk away from my people."

"I told you I wouldn't harm them. I am happy in this world. I have more power than I ever dreamed of. I have women in my bed every night. I am no longer the man I was before, and I no longer need you. Which means I won't hesitate to strike you down next time we meet if war is what you choose. I am only giving you this as a gift to my brother. I owe you nothing and consider you nothing more than a thorn in my side. Make your choice, Anastasia, before I lose my patience." He faded away, and Anastasia turned to Dakota.

He was awake and staring at her. "Please tell me I'm not hallucinating."

"You're not." She climbed into bed next to him.

"So Vincent was really here?"

"Yup."

"And offered you a truce?"

"Yup."

"Well, that's interesting."

"Yup."

"We can't accept it," Dakota said firmly.

"I know, but he doesn't have to." She smiled widely. Maybe they could use this to their advantage, make Vincent think they had a truce when in reality they were just waiting for the right opportunity.

"So he offered you a truce in return for a normal life?" Tony paced Dakota's living room.

"That sums it up."

"And he said he has no plans for Terrenia?" Grey eyes locked onto hers and she shook her head.

"Not exactly. He said old debts had to be paid, but that he personally wouldn't harm anyone in that world."

"Those are some twisted words if I've ever heard them," Elizabeth commented.

"What do you think he has planned?"

"I don't know, but it's not going to be good."

"What are we supposed to do?" Tony asked.

"Nothing has changed. We need to go back to Terrenia and see that everyone is all right. Then we come back here and bring Dakota and Elizabeth home."

"Maybe we should all go back now," Dakota said. "Just in case."

"And if you come down with a secondary infection?"

"It's not like Ana can't bring us back, Mom."

"What if she can't? What if something happens? I've lost everyone, Dakota. I refuse to lose my last son too."

Anastasia opened her mouth but stopped. *Last son?* What the hell did that mean?

"Last son? Mom, I'm your only son," Dakota joked. "Unless of course you have one I don't know about?"

She glared at him. "You know what I mean."

"With Vincent popping in here, I don't know that leaving you two unprotected is our best option." Tony folded his arms over his chest.

"As much as I hate to say it, I agree," Dakota said. "I think the safest option here is for us all to go back. Today."

Elizabeth sighed. "I see I'm outnumbered. I'll go pack all my medical supplies."

52

ANASTASIA

Twenty minutes later, they stood in Dakota's living room.

"We ready?" Anastasia asked. She and Tony had changed into the clothes they'd come to Seattle in—minus the blood, thanks to Elizabeth. Elizabeth had chosen a sweatshirt and dark jeans, and Dakota wore a pair of dark blue jeans and a navy colored t-shirt that made his eyes appear impossibly blue.

He stood from the stool he'd been sitting on and nodded. "Let's do this."

Anastasia closed her eyes and called her magic. The room swirled around them until the portal appeared. Gripping hands, they stepped through, returning quickly to the medical cottage.

The copper tang of blood filled her nose and Anastasia scanned the room. Bloody rags and strips of clothing littered the floor and counters.

"What happened here?" Elizabeth whispered.

Tony ripped the front door open and Elizabeth screamed. Bodies littered the ground outside the cottage. The entire center of the village was covered in death. Eyes frozen open, the lifeless villagers stared at Anastasia as she stumbled down the steps and into the carnage.

"No, no, no." She knelt beside Selena and Sarah. Blood splattered the front of their pale dresses, and Selena still gripped Sarah's hand in hers.

"No!" Tony roared, but Anastasia barely heard him. Why had they waited? They should have come back immediately!

"Check for survivors." Dakota touched her shoulder. "We need to see if anyone made it, Ana."

She numbly stood, her body carrying on when her mind and heart were shattered.

Someone coughed nearby and Anastasia stepped carefully through the bodies. She crumpled to the ground beside Andrew, who gasped for air.

"Over here!" she yelled to Tony and Dakota.

Andrew's shirt was splattered with blood, although she couldn't see where he was injured. His pregnant wife lay lifeless beside him, and Anastasia lifted his head so it was in her lap.

"What happened? Who did this?" Tony asked, kneeling beside them. "Shit, Andrew," he said when he saw the woman lying next to him.

Andrew tried to say something, but he coughed, and blood splattered the front of Anastasia's shirt. "She. Did." He pointed to Anastasia, and it was as if someone drove a dagger into her heart.

"I didn't do this, I never would have hurt any of you! Please tell me what happened." Hot tears streamed down her face.

"You caused this," he said again. "You should have taken the truce." He coughed, and blood splattered her again.

"Vincent." She growled his name, a dangerous threat that she fully intended to follow through on.

Anastasia placed Andrew's head gingerly on the ground and got to her feet. Tony and Dakota stood as well and she spun in a circle, searching.

"Where are you, Vincent? You fucking coward! I know you're here somewhere."

"I'm surprised you didn't sense me before." He appeared before them, and the bodies faded away until they stood in darkness. "Just shows how out of touch you are with your magic. It's embarrassing to be related to you."

Tony made a move toward him and Vincent held up his hand. "If you don't want to die, I suggest you stop right there."

"How dare you," Anastasia growled. She felt the magic pooling in her blood and wondered just what it would take to strike him down where he stood.

"How dare I? I offered you a truce. A way to survive and have at least the chance of a normal life with Dakota, and what do you do? You ignore me!"

"You couldn't have honestly thought I would take that deal." Sparks snapped at her fingertips. "You and I both know you weren't going to keep Terrenia safe."

"I never said I would protect them, only that I wouldn't harm them personally. The Trepidos are going to take this world whether I allow them to or not; it's only a matter of whether I went down with all these poor bastards or not. And let's face it, I've never been particularly fond of this place."

"So it's the Trepidos you owe a debt to."

"Technically, no, that would be their creator, but it was a fairly even trade."

"Thousands of innocent lives for what? Power?"

Vincent's eyes flashed blue for a moment. "Anastasia, you need to go," he warned, but before she could say anything, his eyes were back to silver. "I like power."

"You disgust me," she spat.

"The feeling is quite mutual. You have too much of your mother in you. It's going to cost you your life."

"Your arrogance is going to cost you yours."

"Unlikely."

"Why don't we see, then?" She flung two orbs of light at him, but Vincent waved his hand and they disappeared.

"You are no match for me, child." He flung out a hand and sent her flying back into the dark. Her head slammed into something hard, and she lay for a moment staring up at the ceiling.

"Ana!"

Anastasia got to her feet and stared at the inside of the medical cottage. The bloody rags from earlier were gone, and it looked just like it had nearly every day for the last five years.

"What the hell just happened?" Tony asked, slowly turning around in a circle.

All four of them stood inside now.

The sound of laughing came from just outside, and she rushed to pull the door open. The village was bustling, alive as ever, and she breathed a sigh of relief. They weren't too late—at least, not yet.

"Anastasia!" Andrew headed toward her, Leo and Shane beside him. "When did you get back?" he asked, shaking hands with Tony and Dakota.

"Glad to see you aren't dead," Shane said as he shook Dakota's hand.

"Glad to not be dead," Dakota returned.

"Anything happen while we were gone?" Tony asked.

Andrew shook his head. “It’s been quiet since you guys left. We had the, uh, funerals last night.”

“You okay?” Shane asked and Anastasia looked over to see he was staring at her.

“Yeah, sorry. Just tired,” she responded. “How’s Selena?”

“She and Sarah haven’t been out much.”

“I’ll go see them in just a little bit.” She looked to Dakota. “Let’s get you home, you still need to heal.”

“I’ll catch up with you once we get them settled,” Tony told Andrew as he and Elizabeth followed Anastasia and Dakota through the bustling village.

“So, that was a mind fuck,” Dakota said once they were inside.

“It’s what Vincent’s best at,” Anastasia responded dryly.

Tony hadn’t spoken since they’d stepped inside, and when she looked at him she could see he was barely leashing the rage inside. His jaw was tight, and his eyes narrowed as he stared out the window and into the trees. “He’s been doing that to you?” he asked finally.

“Messing with me?” She snorted. “It’s his favorite past-time.”

“It felt so real,” Elizabeth said.

“It always does. The world he crafted inside the stasis was nearly indistinguishable from reality. I could feel, taste, and smell everything.” Her words choked up at the end when she thought of the little girl she'd left behind.

Dakota, who sat beside her on the couch, reached over and gripped her hand. She curled her feet up and leaned against him, and he wrapped his arm around her shoulders. "I love you," he whispered softly.

"I love you, too."

"I want to check on everyone, see that they're all right." Tony headed for the door.

"I'll come with you," Elizabeth offered. "You two okay?"

"We're fine, Mom." Dakota offered her a smile. "Go on."

She and Tony stepped from the room, and Anastasia pulled away to look at him. "I'm so tired of his mind games," she whispered.

"We'll find a way to stop him." Dakota tucked her hair behind her ear. "But first, I really want to kiss you." He pulled her to him and Anastasia climbed onto his lap to straddle him.

She pressed her lips to his and buried her hands in his thick hair. The melding of their mouths pushed thoughts of death from her mind as she focused on what was before her: life.

53

ANASTASIA

Later that night, Anastasia walked the fence line with Kaley. She had done it so many times over the years, and still, it felt so alien to her now. She looked back toward the training cottage where Gregory wouldn't be waiting for her with a stiff drink to end the day. Dakota would be, and while that was a beautiful thing, her heart longed for her father.

He'd never come back. He'd never watch her get married, or see his grandchildren. All because his brother wanted power. She would never understand the allure of it. All she wanted was to be able to lead a normal life with Dakota, to someday give them both a family. She wanted to see what he would look like with gray hair. Handsome as ever. She smiled to herself.

"Hi, Anastasia," a girl said behind her.

Anastasia turned around. Brady's younger sister, Sarah, leaned against the wall. She hadn't spoken to Sarah or Selena since Brady's death, and the guilt from that alone was heavy.

"Hi, Sarah. Everything okay?" she asked hesitantly. Sarah's long black hair was braided back, and at sixteen, she already had her mother's beauty.

"Yes, it is." She smiled lightly. "Just out for a walk. I've been coming out almost every night since—well, you know."

Anastasia nodded. "I'm so sorry, Sarah. I didn't tell you and your mother before, but I am so sorry." The pain was like a knife in her heart at the thought of Brady, and the tears threatened to fall. She missed him so much.

"Thank you. You have to know we don't blame you, Anastasia. You were the big sister we both never had, and we missed you. I miss you." Sarah wiped the tears from her cheek.

"I've missed you, too, Sarah." Anastasia opened her arms and pulled Sarah in for a hug. It was soothing to her soul to know that Sarah and Selena didn't blame her, but Brady's death still weighed heavy on her heart.

"How is your mom?" Anastasia asked when Sarah released her and pulled away.

"She comes and goes. I honestly don't think she is ready to admit that he's gone. She keeps talking about him as if he's going to walk in from another scouting mission any day. She didn't even go to his funeral." Sarah's voice cracked, and Anastasia touched her shoulder.

"Everyone grieves differently." *Or they just bury it*, she thought to herself. "This is just how she is working through things. It'll get easier, I promise."

Sarah nodded. "How are you doing?"

"I'm dealing," she lied. "Trying to make it through each day, and if I do that, I consider it a win."

Sarah smiled slightly, but it didn't reach her eyes.

The night air chilled, and Anastasia's breath came out in an icy burst. Her skin tingled as the hair on the back of her neck stood on end.

Anastasia spun slowly, searching the night for the source of the change. She turned back to Sarah and started to speak, stopping when Kaley growled low in her throat.

Anastasia spun, shielding Sarah and drawing her sword. "Go, Sarah."

"What is it?" Fear filled her voice as they frantically looked for who or what approached.

"I'm not sure. Get home."

Sarah turned and ran, and when she disappeared into the village, Anastasia focused her attention back to what was around her.

Kaley, still growling, seemed just as confused.

Anastasia opened her senses and felt emptiness. It

was as if the world was void of all noise, and that frightened her more than anything else she might have sensed. That fear was what made her realize what Kaley was sensing. Trepidos.

"Go and get Dakota, girl," she said to Kaley as she sheathed her sword. It would do no good against them and would only allow them to make her a bigger danger than she already was.

Anastasia pulled at her magic and did her best to put up a wall around her people and against the monsters. She wasn't sure how far away they were, but if Kaley sensed them, then she knew it wouldn't be too long until they arrived. She looked down at her hands, blue sparks flew at her fingertips and worked their way up her arm, illuminating her skin as they went.

Shadows crept closer to the edge, and Anastasia held her ground as they crept along the dirt.

"I was wondering if I'd see you bastards again," she growled through gritted teeth.

The answer came from inside her mind. *"We have missed you, baby bird."* It mocked her just as the Brutes did.

"Can't come up with your own insults? Have to steal from the Brutes?"

"We cannot wait to taste your fear."

Something rammed against her mind, a battering of the walls she'd carefully erected around herself once again. "You'll be waiting a long damn time. How about you take form and we see who has the upper hand then?"

"You truly have no idea what we are, do you, baby bird? Or who we come from?"

"I know that I don't care."

The light her body threw off seemed to keep the shadows away, but some were sneaking through her defenses. She heard the terrified screams from behind her and Anastasia knew she couldn't protect everyone when they were spread so far apart. Fuck!

"Anastasia!" Dakota yelled.

She spun just in time to dodge the blade Sarah wielded. "You monsters killed my brother!" she screamed, tears running down her cheeks.

"Sarah! It's not real!" Anastasia pulled her to the ground and shook her shoulders. Moments later, her eyes began to refocus on Anastasia.

"What happened?" she asked, dazed, and the Trepido's chilling laughter filled Anastasia's mind.

"Get everyone gathered in the center of the village!" she yelled to Dakota as she climbed off Sarah and pulled her to her feet. "I can block them, but I need everyone together!"

Dakota nodded and rushed Sarah away.

"You won't win." The hissing voice of one of the Trepidos behind her said.

She turned and smiled at it. She threw her hand up, sending light straight into the dark, and it fell to the ground, its shadow disappearing to reveal its monstrous, goblin-esque appearance.

"Anyone else want to play with me? Or try, anyway," she taunted, hoping to buy Dakota more time.

She walked slowly behind him, wanting to get to the center of the village before the Trepidos did. The villagers would be sitting ducks until she arrived.

Dakota passed the message to Tony and Argento, and Anastasia watched, relieved as everyone gathered. Shadows followed a few of the villagers that were being dragged into the center in a panic, and she threw light at the monsters, watching in satisfaction as the shadows crumbled to the ground. These deaths did not bother her —Trepidos were never peaceful; they were pure evil and, according to Argento, always had been.

"That everyone?" Anastasia asked through gritted teeth. The Trepidos were not going down without a fight; they continued pushing at her barrier, battering every one of her defenses, and it was wearing on her. Her vision swam, but she reached deeper into the pool of magic inside her.

Dakota nodded. "What are we going to do?"

"Make them wish they had never taken Vincent's deal," Anastasia responded.

Carmen walked over to Anastasia and nodded. "I'm with you, Anastasia. I will hold the barrier; you handle the monsters."

"Sounds good to me." She stepped toward the edge

of the circle the villagers had made.

"Be careful, Ana," Dakota said.

She nodded, and after reinforcing her own mental barriers, stepped out of Carmen's light.

"Come and get me, boys," she called.

"You are foolish, girl," one of them whispered.

"Your death will be so satisfying," another said.

Their assault on her mental barriers continued, but she held steady. Something slammed into her, knocking her onto the ground. For a moment, her barrier dropped, and the invasion, the worse kind of mental perversion, pushed into her mind.

Anastasia closed her eyes against the images of the village behind her being destroyed. "It's not real." She held strong and pushed to her feet.

The shadows retreated slightly, pulling back into the night where they'd come, and Anastasia followed.

"She is strong, but not strong enough." The whisper filled her mind, and she threw her blocks back up.

"That all you got?" she asked. "Drop the shadows, show me your ugly selves."

"Ugly, she calls us? Maybe you are the ugly one, human." The distaste in the Trepido's voice made her smile.

"Well then, show me." She continued following them further into the trees, ignoring the calling of her name from behind her. *I will drive them away so I can slaughter them all.*

Once they were hidden by the trees, the Trepidos began dropping their shadows, and soon she was surrounded by monsters. Their gangly appearance was nothing compared to their troll-like features. Oversized noses sat on large, round faces that didn't fit the slenderness of their torso's. Their large arms hung to their knees, before ending in claws.

"Ugly," she taunted.

"I am tiring of her games." One sneered at her, no longer in her mind since they were solid forms.

Anastasia's hand itched for her sword. "Then come and get me."

The annoyed monster began to move toward her, but another threw out its claw.

"She taunts us, and you won't allow me to kill her?"

"She is much too calm," it said cautiously.

"Come on! Going to let him boss you around?"

"Why are you not afraid, girl? You are mere inches from death, and you do not even see it." The monster's claw reached out and stopped just before touching her, in demonstration. "These humans you foolishly protect will all die. You have seen it, have you not? I know you have," he sneered. "I can see it in your eyes. Vincent showed you what we are capable of. We will end it all." It waved its claws around to show her what he meant. "And we are only the beginning. You have no clue what is coming."

"I'm tired of your threats." She pretended to yawn.

"I tire of this as well." The annoyed Trepido from moments before charged her, and she threw her palm out. He crumbled to ash before her, and the other Trepidos began moving angrily, predators stalking their prey.

"Leave her, fools! The old woman is going to give in soon, and then we shall feast!" the leader yelled, but the others did not seem thrilled by the idea of leaving her alone, and in unison, over half of them charged her.

They met the same fate as their comrade.

"You fools!"

All but the leader and one other Trepido turned back into shadows and disappeared into the night.

"We had much better luck in that Seattle. This world isn't worth it," she heard the remaining monster whisper to the leader while he stared straight at Anastasia. She held his cold gaze, not willing to show even an inch of the exhaustion weighing her down.

"Let us go," the leader finally said, then they disappeared.

Anastasia opened her senses, and dropped to her knees, clutching her head. The second she released the barriers, pain assaulted her head, making it feel like it had been split open.

Leaves crunched behind her, and Anastasia turned just in time for her world to fade to black.

54

DAKOTA

Dakota, Argento, Shane, and Tony, raced through the trees, searching for any sign of Anastasia. She had disappeared into the tree line, leaving him staring after her until Carmen deemed it was safe again to leave the center of the village.

The monsters had vanished before she'd even left the clearing, right after they'd knocked her to the ground, but still she'd kept moving, making him wonder if the beasts hadn't drawn her in somehow.

"I don't see her anywhere," Shane called out.

"Nor do I," Argento said. "Perhaps we should head back to the village, just to be sure she hasn't returned."

"You guys go ahead. I'm not done looking yet,"

Dakota told them when they gathered together in a clearing.

"Wait." Tony knelt and pressed his fingers against something dark that had pooled on the ground. "Shit." He held his fingers up, and in the light from the moon above, Dakota saw the dark red stain of blood.

No, God, please no. "Ana!" he called out into the night.

"There is no trail," Argento noted. "We need to go back and gather more warriors."

"We can't just leave her out there!" Shane insisted.

"I agree, but we are no good to her dead. Which is what we will be if we run into those Trepidos again," Tony said sadly. "As much as I hate it—and believe me, I do—we don't have an option."

"You two feel free to go back. I am not returning unless I have Ana with me." Dakota unsheathed his sword and headed for the tree line.

"I'm coming with you," Shane called after him.

"Wait!" Andrew burst into the clearing, breathless.

"What is it?" Tony demanded.

"Elizabeth and Sarah."

Dakota's stomach twisted. "What happened?"

"They're missing."

"What the hell do you mean, they're missing?" Tony stepped toward him. "You were supposed to be watching everyone!" Tony's voice boomed through the trees, but Dakota barely heard it through the hammering of his own heart.

Both people he loved more than anything in the world were missing, along with a young girl whose mother had already lost one child.

What the hell was going on?

"Go back and rally the others," Tony told Andrew "Prepare them for war. We don't know who we're going up against, but we have to find them."

"Where's Anastasia?" Andrew asked.

"Missing," Shane answered.

"God help us." Andrew rushed back toward the village.

"Is it possible the Trepidos turned her?" Argento asked. "They could have easily manipulated her into grabbing Elizabeth and Sarah."

"Then why the fuck is there blood on the ground?" Dakota demanded angrily. "If she had gone willingly, why hurt her?"

"I meant no disrespect." Argento held up his large, pale hands. "Only doing what I can to gather information."

"I know you are, man. I'm sorry." Dakota sheathed his sword and ran his hands over his face.

"Where do we even start looking for them?" Shane asked.

Dakota looked back at the trees. "I have no fucking clue."

Night turned into day, and they still had found no sign of the missing. Exhausted, Dakota, Tony, and Shane returned to the village, while Argento gathered some of his Brutes to continue the search.

They'd checked every inch of forest within a three-mile radius of the village, and Argento had told them they would move out to a full five before the afternoon hit.

"Could Vincent have opened a portal directly into the village and taken her?" Shane asked as they made their way into the village's center.

People were still holed up in their homes, terrified the nightmarish monsters would return.

Dakota looked over at the three bodies covered in white linen and clenched his fists. They would not add Anastasia, Sarah, and his mom to the list of the dead.

"I sure as hell hope not," Tony said. "We need to get some rest; we can reconvene in a few hours."

Tony placed a hand on his shoulder, and Dakota looked over at the other man. "We will find them, Dakota."

"I sure as hell hope so."

55

ANASTASIA

Anastasia opened her eyes, and the assault of light that hit her might as well have been daggers to her temples. "What the hell." She groaned and tried to lift her hands, but they were tied behind her back.

"Thank God, Anastasia."

Anastasia turned. Elizabeth sat beside her, bound to a tree.

"Where the hell are we?" she asked, searching their surroundings. They were sitting at the edge of a burned village, and by the looks of things, it was what remained of Pilke, the first village she and Tony had convinced to pack up and join Terrenia a few years back.

Only the house in the center remained partially

standing, and grass had grown over the dirt paths that the villagers once traveled going to and from their homes.

"I don't know. The last thing I remember, Sarah had come for me because her mother had gotten hurt."

"I was in the trees after driving the Trepidos away." Anastasia closed her eyes at the wave of pain-induced nausea. She'd never had a migraine before, but she was pretty damn sure she was currently experiencing her first one.

Her head felt like someone had taken a jackhammer and was currently hammering it into her brain.

"You got hit pretty hard," Elizabeth told her. "They wouldn't let me tend to you." Her blue eyes, so like her son's, filled with tears. "What are we going to do?"

"We'll get out of here, I promise." The throbbing in her head made it impossible to focus, but she tried to reach down and access her power. Every time she got close, though, pain would radiate through her as she was thrown away from her magic.

"It won't work." Anastasia looked up as Sarah entered the clearing, a dagger in her hand.

"Sarah! Thank goodness!" Elizabeth exclaimed.

Anastasia studied the young girl. She was far enough away that it was impossible to get a close look at her face, but the harshness of her body language and the stiffness in her stance was much like Brady's had been when he'd been under Vincent's control.

"Sarah, what's going on?" Anastasia asked cautiously.

"He's blocked your power." Sarah stepped close enough that Anastasia saw the blackness of her eyes that were void of any humanity, just as her brother's had been.

But she'd brought Brady back, right? Surely she could do the same for his sister. "Who blocked my power?" Anastasia knew the answer, but wanted to keep Sarah talking.

"Vincent. He told me I could get my revenge, for what you did to my brother."

"I didn't do anything to Brady; I loved him like a brother."

"Lies!" Sarah screamed, rushing toward her. "You got him killed!"

"Sarah, calm down. Vincent is controlling you," Anastasia told her, trying like hell to get her hands free.

Sarah brought the blade up to Anastasia's cheek and pressed down. The bite from the blade was quickly followed by the warm sensation of blood dripping down her face.

"I don't need anyone to control me for me to understand you are the problem. You've always been the problem."

"Sarah, I know you're in there somewhere."

Sarah got to her feet and smoothed out the lines in her brown dress. Her dark hair had been pulled back away from her face, and Anastasia tried to see past the young girl on the outside, to the monster she had controlling her.

The only way the three of them would walk out of here together was if Vincent was separated from his latest victim.

The problem was, though, that she currently couldn't access any of her magic.

Sarah strolled over to Elizabeth, her movements smooth like she was gliding instead of walking. She knelt in front of Dakota's mother, who refused to move.

Sarah lifted the blade and sliced Elizabeth's cheek.

"Stop!" Anastasia yelled.

Sarah looked over at her. "Why? You took someone I loved, so I should take someone you love, too. It's only fair. It would have been Dakota, but he said no."

"Who said no?" Anastasia asked.

"The King."

Elizabeth had paled, but turned her focus back to the current threat. "So Vincent wants to be called King now?"

Sarah laughed, the chilling sound so unlike the girl it belonged to. "You have no idea what's truly coming." She straightened and Anastasia tried like hell to access her magic. The pain barriers slammed up in front of her, but she blasted through.

As soon as she felt the familiar pulsing of her magic,

Anastasia dissolved the ropes around her wrists, and pushed to her feet.

Sarah gaped at her, and for a moment, her eyes faded back to their normal brown. She looked down at the knife in her hand and dropped it. "What is happening?" she asked.

Anastasia took the time to slam Sarah's mind with blocks to keep Vincent from re-entering. "You should be fine now."

"I don't…" Her eyes went blank, and blood dripped from the corner of her mouth. She began to fall forward, and Anastasia lunged for her.

"Sarah!" she screamed, catching her just before she hit the ground. "Sarah, wake up!" The young girl's face was completely pale, her eyes wide and lifeless. A single tear slipped down her cheek.

"What the hell just happened?" Anastasia looked up at Elizabeth in shock. How had she just died?

"You happened." Vincent said from behind her.

Anastasia closed her eyes on a long blink. *This ends now.* She set Sarah down and got to her feet, the power humming steadily in her blood.

"You killed her!"

He stood just on the inside of the clearing, flanked by half a dozen pale Brutes. He wore a suit much like the one she'd seen him in back in Seattle, and his eyes blazed silver.

"No, you killed her, dear niece. You shouldn't have

invaded her young mind like that." He folded his hands in front of him and rocked back and forth on his feet.

"What?"

"Young minds are so easily broken. When you invaded her that way, you caused her mind to shut down, and since you are so powerful, it killed her."

Anastasia felt the blow of his words as if he had punched her, and she shook her head. "No."

"Oh, yes." He smiled. "And now I'm going to do what I should have done years ago." He nodded to the Brutes, who started moving toward her. His eyes flashed blue and he shook his head. They returned to silver again. "Tell me, do you still think you're better than me?"

Anastasia reached back for her magic, but was unable to access it anymore. What the hell had he done to her?

"The fact that you haven't answered is telling enough. You slaughtered that girl." He motioned to Sarah. "You could have frozen her, couldn't you?" The mirth in his eyes only caused his words to hit her harder.

"It's because you and I are the same. You wanted to feel the power, and it's time you embraced it."

"I am nothing like you!" she screamed.

"You are everything like me!"

The Brutes closed in around them, and Anastasia reached down to untie Elizabeth. She was ripped away and slammed into the ground before she even touched the ropes.

"Anastasia!" Elizabeth's voice carried through the night, and Anastasia's vision swam.

Vincent wrapped his hand around her throat and lifted her from the ground. "Tell me why I shouldn't just squeeze." He gripped her throat harder and black spots began to invade her vision again.

"You will pay, Vincent," she choked out.

"You know, people keep saying that to me, and yet, here I stand. With not a scratch on me."

She spit in his face, and he wiped it angrily.

"Brat." He threw her back, and she bounced off the Brutes that stood around her. "Finish her, then kill the woman," he instructed. "After that, go and get the boy. There's someone who's quite interested in meeting him."

Without her magic to help her, she was at a loss. Part of her wanted to fall to her knees and beg for death, for an end to all of the pain. But Elizabeth deserved better. She would get Dakota's mother back to him and then deal with picking up the pieces of her soul, if that were even possible at this point.

The first Brute attacked, and Anastasia ducked out of the way just in time to avoid a crushing blow from its fist.

"Mouse is fast."

"Let's play with her first. Then the other," another added and swung a meaty hand at her.

She didn't move fast enough, and its fist knocked the wind out of her. She gasped for air, and before she could recover, another hit her from behind. Everything began to blur together. The pain eventually subsided, and the numbness told her that she was close to death. Elizabeth's screams were the only sound as the Brute wailed on her, and Anastasia briefly wondered why it hadn't killed her yet.

It had called her mouse. It must believe itself to be the cat, and this the game.

Her vision faded in and out until, eventually, there was nothing but darkness.

56

DAKOTA

Blood pounded in Dakota's ears making it impossible to hear anything as they snuck up on a group of Brutes. As soon as the clearing came into full view, Dakota's anger took over.

His mother was tied to a tree, tears streaming down her face as she screamed.

Red-hot rage surged through him and he plunged into the clearing with Shane, Tony, Argento, and half a dozen Brute warriors on his heels.

"Dakota!" Elizabeth yelled, as she struggled to get free. "They have Anastasia!"

He fought, blood splattering him as he moved through the beasts. He saw nothing but a blur of action as he fought his way to the crumpled form in the center.

One Brute hadn't turned his attention away from her, and lifted her broken body by her arm.

She dangled in the air and Dakota yelled out as he attacked. He slammed all of his body weight into the beast, and it dropped Ana back to the ground. His blade cut down through the beast's neck, and a hot spray of blood hit his face.

Dakota lunged for where Ana lay on the ground. Her face was so swollen she was barely recognizable. Blood covered most of her skin and had matted into her hair.

He checked for a pulse and let out a sigh of relief when he felt it, even though it was faint.

Someone freed his mom and she rushed to his side, quickly checking Ana.

"Anastasia, can you hear me?"

Her breaths were ragged gasps.

Dakota lifted her. "We need to get her back to Carmen."

"It's a long ride, Dakota. I don't know that she can make it," Argento said.

Shane whirled on the Brute King. "Then what the fuck do you expect us to do? Let her die?"

"That is not what I'm saying."

"Good. Then let's go."

They jumped on the horses and raced through the trees. Dakota kept checking to be sure she was breathing, but it was faint. He could feel her fading away from him with each minute that passed.

If she died tonight, he was going to die with her.

After what felt like an eternity, the village came into view. Dakota pushed his horse faster and rode straight to the medical cottage.

Carmen sat on the porch, and her eyes widened with agony when she caught sight of Ana's broken body.

"What happened?"

"I will fill you all in," Elizabeth began, "but we have to get her stable. Where's Tilly?" Elizabeth looked around the room.

"I will get her," Argento grumbled and jogged out of the cottage.

"Internal bleeding," Elizabeth noted as she cut open the front of Ana's torn shirt.

Bruises and contusions were everywhere on her abdomen and chest, and the twisted angle of her arm told him it was broken, as was her nose and probably multiple ribs.

"Oh my God," Tilly choked out when she entered the cottage.

"Get me a knife. We have to stop the internal bleeding." Elizabeth grabbed the sanitized blade Tilly handed her and made an incision along Anastasia's ribcage.

Dakota watched, completely helpless, as his mother worked relentlessly to save Anastasia's life. She stopped breathing twice, and both times, his mother performed CPR to bring her back. Each time he held his breath, waiting for hers to start again.

When Elizabeth finally stopped the bleeding and set her wrist, she adjusted Ana's nose and turned to Carmen.

"Is there anything you can do to help her heal? With your magic?"

"She is a healer; her magic should help her heal faster than normal. I'm afraid that if I try and interact with her healing power, I may cause more damage," Carmen said, her face white with fear.

"She doesn't have any. Vincent took it," Elizabeth said softly.

Dakota snapped his head up, his eyes narrowed. "What do you mean, he took it?"

"That's not possible," Carmen said quickly. "Her magic is in her blood… he couldn't have taken it. Unless—"

"Unless what?" Dakota urged, begging for an answer.

"Unless he blocked it, but I don't… Son of a bitch!" she cursed. "He's been playing at this since the day he captured her in Seattle."

"Playing at what?" Elizabeth asked.

"He's been manipulating her mind, toying with her. We all thought it was to take her out by turning her dark. But the whole time, he's been playing at a different game." She fell silent and Dakota held his breath as she pieced the rest of the information together.

"He blocked her magic," Carmen said. "He found the place in her mind where she's most vulnerable, a place that he could exploit and erect a mental wall."

"Is there anything you can do?" Elizabeth asked. "Because I've done all I can, and I really need to sit for a moment, but I can't do that unless I know she is going to live."

"Yes, I can help. But I need you all to leave."

"I'm not going anywhere," Dakota said, crossing his arms.

"Fine, you can stay, but everyone else get out."

Carmen held her hands over Ana, her eyes closed. The magical charge in the room was nearly visible and the drain on Carmen showed in the slump of her shoulders. He wasn't sure what help he could be, but he gripped her wrinkled hand lightly and closed his eyes, willing Anastasia to heal.

He put everything he had into it. He pictured the two of them together as kids, running and playing in the woods at his parents' cabin. He remembered brushing the hair out of her face, wishing he had the courage to kiss her.

Carmen lightly squeezed his hand, and he opened his eyes to stare into her tear-filled hazel eyes.

"I don't know what else to do," she whispered. "I can't undo that block, it's beyond me."

“What do you mean?” he asked, fear getting a fresh grip on his heart.

“If we don’t remove that block, she is going to die.”

“How do we do that?”

“We can’t.”

“Then tell me who the hell can!” he yelled, desperation and grief taking over.

“The Sorceress.”

57

DAKOTA

"Who the hell is the Sorceress?" Dakota's heart might as well have been ripped from his chest. Ana was going to die, and there was nothing he could do about it. "Isn't that what you are?"

"Hardly. There is only one with that title and the power that goes with it. She is the most powerful being in any world, and is tasked with caring for and maintaining peace between the worlds."

"Then where the hell is she? Why isn't she fighting with us?"

Carmen sighed. "Because she's been in hiding for nearly thirty years."

Dakota pinched the bridge of his nose to keep the tears

from streaming down his face. "Great. So our only hope lies with the biggest introvert in all the worlds." He leaned forward to lightly brush a strand of hair from Ana's face.

"Without her magic, she won't last long. Her healing power is what kept her alive when the Brutes had her before—we just didn't know it. Now that it's blocked, I fear she doesn't have long left."

"What about Argento? Their healer? Is there something they can do?"

Carmen shook her head, and what little hope Dakota had extinguished at the pain reflected in the old woman's eyes.

"We have to get her to Jocelyn." Carmen shook her head sadly and covered her face with her hands.

"We need a damn miracle, Carmen."

Carmen reached out and gripped Ana's hand. "We need the Sorceress."

"Well, where is she?"

"She is the only inhabitant on a world that can only be accessed through a portal conjured by a Silvan."

"What the fuck does that mean?"

"Gregory helped her hide, which means only his or Anastasia's blood can open the door."

"This is just fan-fucking-tastic. Ugh!" He wanted to scream, to hit something. Shit, he wanted to bury his blade in the chests of those Brutes all over again, but none of that would bring Ana back.

"We may be able to combine Anastasia's blood with my magic to open the door. But we won't know until we get there whether it's the right place or not."

"Do it," he said without hesitation. Ana was dead if they didn't at least try.

"Go tell Tony and Elizabeth. No one else comes with us, Dakota." Carmen waved her hand and Dakota turned to leave.

"She will live," he said, more for himself than for Carmen. He took one more look at Ana's broken body lying on the table and he willed it to be so. Without her, he was nothing. "Hang on, Ana," he whispered as he headed for the door.

Tony looked up as Dakota stepped outside into the sunlight. "How is she?"

Dakota studied his mother, who appeared to have aged more than ten years in one night. Her eyes were swollen and etched with worry. She needed to rest, but refused to leave. Dakota hated that his news was only going to make things worse. "Mom, can you give Tony and I a minute?"

Elizabeth eyed him. "Dakota, don't you dare cut me out of this conversation because you are trying to ease my worry. I'm a damn doctor; I know she's not doing well."

"It's worse than that." Tears welled in his eyes, so he squeezed them shut. "She's dying."

"What?" Tony's voice was so much smaller than normal.

"Carmen thinks there's a way to save her."

Tony got to his feet, and Elizabeth stood with him. "What can we do?" he asked, ready for any mission that would give Ana a chance.

"We need to go to someone Carmen called The Sorceress. Carmen thinks she may be able to save Ana."

"She's a myth, a legend. We're staking Anastasia's life on fiction?" Tony's jaw hardened.

"Carmen says she's real and we have to leave now."

"I want to go." Elizabeth finally spoke, and Dakota noticed the way his mother avoided his eyes.

"Mom."

Elizabeth lifted her tear-stained face to Dakota's. He stepped toward her and wrapped his arms around her.

"I'm so sorry, Dakota. If she dies—"

"It's not your fault, Mom. This is Vincent and the Brutes that had a hand in it. None of it is your fault, you hear me?" He pulled back just enough to see her face and kissed her lightly on the forehead. "I love you, Mom, and I'm so glad you're all right."

"Dakota, we need to go," Carmen interrupted as she stepped onto the porch. "Now."

"Where is this woman?" Elizabeth asked, leaning into Tony.

"On another world. One that is nearly unheard of

and damn difficult to get to. It takes a hell of a lot of magic to reach her."

"Can you do it?" Tony asked.

Carmen glared at Tony, her eyes narrowing on his face.

"Are you *able* to in your current condition?" Dakota spoke up, not wanting to waste any more time.

Her glare turned to him. "Yes, Dakota. I may be old, but I can still muster up the energy I need to reach her. I just hope Anastasia's blood will be enough to activate the door." Carmen turned to Tony. "You need to keep watch, Tony. Strange things are coming, I can feel it."

"I will."

Carmen nodded. "We should be back within an hour. I cannot imagine she is going to wish us to stay long."

"Good luck," Elizabeth said.

Dakota followed Carmen back into the house and watched as she made a small cut on Ana's arm. Once the blood had welled on the surface, she touched it gently, spreading the blood onto her palm.

Carmen closed her eyes, and the air shifted. Within moments, a portal opened before them, and without hesitation, she stepped through.

Dakota lifted Ana into his arms and held her tightly against his chest as he stepped through the portal. After the now familiar feeling of weightlessness disappeared, he took a moment to catch his breath and then opened his eyes.

They stood in front of a small cottage. The walls were old and fading, as was the railing on the rickety porch that surrounded it.

A light breeze ruffled the tall grass that reached to Dakota's waist and surrounded them completely. There were no mountains, no hint of any other civilization anywhere. It looked as if the place had been deserted. Dakota took a deep breath. The air was fresh, but it didn't carry the sound of birds or any other animals.

What kind of person wanted to live in a solitary world? Was it possible the magic hadn't worked, and the Sorceress didn't live here? A momentary panic filled him. If she wasn't here, what did that mean for Ana?

The door creaked open and he realized that not only did she exist, and still lived in this empty world, but they had also arrived right on her doorstep.

The woman who stepped out looked nearly as exhausted as the old house she lived in. Hair that he imagined had been auburn at one time but was now a faded brown, was pulled back away from her face, and she wore a chocolate-colored dress that nearly matched the color of her eyes. He hated to think it, but there was nothing spectacular about this woman at all.

How was she going to save Ana?

"Who are you?" The woman spoke with a slightly raspy voice, and her curt tone left little wonder as to her current mood—she was pissed that they were here.

Dakota started to take a step forward, but Carmen held her hand up to stop him.

"We met once before, Jocelyn. I am Gregory Silvan's mother-in-law."

At the mention of Ana's father, the woman straightened slightly, the corner of her mouth twitching. *So she did have a heart after all.*

"Carmen. It's nice to see you again. Who is he?" She nodded toward Dakota and crossed her arms under her chest.

"We don't have time for this," Dakota muttered under his breath, and started to take a step toward the cottage again.

"You have time for whatever I deem necessary. You are in my world, and standing in front of my house, remember?" Jocelyn's irritated tone was back, and Dakota's anger flared, and he clenched his hands into fists.

"She's dying."

"I can very well see that," she retorted matter-of-factly.

"Can you help her?"

"I don't know who 'her' is."

"Listen—"

"This is Anastasia Silvan, Gregory's only child. Vincent had her cornered by Brutes and then he blocked her magic." Carmen's voice cracked at the end, and Dakota looked over as a tear slipped down her cheek.

"Please, she will die otherwise. She needs you, Sorceress."

Jocelyn's face softened slightly, but Dakota didn't miss the anger that tightened her jaw at the mention of Vincent. Apparently, she also knew the bastard. "Leave her on the porch. I will take care of her."

"We aren't just going to abandon her on your porch. We stay."

"Then she dies."

Dakota's temper flared again at the nonchalant tone of her words.

"Dakota, she will be safe," Carmen insisted.

"I'm not leaving her. This isn't negotiable."

The Sorceress studied him for a minute. "Very well. You will bring her inside, then you will leave."

"Did you not hear me? I stay with her; I'm not leaving." Dakota stood his ground. He didn't know this woman; even Carmen didn't know her—not really, anyway. He'd be damned if he was going to leave the woman he loved in the care of some stranger. Especially not when she may not live another day and that stranger was so afraid of her own shadow that she hid in a cabin in the middle of a deserted world.

"Fine. But you will leave my home. I don't care if you sit outside, you will not be inside with us. That, too, is nonnegotiable." She put her hand up and then stepped aside so he and Carmen could bring Anastasia inside.

As Dakota passed her, he saw a thick scar that ran

across her throat. The sight of it made him understand her hesitance and fear completely. Someone had tried to kill her. Judging by the ragged edges of the healed wound, they had probably come very close to succeeding.

When they entered the house, Dakota wasn't surprised to see that the inside matched that of the outside. The creaky wooden floors were covered with thin rugs, and tapestries that looked to be made of the same material hung on the walls. A fire roared in a fireplace, but that was the liveliest thing in the single-room cabin.

"Put her on the bed," Jocelyn instructed, and Dakota gently laid Anastasia on the small twin-sized bed.

"I love you," Dakota whispered, kissing Anastasia's pale cheek. He pressed his forehead to hers. "Please come back to me, Ana. I can't live this life without you. We have to experience that future we've dreamed of." He placed another kiss to her forehead, then stood. "If anything happens to her because of you, I don't give a shit how powerful you are—I will come for you."

"You think I'm afraid of you?" Jocelyn's lip twitched in amusement.

Dakota didn't even blink. "You should be. She is my entire world, and the only thing that makes my life worth living. If you do anything other than try to help her, I swear I will kill you, no matter what it takes." He stepped out of the cabin with Carmen on his heels.

"You can return for her in two weeks," Jocelyn said, slamming the door shut.

"What the hell does she mean, two weeks?" Dakota asked Carmen angrily.

"I don't know," Carmen said, and took a seat on the steps leading up to the porch.

"What are we going to do if she dies?" Dakota said, voicing his deepest fear, hoping it might in some way diminish it. Instead, the lump in his throat grew painfully and his chest tightened.

"We can't think like that." Carmen smiled. "Anastasia is as strong as they come, and Jocelyn will take care of her."

"How can you be so sure?" Dakota looked back at the door the woman known as the Sorceress had slammed only moments before. "I don't mean to sound ungrateful, because I am beyond glad that she is willing to try and help, but, Carmen, why would someone so powerful be in hiding here? Why not at least come and help us? She has to know what's going on out there, with Vincent."

"She's not the same as she used to be. Years ago, she would have." Carmen took a deep breath. "She used to be so beautiful, so vibrant when she was young. But she ended up falling for the wrong man. It was such a shame to see, Dakota. The day I met her, I said to myself, 'What a wonderful choice the universe has made to carry on the Sorceress name.' She was a spitfire."

Carmen laughed sadly. "But the next time I saw her, years later…" She shook her head. "She was bright and passionate like fire; he was ice, frozen down to the very heart that beat beneath his chest."

Carmen clasped her hands together and an orb appeared with an image inside it. The woman who stood before him encircled by magic was absolutely gorgeous. Her auburn hair shone brightly, and was only outmatched by the huge smile that spanned across her face. He could see the similarities, sure, but it was hard to believe that the woman inside the house behind him had once been the woman he was looking at now.

Carmen slammed her palms together and the light exploded. "It was only a matter of time before he snuffed out her light."

Dakota couldn't do anything but shake his head. What type of man would it take to dull the light he had seen within the woman Jocelyn had once been?

Carmen got to her feet. "I am going to need rest. I imagine you are not coming back with me?"

He took one look at Carmen's weary face and knew he couldn't let her travel back alone. "You believe she will be safe?"

"She will be, Dakota. I promise Jocelyn will not harm her. She owes Gregory her life, and she will come through for him."

"Then I will take you back, but I want to come back

here tomorrow. That'll give me enough time to gather some things I'll need."

"Okay." Carmen offered him an exhausted smile. "What do you say you escort an old woman back to town?" She offered him her arm and he looped it through his own.

Dakota couldn't help but smile. "I would be honored." Carmen conjured a portal in front of them.

He took one last look at the house and his jaw tightened.

"I love you, Ana," he whispered, then he stepped into the light.

Find out if the Sorceress can save Anastasia in Vengeance of the Phoenix! Available now!

ALSO BY JESSICA WAYNE

Fae War Chronicles

Ember is dying.

But as she will soon discover, some fates are worse than death.

Accidental Fae

Vampire Huntress Chronicles

She's spent her entire life eradicating the immortals.

Now, she finds herself protecting one.

Witch Hunter: FREE READ

Blood Hunt

Blood Captive

Blood Cure

Curse of the Witch

Blood of the Witch

Rise of the Witch

Blood Magic

Blood Bond

Blood Union

Cambrexian Realm : The Complete Series

The realm's deadliest assassin has met her match.

The Last Ward: FREE READ

Warrior Of Magick

Guardian Of Magick

Shades Of Magick

Rise of the Phoenix: The Complete Series

Ana has spent her entire life at the clutches of her enemy. Now, it's time for war.

Birth of the Phoenix

Blood of the Phoenix

Vengeance of the Phoenix

Tears of the Phoenix

Rise of the Phoenix

Tethered

Sometimes, our dreams do come true. The trouble is, our nightmares can as well.

Tethered Souls

Collateral Damage

For more information, visit www.jessicawayne.com

ABOUT THE AUTHOR

Photo Credit Mandi Rose Photography

USA Today bestselling author Jessica Wayne is the author of over thirty fantasy and contemporary romance novels. The latter of which she writes as J.W. Ashley. During the day, she slays laundry and dishes as a stay at home mom of three, and at night her worlds come to life on paper.

She runs on coffee and wine (as well as the occasional whiskey!) and if you ever catch her wearing matching socks, it's probably because she grabbed them in the dark.

She is a believer of dragons, unicorns, and the power of love, so each of her stories contain one of those elements (and in some cases all three).

You can usually find her in her Facebook group, Jessica's Whiskey Thieves, or keep in touch by subscribing to her newsletter.

Stay Updated:

Newsletter: https://www.jessicawayne.com/free-books-by-jessica-wayne
Website: https://www.jessicawayne.com
Readers Group: https://www.facebook.com/groups/jessicaswhiskeythieves

facebook.com/AuthorJessicaWayne
twitter.com/jessmccauthor
instagram.com/authorjessicawayne

CONTEMPORARY ROMANCE BY J.W. ASHLEY

The Corrupted Trilogy

They're being hunted and the only way to come out of it alive, is to put their badges aside.

Rescuing Norah

Shielding Jemma

Targeting Celeste

Olive You: *Six best friends and their hunt for true love (or something like it anyway).*

Long Road Home: *Coming home was always part of the plan. He was not.*

Home For Summer: *He thinks she's a spoiled brat. She thinks he's a stick in the mud. Turns out, they're both wrong.*

Way Back Home: *Facing your past is always the hardest part of moving forward. Especially when you've kept a secret for five years.*

Home At Last: *Rule #1: Never get tied down. Leo smashed through that like it was a pane of sugar glass*

AND HE'S AN ACTION STAR WHOSE MISSION IS TO TAKE ME DOWN... REPEATEDLY.